Crest of the Fallen

Johnna Dee

Other books by

Johnna Dee:

Calpa Series - Cowritten with Krysta Lyn

- The Clan of Mist
- The Clan of Deception

Crest of the Fallen

Johnna Dee

Book 1 in Ascelin Series

This is a work of fiction. Names, characters, places, and incidents either are the product of the author's imagination or are used fictitiously. Any resemblance to actual persons, living or dead, events, or locales is entirely coincidental.

Copyright 2023 © Alstroemeria Publishing LLC

Alstroemeria Publishing is the entity under which author Johnna Dee independently publish under.

All rights reserved. No part of this book may be reproduced or used in any manner without the prior written permission of the copyright owner, except for the use of brief quotations in a book review.

To request permissions, contact the authors
at info@alstroemeriapub.com

Hardcover: 978-1-959356-04-2 | Paperback: 978-1-959356-05-9 | EBook: 978-1-959356-06-6

First Paperback Edition: March 2023

Edited by: Alstroemeria Publishing
Cover Art by Johnna Dee

Physical books printed by Ingram spark and Hero and Villain Designs.
alstroemeriapub.com

Thank you to all my backers who
helped make my dream of my
first book come true!!
Thank you to my friends and
family who supported and listened to me drone on
and on
about book stuff!!!
I appreciate you all so much and
would not have made it this far !!

Chapter 1

Feya sat in the corner, trying to stay hidden. She was trying to be as small as she could be. The house was dark except for the flickering lights coming through the windows cast by the flames of other buildings burning. She could barely see her mother, Elida, who was a few feet away.

She felt the warm blood dripping from the wounds in her neck. The wounds stung from where the vampire had sunk his teeth into her delicate flesh. She clutched the wound with her hand, trying to stop the flow of blood from draining out.

A burst of flames lit the room up showing as her misty green eyes saw the horrors in front of her. She watched the vampire draining her mother's life force, her blood dripping from his chin. The light slowly left her mom's eyes, eyes that were as green as hers.

In all seven years of life, she had never experienced something like this before and wasn't sure how to fight him. In the doorway lay Oren, her father. His blonde hair stained crimson red from the pool of blood he laid in. A huge gash slashed across his throat where the vampire had ripped it open. He tried his best to fight off the vampires, but he was not a warrior. He was simply a farmer. It had not taken long for the vampire to take her father out. She looked at her father's prone body, his blue eyes glazed

over, staring vacantly through her.

She looked up as the vampire came towards her. Blood dripping down his chin, his white shirt and tan pants drenched in the blood of her family, her clan, and herself. Her lip quivered, as tears welled up in her eyes, because she knew she would soon crossover and be with her parents. She tried to suppress the sob as fear clenched her chest. She was not ready to die. Her eyes never left the vampire's face as he approached her. She stared deep into those eyes as black as midnight as he continued to walk towards her.

Suddenly, the vampire stilled. His black eyes grew wide. Feya flinched as she glanced away as a sword pierced through the vampire's chest. As the sword was withdrawn from his heart the vampire fell to his knees. A fae warrior stood behind him. Dark red blood dripped from the sword to the ground to mix in with the blood splattered across the floor. The warriors had finally made it to Feya's village and her family's hut. The fae warrior stood there, covered in blood and cuts, his brown eyes weary. She doubted he noticed her before he ran out of the house, never looking her way. It did not matter though; she knew it was too late for her, as it was too late for her parents. Her family was dead, and she had been bitten. They would not let her live.

Feya sat for a moment and reached out to touch her mom's hand. It was growing cold fast. Her fingers trembled as she pulled her hand back.

Her head spun for a moment as she stood up. Slowly, she crept out of the house, looking both ways, in hopes no fae warrior or vampire would see her. She could hear the clanging of swords and screaming as she snuck out. She tried to stick to the shadows. The moonlight and flickering flames lit the path as she crept out to her friend's house.

She wanted to say one last goodbye to her dearest friend, Elwyn. The tears came hotter and faster down her face as she clutched her neck. She looked up at the moon, praying for guidance to the goddess Arianrhod.

Once a fae had been bitten by a vampire, their life would be ended in a sacrificial ceremony. They cannot cross over to

the other side and become a mix of fae and vampire. The horror stories the elders told of those who crossed over were nightmare filled. All the evil stories they had told her made shivers run down her spine. Stories filled with blood lust and rage, of half fae half vampire creatures killing anyone and everyone in sight as soon as the blood rage hits them. She was not sure how much time she had before she turned. The fear of what would happen, filled her with panic, her breath came out ragged.

The last of the vampires who had attacked her clan were being pushed out of town. Bodies of both vampires and fairies scattered the grounds throughout the village. Biting down on her lip to stay silent, she felt a trickle of blood slide down her chin. She focused on the path. She had just a small way more to go to say her last goodbye, then she would turn herself in to the elders.

She got to Elwyn's hut without being noticed. She covered her neck with her hair the best that she could, to hide the trail of drying blood. Looking down, her own blood soaked her white dress, making it look more red than white.

She tapped on the window and whispered Elwyn's name. A moment later, she saw his blue eyes peek out the window, then vanish. Fear clutched at her as she wondered if he would talk to her. The wait felt like an eternity as she watched to see if he would open the door. *What if he knew what had happened, and hated her?* She wondered. Silent tears welled up in her eyes.

It took only a moment before he opened the door and let her in. The hut was dark, no candles lit and no fire. The curtains were drawn making it even darker inside. His parents were gone to fight the hoard of vampires. Turning, she heard him closing the latches on the door and locking them in.

"Feya," he whispered, worriedly. "Why would you leave the protection of your house? You know better. What if something had hurt you coming here?"

"My pa… parents," she stammered, tears streaming down her face. Trying to finish the sentence, she swallowed, hoping to clear the lump building in her throat. She looked at her feet. The room was so dark she could not see her bare feet. "A… are dead."

"Feya." he whispered, pulling her into a bear hug.

He was two years older than her and her best friend. She started sobbing into his arms. Grief washed over her as she tried her best to stay quiet. His hand accidentally touched her neck. Wincing from the pain that shot from it, she pulled back.

He cast a spell, and a flicker of flame lit up his fingertip. His dark blue eyes shone in the flickering flames as she stared into them. His other hand brushed the hair away from her neck.

The tears came faster. Her breath was ragged and choppy. She knew that he would have to tell everyone. She did not blame him. It was what needed to be done before the blood rage took over her.

"Run." he whispered.

She looked up in surprise. "What?" she stammered.

"You need to run, and run now!" he whispered. "Go!"

He released the spell, and the room went dark. She followed him to the door. He opened it up. His hand clutched hers for a moment, before he released it.

"Stay safe, Fe." He whispered. She saw tears streaming down his face.

"I will, Elly." she whispered back.

Turning to leave, she felt the panic riding in her. Where would she go? What would she do when the blood rage hit her?

"Be extra careful," he said, looking around. Making sure no one was watching them, "Stay off the main road."

She nodded. He brushed his hand down her check. His eyes glistened with tears.

"I'll find you again one day, I promise," he whispered. "Go now before my parents come back."

She flitted out the door. She ran as fast as she could. Pausing a moment at the edge of the forest, she looked back at the village she had never left before. Some faes were putting fires out, some were tending to the wounded, and others were rounding up the faes who had been bitten by vampires. Turning before anyone saw her, she entered the forest. The oak trees

were a blur as she tried to get as far away as she could. When she could no longer run, she fell to the ground sobbing.

A million thoughts ran through her head as she ran. *Why would he let me go? What if the hunger hit me? Where would I go? How would I take care of myself? Will I need to kill to survive?*

Lost in the forest, she sobbed. Not sure where to go, or what to do. With each dark thought, a sob escaped her. She crawled to a great old oak tree, leaning on the tree for support. No longer able to stand, the adrenaline had left her. The loss of blood made her cold and her vision blurry.

She heard a branch snap. She looked up, startled; a vampire walking towards her.

This is the end, she mused. There was no way he would save a little fairy girl. Her life would be ending soon.

The vampire held out his hand, speaking softly, he said "Hey, little one. You're a long way from home."

She stared at his hand, then up at him, startled. His amber eyes glowing. He seemed gentle, but the fear gripping her made her wary.

"I won't hurt you, little one," His voice was so very soothing. "I am going to help you heal. My name is Aethelredd Ascelin. You are very special, little one. I'm going to take care of you. You don't need to be scared anymore."

"I am Feya," she whispered. Her voice felt hoarse from all the tears.

Was he going to drain the last of my blood? She thought, *should I try to fight? Can I even fight?*

He bent down and gently examined her neck. He sliced his hand open and smeared his blood on her wound.

"Won't that make the hunger come?" she stammered.

"No, little one," He whispered, "You are different. You need not worry. Open your mouth."

She obeyed his request. Fear wracked through her body, but she was more scared of death than him.

her mouth. Suddenly, a warmth spread through her body. She felt like she was floating. Her head spun with a dizzy euphoria. Then an intense pain wracked her body, like she had nothing she had ever felt before. The pain racing through her body caused her to black out.

He drizzled some blood into her mouth. "That wasn't so bad now, was it?"

She nodded, disgusted by the coppery taste that was left in

Chapter 2

When Feya woke, she was in bed, snuggled up under layers of blankets. A small fire was lit, warming the room and providing dim light. She looked around, confused about where she was. The four-poster bed she laid on was so comfortable. The blankets were very soft, she had never felt so comfy. Across from the bed was a dark wood dresser and wardrobe.

A breeze drifted in through the window. Taking a deep breath, she could smell the wet grass that wafted in through the windows. She missed the smells of the forest. Trying to sit up, she felt dizzy, falling back down onto the pillows.

"Don't get up, little one." Aethelredd said from the corner. She looked at him, startled. "You are at my manor. We have some people downstairs who would like to meet you. Do you think you would be up to it?"

Once the dizziness settled down, she nodded tentatively. He walked over to her and held his hand out. "If you feel scared or sick, just let me know. I am going to take care of you. This is your home now. You are part of my clan."

Slowly, she sat up, the dizzy sensation was lessening. She looked up at him with her big green eyes, filled with sadness and fear. She had so many questions she wanted to ask, but fear clogged her throat.

She slowly climbed out of bed. Looking down, she saw her blood-soaked dress was gone and in its place was a clean white nightgown.

Aethelredd held out his hand to her. Staring at it a moment before she grabbed it. Clinging to his side as they walked down the manor house stairs. She had never seen a house this big. She surveyed the dark red walls as they walked down. Paintings of various people littered the walls. A brown carpet runner covered the wooden stairs. At the bottom of the stairs was a grand entrance with a dusty chandelier. Hearing what sounded like a slight drumbeat in the room off to the right, startled her. Looking up, at Aethelredd in confusion.

"What is it, little one?" he whispered.

"Why are there quiet drums, Mr. Aethelredd?" She asked, confused.

Laughing, Aethelredd shook his head. "Those aren't drums. They are heartbeats. You can call me, Redd."

She nodded, confused why the quiet drums would be heartbeats.

A musty smell hung in the air, like the windows were rarely opened. She had been so accustomed to the fresh smells of the forest that surrounded their village. It was so strange not to smell it.

"We will decorate your room when you're up to it," he smiled at her. Shoulder length red hair fell over one of his cat shaped amber eyes. His cat-like smile spread across his face. His triangular jaw and Grecian nose shone in the firelight.

She looked back at her feet nervously. She didn't know if she should run or stay. *If I ran, where would I go?* She mused. Deciding to stay because she had nowhere else to go. She had never left her own town before. Had never gone past the edge of the forest. She rarely saw outsiders. The only people she had ever seen were her clan and the occasional visitor, which was usually another fairy.

"You ready?" he whispered.

She looked up and nodded. Unsure if she was ready or not. She clung to his hand, fear raging a war inside her as they entered the room.

"Hello, Cardinal Joseph." Aethelredd said.

Cardinal Joseph looked stern as he sat in front of the fireplace. He wore a red cloak that hung down to his feet. His face was stoic, brown eyes and brown hair. His plump face glistened in the firelight.

"What is he?" she mumbled.

"He is a human," Aethelredd said, laughing.

She had never seen a human before. She looked him up and down, trying to figure out what humans were like. He smelled like dusty old papers. The drumming noise sounded unsteady compared to Redd's. The human frowned at her. She hid further behind Redd's leg.

"How do you know you can train this little slip of a child? She doesn't look like she is worth the effort, even." The human asked, annoyed.

Burying her face in Aethelredd's leg, she hid from the human's cruel gaze. The fear winning, tears started rolling down her cheeks. She squeezed his hand tighter.

Then she noticed two other human men standing behind the human, hidden in the shadows. The firelight did not reach out to them.

Aethelredd laughed. "It will not be a problem."

The Cardinal looked at her, waved his hand dismissively. "Do as you wish, then. As long as she does not become a liability and you get the job done."

Aethelredd smiled down at her. She tentatively smiled back, her cheeks stained with tears. He picked her up, and she clung to his neck.

She listened as he talked to the cardinal and his men for a while longer. They discussed Aethelredd's next mission, to find a missing book. Soon, the cardinal and the two men left.

After they left, Aethelredd picked up Feya. He carried her over to the chair by the fire. Sitting down, he set her down on his lap. Picking up a book on the table next to the chair, he began reading her a story. She had only seen a book once before. The village elder had smacked her hand when she had reached out to touch it. Tentatively, she reached a finger out and gently touched the page.

Pulling her hand back, she looked up at him. He smiled down at her and tapped her nose with his finger. She no longer felt fear. She rested her head back on his shoulder and listened quietly until she fell asleep again.

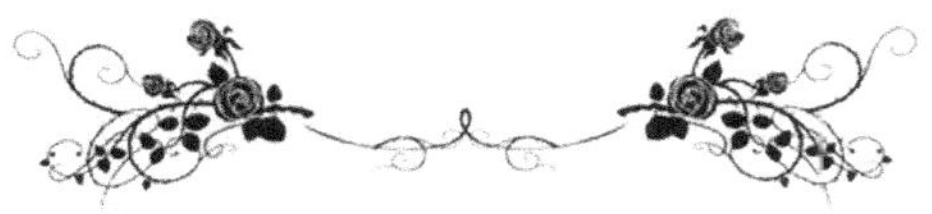

She woke up the next morning in her bed. The sun was out, she could see it through the crack in the window. It stung her eyes a bit. She felt restless. Not wanting to be in bed anymore, she jumped up, figuring she could explore the castle.

She stood up, catching a glance in the mirror, noticing her neck was completely healed. She walked closer to the mirror to get a better look. It was like they had never attacked her. No trace of the bite. She stood there a moment, looking at herself. Opening her mouth, she examined her canine teeth as she gritted her mouth. She thought they looked a little longer and sharper, but just barely. Touching her tongue to her canines, she realized they were sharper. Staring in the mirror a moment longer before turning away.

She snuck out to wander around the upstairs of the house. There were five bedrooms. No one was in any of them. The interior of the rooms was dark and somber. She went back to her room and noticed the sun was setting in the sky. She snuck a peek out the window.

Would I turn to dust if the sun hit me? She wondered.

Just in case, she closed the curtain fast Sitting there facing the curtain, her mind started drifting. She pictured her mother and father. Tears welled up in her eyes. She felt an overwhelming sadness.

She turned around and saw Aethelredd leaning in the doorway. He smiled down at her.

"Come down, little one," he said, then turned and walked

away.

She followed him down the stairs. To a dining room. A plate was set with eggs, toast, and bacon.

Tears slid down her face, as her mind wandered. From now on, she would only drink blood. She'd never have her mother's cooking or her dad sneak her a piece of candy.

"What's wrong, little one?" He asked. She shook her head.

He bent down and brushed her black hair out of her eyes. Her big green eyes glistened with tears as she pretended to be brave.

"Tell me." he said, gently.

"I can't eat food anymore," she started, then the tears started falling. "I miss my mom and dad."

He picked her up and rocked her for a while, comforting her.

"Remember when I said you were special?" He said, looking down at her.

She nodded.

"You are of two worlds now, little one." he said, laughter filling his voice. "Part fairy and part vampire is what you are. You are a part of my clan now. I will train you and keep you safe. You will eat normal food, but sometimes you will crave blood. I will teach you how to appease this appetite."

"Will I die if the sun hits me?" She whispered.

He laughed, "No, but it will hurt your eyes."

He rocked her for a moment longer. "Are you ready to eat?"

She nodded.

"We will start your training next week." He said. "Tonight we have some people coming by to show you some options to decorate your room."

"I get to pick?" she asked tentatively. Grabbing a piece of bacon, she started scarfing the food down. She had not realized how hungry she was. Trying to remember when she had last eaten. It was dinner before the vampire attack. Her mom had made a honey cake. It was her favorite treat and her mother would never make it for her again. Frowning, she looked back down at her toast.

"Yes, you do. Whatever you want." He smiled down at her. Tapping her nose gently.

She smiled back. A smile that did not reach her eyes.

Chapter 3

Feya sat tired. Aethelredd made her train all night long. Falling into her bed, her whole body was beyond physically exhausted, but her mind was running rampant.

It had been thirteen years since Aethelredd had adopted her. He was her sire and her father. She barely had memories of her birth parents. She tried to remember her mom's voice, her father's laughter. No memories came flooding back. She could no longer hear it. She was slowly forgetting them. A twinge of sadness went through her soul. Only vague memories came to her now. Sometimes she would see something, and think of them wistfully. Or the scent of a forest would remind her of the village she grew up in. She had few memories of the village and the people. She remembered Elwyn for his kindness, but the rest of the fae's faces were fading away.

Her life was nothing like her parents had planned for her. She wasn't sure the person she had become would like the life that had been planned out for her old self. But it did not matter. This was the life that was destined for her. She had trained for years for this, and she was ready for her first mission.

Her father, Redd, was finally taking her on her first mission tomorrow. Her father worked for the Vatican. A soldier of fortune. He and his ragtag band of misfits had made a family of their own. Misfits that their own clans had shunned.

Her father's entire clan had been wiped out during a war

long ago. Cardinal Joseph had brought him into the fold to work for the church. He had worked with them ever since. Feya, the youngest and the first Redd, had been brought into the fold. He had raised her since that day he found her in the forest.

The next one Redd brought into the family was a wolf shifter. He never talked about why he left his clan, just grumbled too many alphas. He was the biggest wolf shifter she had ever seen at 6'8" tall and broad shouldered. His blue eyes shone with a gentle kindness. He had wild gray hair and when he shifted, he had the softest gray fur. He was not someone you would call book smart, heck he could not even read. He was the strongest, most loyal magical creature she had ever met. Her uncle Leo Ascelin.

Then there was a fire witch, banned from her clan for refusing to obey an order that she decided was wrong. No matter how much Feya asked, she refused to tell her what it was. Her golden blonde hair hung down to her knees. Her golden eyes sparkled like fire. She was a sassy little firecracker at 5' tall. Her aunt Aguya Ascelin.

A human walked among them too, but he was not family. A guardian of the guild is what the church called him. A dour man, always serious. He wore the black cloak of his calling. His mousy brown hair and eyes. Eyes that always followed her, filled with annoyance. He stood a few inches shorter than her 5'8". Father Thomas.

Father said that human priests would come and go due to the nature of their life spans, and not to get attached to them. There was no possibility of that happening with Father Thomas. She despised everything about him. He would always frown at her and reprimanded her repeatedly.

Then there was her father, Aethelredd Ascelin. Everyone called him Redd. He had brassy red hair and amber eyes. He stood about four inches taller than her. Lean build, but scary strong when he was cross.

She would rest for the day. In the evening, she would go on her first mission for the Vatican. She was excited, which made it hard to sleep. Her mind was running a mile a minute. She tried to calm her thoughts, but the excitement would not go away.

She woke up the next evening refreshed and ready for the night. Stretching, she got up and got dressed. Corsets were the thing she hated most about fashion. She would never get used to this. Pulling the strings tight to her black corset. Even though her wings were bound with a spell, the corset still felt like it pinched them. Her father told her it was all in her head and that they would be fine.

She pulled on her black skirt and blouse. The puffy sleeves of the blouse billowed out. Quickly, she threw her long black hair up in a loose bun. She looked in the mirror at her rosy, pale complexion. She remembered her skin being a bit tanner before she transitioned. Probably from being in the sun all the time. Rarely did she go out during the day anymore. She would get blinding headaches from the sun. So she stayed with her father in the night. They all lived in the night. Their small dysfunctional family.

Her black hair made her skin look paler on her diamond shaped face. Her almond-shaped green eyes shone brightly in the candlelight. The corset made her slight hourglass figure more prominent. Her ample bosom squished a bit from the restrictive binding.

She went downstairs. So far, her father was the only one up. Breakfast was already on the table for her. She smiled at him lovingly. Every evening he made her breakfast, since the first day he brought her home.

"Let's go over the rules again." He started, "First…"

"Do we have to?" she interrupted him. Smiling her sweetest smile at him, while taking a bite of toast.

"First," he continued, gazing at her intently. "You are to stay behind one of us at all times. Second, if things get hairy, you fly your ass out of there. I don't give two shits who will see you. Third, be careful, don't wander off, and don't run your mouth. Fourth, do as you're told. Clear?"

"Yes, father." She muttered. Blah, blah, blah. He had said the rules so many times she could recite them in her dreams. "There is one minor problem though…"

Redd stared at her sternly, waiting for her to continue. She was determined to take her time. She loved to pick on her father whenever she could. Taking another bite of toast, she slowly chewed on it.

After a moment, he huffed. "Well?"

"Well," she sighed. "The corset is quite constricting. How will I get my wings out with it on?"

He stared at her, dumbfounded. She knew she would not fly off. She watched as Redd mulled over this new dilemma. The wheels turned in his head, as he tried to find a solution.

She could hear Leo's steps coming down the stairs, and smell his blood. She thought it was funny that she knew the smell of her family's blood, the sound of the heartbeats. One of the special traits she picked up after turning.

Father had hired a rogue fairy, Lena, to teach her as much about her fairy side. Plus, to learn as much as she could about magic before Lena left. Aguya was teaching her all about fire magic.

There was a long way to go and much to learn still. She didn't miss the fairy teacher. She was always so scared of Feya. It was no surprise when she disappeared one day.

She had been twelve years old when she saw Lena's wings. They were like gossamer, shimmered in the firelight. So delicate and soft, she had thought if she touched them, they would crumble. She had released the spell that bound her own wings as well and was so proud to show them off.

They were kind of more like bat wings. She had four wings. Each wing had arms that stretched across the top. A sheer green, gray membrane stretched between them. Before the change she had wings like Lena's, but they had changed after she turned. . She had gone through many changes that day. Her senses, her hearing etc. had changed.

She remembered thinking that her own wings were pretty.

Her dad, aunt and uncle told her how pretty and unique her wings were.

Lena had recoiled in disgust at her wings.

It wasn't till then she realized how different she was. Knowing that she would never fit in the fae world or the vampire world fully, made it hard for her. She was an outcast and would always be one. She tried to hide from her family how much it stung her. Not wanting them to know how insecure she felt about her wings and knowing she would never belong in either world truly.

She finished her food and heard Aguya's heartbeat coming closer, before she smelled her blood. She had such a quiet step. It was always so hard to hear her.

Grabbing part of the paper to see what human news was happening, nothing caught her interest, and she rustled through the page. She set it back down, frustrated.

"When do we set out?" Feya asked, looking at Redd.

"As soon as Father Thomas arrives." He said, reaching over to push a stray strand of hair that had come loose from Feya's bun.

He had tried his best to raise her to be a proper young lady, but failed. What was a bachelor of one hundred years to know about raising a girl? Her dress was askew, her hair fell out of the bun within minutes of her styling it. She was always finding new ways to sass everyone.

Since the day he took her in, he felt protective of her. He hadn't wanted to introduce her into this world, but the church was pressuring him. Figuring he would just take her on only the soft missions. Nothing that would put her in harm's way. She was his only sire, after all. Plus, he had no intentions of ever creating another sire.

He had promised he would not sire another after the war

where he lost his clan. Then he saw this tiny little creature run past him. Another vampire had bitten her, causing her to lose a lot of blood. She was weak and close to death.

She had been so small and tried to act so bravely. Her own blood saturated the white dress she wore. She had left a trail so strong, even a toddler could follow it. He had to get her out of the forest, and fast. Before they started hunting for her. Fae did not treat turnlings well.

All plans to recruit a new team were gone after that moment. He knew if she stayed with her tribe, they would have sacrificed her, or she would have died from blood loss in the forest. He could not let them hurt her.

Watching as the magic grew in her daily. Trepidation filled him as she had difficulty controlling her powers. Aguya could only show her so much. He needed to find a new fae to teach her. A fae who was not scared of them all. The last one he hired had damaged Feya's self-esteem. If the twat had not run off, he might have done something he regretted.

Most strays were a little dormouse or a hawk. Neither would work well with any of them. He was widening his net. She needed a teacher fast. She also needed a mother figure, since Aguya did not have a mothering bone in her body.

Looking up as Father Thomas walked into the room. He waited for the day that he could drink that bastard's blood. He was such an insufferable little prick. Always looking down his nose at them. Most of the people the church sent were.

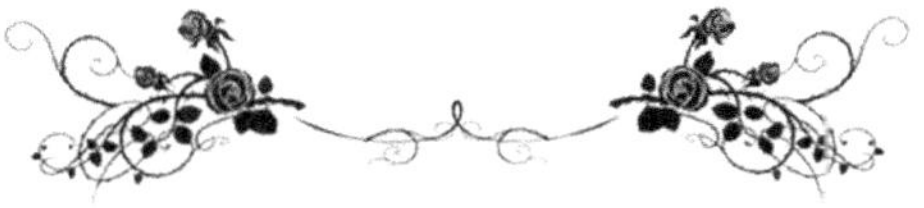

Feya stood behind her father. As he negotiated for the holy relic with a weaselly troll who kept looking over his shoulder to the right. She tried to sense if someone was there, but no scent of blood came to her. She could not hear any heartbeats, voices, or footsteps either.

Redd looked at the troll again and sternly said. "Give us the ring of Saint Edward."

Glancing back at her father, she could tell he was starting to get annoyed with talking to the troll. It was supposed to be a simple mission of a stolen holy relic. She knew he had chosen a simple assignment since she was there, but she didn't mind. She was happy to be part of a mission finally.

She smelled the stranger's blood as soon as he entered the building. Troll's blood smelled of elderberry. She wondered if she would like the taste of their blood. Would they taste like elderberries? She mused.

"Father," she whispered.

"I know, little one." Redd growled. "Looks like your friend has finally decided to join us. Does he have the ring?"

The weaselly troll shuffled from foot to foot. His eyes downcast to his hands. "I didna kno a thing about a ring or a frien comin." His thick cockney accent making it almost impossible to understand him.

Redd stepped closer to the troll. She could sense the anger radiating from her father. "Leo, go greet our guest."

Leo walked off to the right to greet the incoming troll. A second later, the troll came sliding across the floor on his belly. Redd stopped him by putting his foot on his back. The troll lay unconscious on the ground.

Maybe there will be some excitement after all, Feya thought. She took her gloves off to make casting easier if she had to. Her spells were too weak to cast without a little help. One day, she would not need her hands for her spells.

"Are you going to talk willingly or…" Redd growled.

She noticed the heat rising as Aguya powered up her flames. The troll's eyes grew as big as saucers as he looked up at Redd. The troll tried to take a step back, bumping into the wall.

She smelled the blood of the trolls long before she saw them or heard them. "More are coming. They aren't in the building yet."

She tried to focus on their heartbeats to count how many there were. "At least fifteen trolls, father."

"Get ready for rule two, little one." Redd said.

She bit her lip to hide her smile, knowing she wasn't going anywhere.

Redd grabbed the troll by his throat. She could sense the blood rage growing inside him. "Give me what we came for or else."

"It... it's in… in the basement." the weaselly troll finally said. His eyes filled with fear.

Redd smiled, then sank his teeth into the troll's neck. Drinking his fill. The smell of copper and elderberries filled her senses.

The thirst came to her, she closed her eyes for a second to control the urges racing through her. Opening her eyes again, she looked back at her father.

"Aguya," Redd said, blood dripping from his mouth. "Take Leo and search downstairs."

"I'd rather take Feya. She can cast a search spell and save us time." Aguya said. Her hair flew around her like fire licking the air. Sparks flew from her fingertips.

"No." Redd said. "She is flying her ass out of here."

Before he could finish the statement, Feya was already running down the stairs.

"Dammit, Feya!" Redd yelled. "Get your ass back up here immediately."

She got to the bottom and started her spell. Remembering the drawing of the ring she had seen, she closed her eyes for a second. She pictured the ring in her mind and felt the pull as she called forth to it. She went down the hall. Second door on the right. It sat in a pouch on the table. Scattered with other books. One caught her eye. It was a book of fae magic. She didn't have time to think, so she grabbed the book.

She knew her dad would be mad, but there was no way she was going to run from the battle. She would stand her ground.

Aguya was waiting for her at the bottom of the stairs. She

could hear the battle raging upstairs. She was fine until she entered the room and smelled the blood. All the blood. She felt the thirst swelling up inside of her. She was no longer able to control it.

Grabbing the closet troll, his back was turned to her. Sinking her teeth into his neck, she injected him with venom to paralyze him. She drank her fill. His blood had a slight taste of elderberries, after all. She let him go when she was done. Watching as he fell to the ground by her feet. She felt the strength that came after drinking blood. A rush of adrenaline coursing through her veins.

She was ready to fight. Looking up, she saw her dad was standing in front of her, with a disapproving glare. She was not getting the fight she had wanted; after all it seemed.

He scooped her up and ran out of the keep. Jumping into the carriage, they raced down the road to where Father Thomas was hiding. She stayed in the carriage, not wanting to get a disapproving look from Father Thomas once again. She knew her face and neck were drenched in the troll's blood. Looking down, so was the front of her shirt. At least the black hid most of it. He would not think a lady should be covered in blood, no matter the reason.

Through the window, she could see that Redd gave him the ring in a small bag. Clutching tight to the book, she smiled to herself. At least one good thing would come from the trouble she was going to be in. She had dropped it during the melee, covering it in blood now. Trying to clean it off, she used part of her skirt that was dry to wipe it. It kind of helped. She wanted to open it up and read it, but was scared she would smear blood on the inside of the book.

Redd got back into the carriage, soon after Aguya and Leo joined them. Everyone stayed quiet the rest of the way home. She knew he would yell at her when they got home. Until then, she would relish the quiet. Looking through the window, she watched as the countryside flashed by. Doing everything she could to avoid eye contact with her father.

Chapter 4

Feya opened her curtains to look out of her hotel room. The sun was rising, just a peek above the skyscrapers. She surveyed the skyline of New York from the window. The orange rays surrounding the dark buildings.

She spent so much time in the night, she sometimes forgot how beautiful the sunrise was. The light rays painted the skies vividly behind the buildings. Splashes of oranges, reds and yellows painted the sky like a Monet painting. Staring intently, she sipped her chamomile tea, admiring the display.

They had just finished their latest mission just a few hours ago. She was enjoying the quiet before her nap. Dad had told her there was to be a few weeks off. They could all use the vacation. It had been back-to-back missions for the last couple of months.

The skyscrapers appeared to touch the heavens as the color of flames licked them. She took a long sip of her chamomile tea. Twirling the golden brown liquid in her cup, watching as it swirled.

She knew Aguya would be here soon. Aguya wanted to go shopping for clothes. At least she had time before that to take a nap. Dad would be asleep all day. No matter how long she had been alive, it still hurt her eyes to be in the sun, but with sunglasses, it made it easier. As long as she kept the sunglasses

on, the headaches stayed at bay.

Turning from the window, she went to rest.

A few hours later, Aguya came knocking on her door. Feya was already dressed and ready to go. Dark jeans and a band tee that had seen better days, she could not even remember which concert she had gotten it at, or if the band was even still together. Her jet black hair fell in waves around her shoulders. Her pale skin looked like porcelain, with her rosy cheeks. She put on a bit of mascara to highlight her green eyes.

"Is Brady going?" Feya asked.

Aguya sighed and nodded.

Feya winced, knowing the struggles to come. Brady was a fairy that Redd had found to train her. She was a boxy little thing. Brady would always stop to look at a shiny object, figuratively speaking, of course. A minute later, her red curly hair bouncing over her ample bosom, entered the room. Her light gray eyes sparkling. She brightly smiled at them.

A hoard of vampires had wiped out Brady's tribe. When she first arrived, she had been iffy around Redd, but had taken Feya in like she was her own child. Sometimes it was like having four parents, two moms and two dads.

"I am ready when you guys are." Brady said.

Feya stood up and put her sunglasses on.

Aguya took another sip of her coffee, her eyes shooting daggers at Brady already. Feya noticed the flames of annoyance coming off of her. Aguya didn't mind Brady, unless they were going shopping. Aguya had very little patience for anyone. Where Brady was always wanting to amble about and would get shiny objects at the drop of a dime.

They walked outside and went to a nearby shopping district. Feya liked to look at all the colors and designs in the window displays. She rarely went out during the daylight. It was a wonder to see these things without all the false lights shining on them. Everything always seemed much more vibrant during the day, in the natural light.

Aguya and Brady bickered as they walked next to her. She

kept on walking faster, trying to get away from them. Her long strides made it easier to escape the squabbling.

A boutique that had some silk blouses in the window display caught her attention. Debating if she should go inside to buy a blouse, she chewed on her lip.

Then she caught a scent, a scent mixed in among the many human smells. A smell she had not smelt in a while. Blood that smelled like a mix of strawberries, jasmine and plums. It was fairy blood.

Faes rarely went into big cities often. They tended to stay close to nature, forests, and jungles, anyplace where there were fewer humans. She turned around, searching through the throngs of people. Looking among the humans who were walking and talking was a feat.

It took her a moment to see him. He had been watching her from across the street. From the look of it, he had been in a fight recently. Bruises and cuts covered his arms and face. Her eyes locked with his dark blue eyes and then recognition set in.

"Elwyn," she whispered.

He smiled at her and winked.

Aguya grabbed her arm, spinning her around. "I am done. I can't shop with her. It is like walking with a snail." When she was angry or frustrated, her Baltic accent would come out. "She is slow, and she argues about…"

"Just a moment," Feya said, interrupting her. Turning, she searched the crowd for Elwyn, but he was nowhere to be found. She couldn't even smell him anymore.

Brady caught up to them. "Why are you always in such a hurry?" She asked Aguya, exasperated.

"Why don't you two go back to the hotel?" Feya said she wasn't ready to leave. She wanted to track Elwyn down.

Why was he hurt? She wondered. Why did he not have a fae healer tend to his wounds? How had he found her after all these years?

"Brady," Aguya said. "She is right, you should go home."

Feya searched for his scent, but could not find it. Her nose was not as good as Uncle Leo. It was hard to track it down in the middle of so many humans. Right when she was about to give up, she caught the scent. She looked over to a bench where he was waiting for her, Elwyn Altalune. When she caught sight of him, he smiled at her.

"Feya," he said, standing up. "You're all grown up."

"Thanks to you," she said. She surveyed his face. She had never thought she would look into those deep blue eyes again. "You've done some growing over the years, too."

Running his hands through his tousled chestnut brown hair. His dark blue eyes sparkled with laughter at her, his blackened eye making the color pop even more. A chiseled rectangular chin had matured him since they were kids. Accentuated by his busted lip, his smile was a little lopsided. He towered over her by at least eight inches. A muscular build emphasized by the tight black shirt he wore. His jeans fit snugly and taut. The smell of a citrusy cologne he wore wafted back to her over the scent of his blood.

"I am glad you got away safe," he whispered.

Smelling Aguya and Brady coming towards them, and knowing she wanted to talk to him privately, she grabbed his hand and started dragging him away.

Warmth spread from his hand to hers, causing a jolt of electricity to shoot through her from the touch of their palms. She gently let his hand go, confused by this feeling. Biting her lip, she looked back to see if the girls had caught up with them. So far, they had not.

"They are coming. Let us walk and talk." she said. Looking over her shoulder, she knew they were still a ways away. "How have you been?"

"Good. You?" he said, smiling at her.

"Good." She laughed.

Excitement washed through as she looked at him. She had not realized how much joy she would get from seeing him. It had been a while since she wondered what had happened to him. Every once in a while, a thought of him flashed into her mind.

Wondering if he was alright, happy, married and so forth.

Walking quietly for a few blocks, they twisted and turned through the streets to lose her tails. They stopped at a coffee bar and sat at a booth away from the window. She sat watching the door. She wasn't sure how much time she had before they found her. After all these years, they were still very protective of her.

Sitting across from her, he rested his elbows on the table. Looking into his blue eyes, nostalgia washed over her. A flood of memories came back. Remembering the times they played together in the forest, her birth father sneaking them candy, running wild through the village, and him saving her life.

Looking away, she wondered where to start the conversation. They hadn't seen one another in a long while.

"I told you I would come back for you one day," he said.

Startled, she looked back at him. "Yes, you did." she laughed.

"Sorry it took so long," he said. "How are you? What have you been up to?"

"Doing good," she said, twisting her hands in her lap nervously. "I have been working with my father. I mean the father who adopted me. Ummm… his name is Aethelredd. People call him Redd. Ummm… yeah. What about you? What have you been up to?"

She felt foolish for stuttering so much. Plus, she hated explaining what they did for a living to people. Most looked down on mercenaries, even if most of their jobs came from the church. Since it came from the church, some looked down even more.

"I have seen better days." he laughed. A self-deprecating grin spread across his face.

"I can see that." She said, laughing back. "What happened to your face?"

"Someone in the fae court has hired henchmen to kill me," he grumbled, as his face lost all the laughter and became more serious. "I have been keeping tabs on you and your family for a while."

"Oh?" she said, confused.

"I need to hire you and your family to find out who is trying to kill me," his eyes filled with rage and anger.

She felt disappointment hit her like a brick. Sighing, she looked away. The disappointment she felt knowing he wasn't here to just see her hurt more than she had thought.

Tilting her head back, she closed her eyes. It was time to treat this like the business transaction that it was. Taking a deep breath, to steady herself. She sensed Leo was coming for her. Hearing his strong heartbeat mixed in with humans. Smelling the earthy, musky smell of his blood approaching. She had been gone too long. After all these years, Dad was still protective.

"How much?" She said her voice was ice cold.

He seemed startled by the change. "How much what?"

She smiled a bitter smile, leaning forward. "How much are you going to pay us?"

She heard Leo's heart rate racing thirty seconds before he stormed in. She waved at Uncle Leo nonchalantly. He walked over to lurk over them.

She patted the bench next to her. Leo sat down, quietly. His bulky frame pushed her up against the wall.

"Well?" she said.

Annoyance crossed his face before he spat, "Half a mil' for two weeks of your time."

"I will get back to you after I discuss this with my associates," she said coldly.

"You do that," he said, anger radiated through his voice.

"Once we have made our decision, where can we reach you?" she said icily.

He gave the hotel name and room before standing up and leaving.

Sadness clenched her chest. Confused as to why, she had always figured they would never see each other again. So being this upset was puzzling her. Shaking her head to brush the thoughts away, she looked over at Leo. His stern expression caused her to roll her eyes.

Leo stood up and looked down at her. "You should not have wandered off like that."

She sighed, knowing that Brady had woken her father up, if they had sent Leo to search for her.

"I can handle myself," she mumbled. "I don't need you to babysit me."

"Redd will refuse his deal," he said sternly. "You are never to talk to him again. He is fae, you know the rules."

Leo stood up, walking out of the cafe. Just expecting her to follow along. She debated staying here and ordering food instead of following, just to be ornery. Sighing, she stood up, complying instead.

Her feet felt like lead as she slowly trudged behind Leo to the hotel. Dreading the discussion to come.

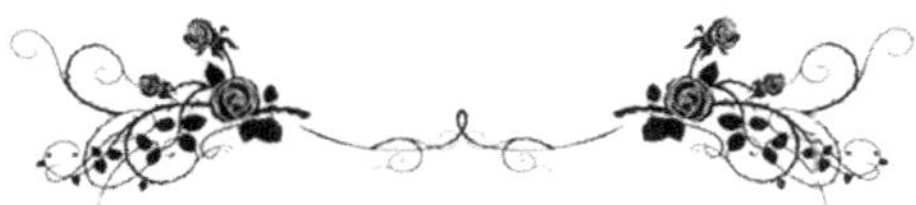

Elwyn watched them leave the cafe. He stayed upwind. That way, the wolf shifter would not smell him. Every time he had observed them, it had been from a distance. When Leo, the wolf shifter, had walked up to them, it had surprised him. He felt off guard. Seeing the shifter from a distance did no justice to how big he was. He was the biggest shifter he had ever seen.

He knew the moment he had angered her. He regretted being so forthright. How could he tell her the truth? Two years ago, he had seen her. He had been dealing with this bloody war that was on the cusp of starting in the court. He had not wanted to bring her into this mess. The situation was escalating. He needed the help of her family to find out who was after him and the queen's men.

He would gain her trust and make her understand what was going on. He needed to find out who was trying to take him down. End this war that had been brewing first. He sighed,

Turning, he walked back to his hotel. He would take some time to figure out a plan of action.

Chapter 5

Feya followed Leo to her father's hotel room. She looked into her father's amber eyes, seeing the rage and anger burning in them. Sighing, she straightened her shoulders to gear up for the argument. No matter how old she got, he still knew how to make her feel like a disobedient child.

"What the fuck were you thinking?" Redd yelled. As he paced the room like a restless tiger. His red hair was a tousled mess since they had woken him up early. "You know better than to wander off with a fairy. A fairy!! Was there any thought in that brain of yours that said this might be a bad idea? Did you forget what the hell they would do to you if they find out what you are?"

"No." she muttered, rolling her eyes. "Elwyn…"

"I don't care who he is!" Redd interrupted. "You know the rules. We do not take jobs with any fae folk. We do not associate with the fae. At all costs, we avoid fae."

Leo coughed.

"What?" Redd turned to Leo, frustrated.

"He wants us to do a job, for half a mil. He asked her to talk with us." Leo muttered. Looking down at his feet as he tried to fade into the background. Shuffling back and forth nervously, Leo glanced up at Feya quickly.

Feya felt frustrated that Leo would throw the info out, then try to run away to hide. Glaring at Leo, she hoped he sensed her displeasure at him.

Redd turned his gaze back to her.

"No." he whispered. The whisper held more power than the yelling he had done.

"Hear me out!" She said, frustrated. Glancing back at Leo, she gave him a look filled with the betrayal she felt. He was slowly making his way to the door. She wondered how he could abandon her so easily. Especially after throwing her under the bus like he did.

"No." Redd said.

"He is the fairy that…" Feya started, frustrated. Wishing he would listen to what she had to say. She knew it was pointless, but she tried anyway.

"No." Redd said. "You will not see him again. You will not talk to him again. As we have discussed before, you will avoid all fae folk. This is for your safety, little one. I don't care who he is or where he came from, I only care that you are safe. The best way to keep you safe is to keep you from fae folk. Do you understand me?"

"Just hear me out!" Feya exclaimed. Her voice filled with frustration that her father would not listen to her side of the story. Hoping she could get him to understand that Elwyn already knew what she was. Her anger at Elwyn was gone for the moment, and replaced with frustration with her father.

"No." he growled. Slicing his hand in the air to end the conversation.

She sighed, knowing that she would not win this battle. There wasn't any talking to him when he was this angry. Best to give in and talk when he was calmer. Just walk away, she told herself, try again later.

"Sure." she mumbled.

"Do you?" he yelled again.

"Yes!" she yelled back. Her hands clenched into fists at her side.

"Good." he yelled. His amber eyes filled with anger. "Go to

your room and do not leave without myself or Leo. Alright?"

Turning before she rolled her eyes again. It seemed like they would never comprehend she was an adult, no matter how old she got.

"Feya?" Redd growled.

"What?" she said, stormily. Turning back to her father.

"I said, alright?" Redd growled. "Do you understand?"

Rolling her eyes to his face this time, she said, "Sure."

Storming out of the room, slamming the door shut as she exited. Hoping the door slam would bring her some relief, it did not. Her anger and frustration were still there. She went to her own hotel room.

Feya paced in her hotel room. The room felt so small as she stormed back and forth. Restless after the ass chewing she had received. She was a grownup and yet they treated her like a delicate little butterfly still. No matter how old she was she would always be considered an adolescent.

She had proven herself in battle after battle as being capable. Yet she will always be treated like the child of the group.

She stopped pacing for a moment and closed her eyes. Seeing his eyes, his smile, and his dimples so vivid in her mind. She couldn't get Elwyn out of her head. He was haunting her thoughts. It stung that he had come to her for her family to do a job, and not just to see her.

Sighing, she started pacing again. He was her childhood hero and crush. No wonder she had these unresolved emotions for him. If she was around him long enough, the affection would fade away. Sure that once she got to know the grownup Elwyn, she would probably just end up disappointed. At which time, she would return to being herself again.

She debated the job Elwyn had offered. Her father would never accept it in a million years. He had told her she was forbidden from seeing Elwyn or any other fairy. Her father was always careful around other fairies, and magicals that he introduced her to. As far back as she could remember, he was overprotective of her. He feared they would find out she was a half blood, a turned one, and would have her executed.

She had to admit it was a fear she also had. On one occasion, she got to see firsthand what they did to a fairy that a vampire had bitten. The vision of it burned in her mind for all her days. She thought Elwyn would not do that to her. She owed him her life. He could have turned her in that night, but he did not. He had looked at her so gently. She knew he had no intention of hurting her.

Sighing, she flung herself onto the bed. Staring up at the ceiling, her thoughts were chaotic. She owed him her life. She would have let them kill her, if he had not told her to run. That night she would have turned herself in, to being tortured to death by the faes. His words and actions saved her life. Plus, learning that all the fables of halflings were untrue made it easier.

What if she helped him out? That would solve two problems she had. Get him out of her head and prove she could be around faes and magicals without getting caught. She could just sneak out to help him and not tell anyone. Maybe prove once and for all that she could hold her own out in the real world. That she did not need to spend her entire journey in life hiding in the shadows. She could control her blood lust. That she could act normal, just like other faes.

How would she escape, even? This was a stupid idea. She would have to tell him no. Maybe she could offer one of father's homes as sanctuary to Elwyn.

Then I could visit him and… and what? Feya mused. Magically get over her affection once she got to know him? See that he is not the magnificent male that she remembered from her childhood.

Wishing she didn't owe him would make things so much easier. She should just turn it down, like her father had yelled. *More like dictated,* she thought.

Jumping up, she decided to sneak out to get some dinner. There were a few hours until the sun went down. She stood by her door, closing her eyes while listening for their heartbeats. Smelling for their blood.

Her father was in his room, pacing. Obviously still irritated

with her. Aguya was in her room, resting. A long day of ratting people out must have made her tired. Brady and Leo were in Brady's room. It seemed like they were talking.

She quietly opened her door. Her shoes in her hand as she creeped down the hallway to the elevators. Looking down the hall, she listened again for the heartbeats as she pushed the button to go down.

She jumped, startled, when the doors opened. Almost squealing in shock before her hand clamped over her own mouth. Surprised to see Elwyn walking out of the elevator.

Pushing him back into the elevator, she pushed the button for the first floor. She glared at him as the elevator doors closed.

"What are you doing?" she whispered. "My father will kill you if he finds you running around here. Do you have a death wish, or are you stupid?"

"How about stupid?" he laughed. "I came up to see you. I figured we could spend some more time getting to know one another."

Deadpan, she mumbled. "You shouldn't have. I told you I would let you know the answer when everything had been decided."

Slipping her feet into her sandals, as the elevator took them down. Once the elevator doors opened, she hurried to the front doors.

"You can go back to your hotel now," she said, exasperated. "We will reach out to you once we have made a decision."

Deciding she would just pretend he wasn't there, she walked outside, ignoring his presence. Earlier, she had seen a burger joint down the street. She could go for a burger right now. Make some time for herself to sit and think.

The sunlight reflecting off the windows of the buildings hurt her head as she realized she had forgotten her sunglasses. The sun would be down soon, at least.

She felt him following behind, but continued to pretend he was not there. Hoping he would take the hint and leave her

alone. She just wanted a few moments of peace and quiet, before spending the night being lectured.

Entering the burger joint, the waitress greeted them and walked them to a table. The table was old, the gray laminate chipped and faded. The dark blue bench was well worn from overuse, the color a graying blue in spots. Sitting on the bench, she sank down and watched as Elwyn sat across from her.

So much for tranquility and silence, she thought. Glaring at Elwyn before glancing around. Most of the tables were filled with humans. The noise sounded deafening with the headache that she had brewing. Glaring at Elwyn again, as he continued to grin at her as if he was an idiot.

"How long until someone finds us?" he asked, leaning on the table, resting his elbows. His smug grub was getting on her nerves. "Maybe we have time to catch up? Talk about old times, new times."

"Are you obtuse, or am I not making myself clear?" she said, frustrated.

"I'll go with obtuse," he said calmly. He leaned back in the bench, his smirk coming across extremely cocky. "So the night your parents died, so did my father. It was quite the battle. Your parents had a beautiful funeral pyre. So did you, for that matter. Everyone loved your parents and you. They had such nice things to say. Everyone thought you died. I never spoke up or told them otherwise."

"Oh…" she muttered. A twinge of guilt hitting her. She had not thought about what might have happened to others, or the impact of that night. She had been so absorbed in her own loss, her own fears. "I am sorry for the loss of your father."

"It was rough for a long time," he said, the laughter gone from his voice. A bittersweet smile crossed his face. "I lost him and I lost you."

She stared down at the menu in front of her. At a loss for words, she tried to focus on what to eat. Muttering the only words she could think of, "Your father was a great man."

He laughed a quick, dead laugh. She looked at him, about

to ask more, but the waitress showed up.

"My name is Michelle and I'll be your waitress. Whatchya guys havin'?" she said, in her soft southern twang. Her blonde hair bounced in the ponytail as she tapped her foot to the music playing on the jukebox.

Feya glanced back at Elwyn before telling the waitress her order. "Cheeseburger and fries. Rare. Strawberry milkshake, too, please."

"I'll have the same, but medium." Elwyn said, handing the waitress the menu.

Sensing his eyes on her, she looked up. The moment her eyes locked with him, the bolt of electricity shot through her. For a moment she forgot herself, her anger at him, everything. Their eyes locked for what seemed like an eternity to Feya.

Feya turned away, embarrassed, her cheeks flushing. Not sure what to say or do anymore. Her thoughts and emotions were a jumbled mess.

"I've thought about you over the years." he whispered. His blue eyes searched her face.

The blush spread down her neck. Smiling a half smile, she said. "I thought about you too." she mumbled. Trying to not say too much about the war going on inside her mind.

He laughed. "Even if your family doesn't help. I'd like you to come visit me sometime."

She searched his eyes, trying to see if he was sincere or not. All she saw was sincerity. She wanted to agree and mean it, but she knew her family would never allow that. Breaking the rules would be the only way she would see him.

"That would be nice." she said. Her mind wandered back to the thought of: what if she took the mission herself? Prove she could handle herself. Payback for the debt she owed him. Get rid of this nervous feeling he caused her to have. Then go back to her normal life. Her father would have a fit if she did that. Sighing, she looked down at her hands in her lap.

"How is your mother?" she asked. She needed a few moments to think about what she should do. Collect her thoughts.

She listened, as he talked. Telling stories of the people she grew up with. Not remembering most of the people, having vague memories of others. She enjoyed hearing the tales of the people from their village. It made her feel nostalgic for a time and place she had thought long dead.

The waitress dropped their food off at the table.

"Tell me what you have been up to?" he said, swirling a fry in ketchup.

"Father found me in the woods that night," she started tentatively. Not sure how much she should tell, or even what she should tell. "He took me to his home and raised me. He likes to adopt strays. Magicals that have no clan or have been abandoned by their people. He took us all in and we became a family."

"You seem like you're happy," he said, smiling. "I am glad he found you. I worried about you for the longest time. Sending you in the forest that night was the only thing I could think to do. I had nightmares that you got hurt, or worse."

"It was a scary time for us all." she said, reminiscing. "I barely remember much from before that. I always remembered you and what you did for me. You saved my life that night."

"We were both quite young," he said softly. "And I would save your life all over again if I had a choice. I never once regretted that."

"If I take this job," she said. The words coming out before she had fully formed the thought, surprising her. "I will need full disclosure of everything you have."

Knowing her family would be mad, but maybe it was time to see what she could do on her own. See if she could complete a mission on her own, instead of always being the child who was dragged along. She had been hiding in the wings for so long for fear of what might happen. Only being taken on certain missions that her father thought would be safe.

Debating if she should go back to get her belongings, or just buy what she needed. Not going back meant getting all fresh supplies and not having to sneak out again. If she bought what she needed, she could get cash out. She would have to not use any of her cards until she was ready to be caught. She would need to turn her cell off. Use runes to hide herself from tracking spells. This would be quite the undertaking. The irony is, it is all the tricks her father taught her to keep her safe.

It was decided she would go shopping as soon as the sun came up and the stores opened. She would get what she needed, and grab as much cash as she could. Hopefully, they would forgive her and understand when it was all said and done.

She needed to prove herself to them and more importantly, herself. She could blend in with the fae, could pretend she was a normal run-of-the-mill fae. All she had to do was not go into a blood rage, hide her wings, and not forget her sunglasses. That should all be easy enough.

"Alright," he said, his blue eyes twinkling in the lights.

Chapter 6

Feya and Elwyn left the restaurant to go back to his hotel. She followed a few steps behind, calculating what she needed to do next.

Feya turned her phone off so they could not use it to track her. Nerves and excitement battled inside of her. She took out a pen she had in her purse, writing a rune on both of her wrists to hide her from vision spells. This was the first time she had done something like this. She had never been on a mission without her family. Scared she would fail, and excited about the new mission all at once. Part of her was excited to be with Elwyn as well. She closed her eyes and pushed that thought away.

Once in the room, she asked. "Well, tell me what you know?"

"Are you sure you don't want to tell your family about this?" he asked, softly.

His eyes gently locked with hers, noting the concern in them. Did he also not think I could do this? She wondered.

"They will just get in the way," she said, coldly. Raising an eyebrow. "Plus, how would you get any of them through the fae vale? Would the fae be happy to have a vampire, a fire witch, and a wolf shifter in their midst? I bet that would go over well."

He nodded and sat on the edge of the bed. Staring down at his feet, he patted the spot next to him. "Get comfortable. I will tell you what I know."

She looked around and decided the chair in the corner was a better spot to sit. She kicked her shoes off and curled up in the chair. The idea of sitting next to him had sent a thrill through her. She knew she needed to get her emotions under control.

Sighing, he stared at her for a moment before starting. "After my father's death, my mother remarried. He was a duke, right hand to king Buer and queen Cassada, Healfdene Gadelica. A few years ago, the king passed away in a tragic hunting accident during the hunt for the golden deer. His horse bucked him and he landed amongst a group of riders, he was trampled to death. The best healers were called in, but none could save him. Since then, there has been some talk of an uprising for the last couple of years. Many were upset that he gave the queen the throne instead of her son or another male. Many are stuck in their old ways and don't see what good she has done. They think a male should hold the throne and rule us. About three months ago, Healfdene was poisoned."

"I am sorry for your loss." Feya said, softly. Watching his nervousness made her want to reach a hand out in comfort.

He nodded, his hands twisting nervously in his lap, as he continued his story. "It devastated Mom. She stayed in her room for weeks, mourning, barely coming out. Since then, the talk of an uprising has gotten louder. Two weeks ago, the queen's cousin, Bayard, was murdered in a hunting accident. It was too much of a coincidence knowing how the king himself died. It was also at the annual hunt for the golden deer of luck. Bayard had left the pack to hunt the deer alone, and we found him with an arrow through his throat. The arrow did not belong to anyone in the hunting party. The feathers do not match any known clan either. We could not figure out who was in the shadows orchestrating this. Rumblings of a war have gotten stronger since. Last week someone attacked me in my room. It seems I am next on the list..."

"Is that where your wounds are from?" Feya asked, when he paused for a breath. Examining his wounds, most seemed superficial.

"Yes," he muttered. "Do not worry about me. The other fae did not fare as well."

Laughing, Feya nodded. She was glad Elwyn did not get hurt too badly. Though she doubted he would tell her if he had. She wanted to ask why he himself had not gone to a healer, but wanted to know the rest of what was going on more

"We have been racking our brains, sending out spies, and so forth. The list is long for those who would love to take the throne." He stopped, looking at his hands as he unclenched them. "I need your help to find who is trying to start a war with the queen, who killed my stepfather, who is after me, and who killed Bayard. Your family has hunted down betrayers of the church in the past. I was hoping your experience would help us find out who our unseen enemy is."

He looked at her, his eyes searching hers. "I need you to be careful, though. I would hate myself if you got hurt."

Feya turned away from him, laughing. "This isn't my first mission. You shouldn't worry about me. I have been in many battles and know how to take care of myself. I was in training a week after I left our village. This is nothing out of the ordinary for me. So why has the queen chosen you? Are there other fae hunting the perpetrator?"

She looked out the window for a moment before turning back to him. "Do you have a list of who you think did this somewhere, or are you going to recite it?"

He laughed. "Promise you'll be careful?"

Rolling her eyes, she ignored the comment. "The list please."

"The promise, please?" He said, sternly. A false frown spread across his face. It was so easy to fall under that charming spell, but she knew better than to let that happen.

Raising her eyebrow, she stared at him for a moment, hoping he would give in. He was more stubborn than she remembered. Relenting "Sure." she shrugged. All the while knowing she would do what she needed to do to get the job done.

"That's not much of an answer," he mumbled.

She shrugged. "I answered."

He sighed and looked away. "The first one is Eleazer, Lord

of the northern clan Frecia. He has been fighting every decision the queen has been making since the king's death. Every time the queen's court is in session, he will talk over her, belittle her decisions, and so forth. He has been open with his attacks. So I don't think it is him, but he is worth looking into."

Running both his hands through his hair he paused for a moment. "Next we have Raisa of Clan Anaris. She was upset when the queen refused to marry her to the queen's eldest son. Her anger and hatred has been boiling over lately. She has made some veiled threats. Constantly smearing the queen behind her back. Someone previously accused her of murdering her husband, but no proof could be found, so charges were dismissed."

"Then there is Reece Pellings of Clan Ailil. He has started several skirmishes, but always straightforward with his anger at the regiment. When the bi-annual meeting of the clans is in session, he will start fights with anyone he can piss off." He stood up and started pacing around the room.

Pausing a moment at the window, he stared at the dark skyline before continuing. "Aelfric Tyronoe of Clan Lutin made several passes towards the queen after her husband's death. She has turned down all his advances. He seems bitter about it and doesn't hide his resentment. Mostly childish behavior. He has quite a vast army at his beck and call. He has spent years growing it and training them to be quite a force to be reckoned with."

He walked away from the window, stopping in front of her. Looking down at her in the chair, he searched her eyes. She tried to think what he could possibly be looking for within her eyes.

His voice lowered. "Last and not least, Nerine Irodiada of clan Cvilidreta."

She waited for him to continue, but he just stared at her.

"Is that supposed to mean something to me?" she asked cautiously. Searching her memory, she tried to see if anything came to her. No sense of recognition came to her at the name.

"She is your mother's cousin." he said softly.

"I still don't remember her," she shrugged.

He laughed. "She has always wanted to be the queen herself. Several failed attempts at marriages and affairs with high-ranking members of the court have gotten her nowhere. She even tried to start an affair with the king himself right before his death."

"That's it?" she said, skeptically.

"No, not by a long shot." he laughed nervously. "Those are just the top ones on our list. Plenty of people hate the queen and her rule. We are just having trouble linking any to these murders. These are some people who attended the hunt, but anyone could have entered the forest and killed Bayard, to be honest. We have brainstormed over this time and time again. We have suspects, but no one who stands out. None that can be linked to both murders."

She nodded. "If you think of anything else, please let me know. What about those that attacked you?"

"He died from his wounds before I had a chance to question him." Elwyn said, laughing.

"Alright." Feya said. Staring down at the floor, as she processed all that he had told her. "I want to run some errands as soon as the sun rises. I need to pick up some things for the journey."

"You want company?" Elwyn said, smiling tentatively.

"Umm…" she said, uncertainly. Glancing up, her eyes locked with his. "Sure, if you want to join."

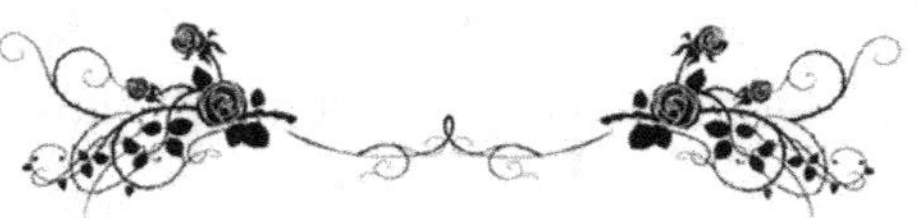

As soon as the bank opened, she was there withdrawing cash. Grabbing enough cash to travel and buy all her luggage and supplies with. She would have to use magic to pass off her travel passport as a random name. She would need one that they could not associate with her and one that was common, like Sandra Smith or something.

The teller handed her the cash she needed. Leaving the bank, she knew she needed to get a pair of sunglasses soon. She did not want to be in misery by the time they started on the plan.

Elwyn waited across the street for her to leave the bank. His cheery smile made her attitude grumpier. All last night they had discussed what he had known was happening. After a while, they each retired to one of the two queen beds in the room.

She had found it hard to sleep all night. Tossing and turning. She should have been tired since she had hardly slept during the day. Her normal routine was off, and she felt a bit exhilarated. Trying to tamp down the feelings so she could focus on the task at hand. She looked both ways, then walked across the street to where Elwyn stood waiting.

She turned her phone on one last time. It started dinging with alerts. Everyone was looking for her. Seeing the worried messages, she closed her eyes and blocked it out of her mind.

She sent one last text before she turned her phone off again. She went to the group chat with her family and sent it.

I am fine and am taking a vacation for a couple of weeks. Don't look for me. I'll see you back home soon.

She turned her phone off. Knowing that the text probably wouldn't help much, but she sent it anyway. They would not believe she was on vacation. Hopefully, they would stress less, knowing she was safe at least.

The sun shone on Elwyn, highlighting the lighter streaks in his brown hair. His smile made her heart skip a beat. Shaking her head to brush the thought away, she needed to quit letting his charm and handsome looks distract her from what she was doing.

"I need to get some clothes, toiletries, and stuff," she said as she walked up next to him. They walked down the street quietly until they got to a pharmacy.

He followed quietly as she went through the makeup and skin care aisles. Aguya had taught her years ago how to make

her own skin care products, but there wasn't time for that. She picked some randomly, hoping they would work for the time being.

"Clothes next?" he asked, looking down at her. Something in his eyes made her breath catch.

"Yeah." she breathed.

She watched as he hailed a cab. He directed the cabby to take them to Fifth Avenue.

"I am on a budget." she mumbled. She didn't think she had enough cash for extravagant clothes and did not want to use her cards. "We should go somewhere else."

"It is fine," he said, smiling at her. He brushed her hair out of her face. A bolt of electricity shot through her. Her blood raced through her veins. Her heartbeat sped up. "I got this. No worries. Part of the commission for taking the job."

Nodding, she turned away to look out the window. It was just a job; she reminded herself again. Quietly, she counted the cars that passed as she concentrated on steadying herself and her racing heart.

Chapter 7

Aethelredd read the text message for the hundredth time. He knew she was not taking a vacation. Feya was a fool if she thought he would believe that crap. Running off to help that damn boy, Elwyn, is what she had done. Turning her phone off so they could not track her that way.

He had already reached out to their current priest, to let him know they could not pick up any missions for the next month. He had tried to balk, but Redd would not back down. Just another priest in a long string of priests. He stopped remembering their names even.

Aguya and Brady were working on a tracking spell to find Feya. Unfortunately, Feya was the one who cast those spells, so he had little hope they would pinpoint where she was. Knowing she also knew how to evade those spells made it that much harder to find her. Fearing something bad would happen to her, he had spent hours training her to hide. He had trained her well, it seemed, because she was hiding from them. So he only hoped that they would get close. Close was all they would need to sniff her out.

He felt his stomach churn, not knowing where she was, or what she was doing. He dreaded what would happen to her once she crossed into a vale. Faes were not always the most forgiving of creatures. If the thirst hit her, and they found out, they would kill her. Plus, once she crossed one of the vales, finding her would be ten times harder.

He was unsure if Brady could get them all through a vale. Even if they figured out which vale to cross. He knew he should not have been so harsh yesterday. It would have been beneficial to have listened to her. He would have known what she was doing if he had. Not knowing who the boy was, how she knew him, or what they were doing, was eating him alive. Leo had gotten little of the conversation they had been having. Only catching the tail end of it. Which provided little detail to go from.

Why were they taking so long to cast this damn spell? He thought. The longer they take on the spell, the more chances of losing Feya's trail. Impatiently, he jumped up and stormed into Aguya's hotel room.

"Well?" he said, frustrated. Angrily slamming the door shut behind him.

Aguya glared at him, sparks flying from her golden eyes. He stared back, his rage barely in check.

"It would go better if you let us be," Aguya said heatedly. "If you keep interrupting us, we will never get this done."

Brady twisted her hands, tears shining in her gray eyes. "She cast a blocking spell. We can't find her."

"Fuck!" Aethelredd savagely uttered. He regretted training her magic of any kind. "Keep trying."

"We were," Aguya growled. "Until you interrupted us."

Redd caught sight of Leo standing in the corner nervously. "Go out and look for her. See if you can locate a scent trail or something. Use that damn nose of yours for some good here. Don't just stand there like an idiot. We need to stop her before she crosses over into one vale or another. She can't step foot into any fairy realms."

Redd stormed out, Leo hot on his heels. They stalked out of the hotel, each heading in a different direction, hoping to find something to track her or some kind of clue.

Feya looked around the plane nervously. Elwyn had gotten up to go to the bathroom, leaving her alone. Rarely was she alone with humans, let alone a plane full of them. The only other humans she had been around were usualy officials of the church. Here she was on a plane in the clouds, with nowhere for her to go to hide if the thirst hit her.

Wishing she had her phone or something to distract her. All she could hear were their heartbeats. So many beating hearts. She could smell their blood, the scent of a tangy sweet nectar. Closing her eyes, she tried to hear the wind outside the plane, focusing on anything else. She took deep breaths out of her mouth, trying to steady herself.

She felt a hand touch her arm delicately. Startled, she jumped. Looking up, she saw the concern in Elwyn's eyes.

"You alright?" he whispered, worriedly. His eyes scanned her face.

She shook her head, then changed her mind and nodded.

"What's wrong?" he whispered in her ear.

The warmth of his breath on her ear and smelling the citrusy musk of his cologne helped to calm her. She nibbled her lip nervously, trying to figure out what she should say to him.

"We rarely take planes like this," she paused, not sure how to explain. "We have a private jet we take. I've never been trapped in a box with so many…"

"Yes?" he asked.

"Humans," she mumbled. Glancing around the plane, their faces blended together. When Elwyn laughed, she glanced back at him. He gently grabbed her hand.

"How worried should I be?" He questioned, concerned.

She glared at him before rolling her eyes. "I am not that bad. It's just the sun and their noise is getting to me. I need to be distracted or something."

She glanced down at their joined hands. He made her feel warm and secure. Thinking she should pull away, but needing comfort at the same time. She had not realized how sheltered she had really been. Her father had kept her away from so many humans and other magical creatures her whole life. Self-doubt crept in as she continued to stare at his hand. Maybe her father had been right in always keeping her in the background, only allowing her to do simple missions.

What if I fail? She thought, racked with self-doubt. *What if I can't do this alone? What if I fail and Elwyn gets hurt?*

Looking up, she saw Elwyn pull his ear buds out of their case and handed them to her. Pushing her self-doubt away, she put them both in her ears and listened to the music he played. The soft melody slowly lulled her to sleep. The lack of sleep was finally catching up with her. Her head falling to his shoulder, her grip on his hand gently loosening.

Elwyn looked down at Feya's hand. It seemed so small to him. He regretted letting her take on this mission, fearing something might happen to her.

When he got back from the bathroom, she looked like she was having a panic attack. Clutching the arms of the chair, she had been taking deep breaths. Before that, she had always seemed so normal everywhere they went. He had forgotten that she had turned. A flutter of panic had hit him that if she got the blood rage, what would he have to do? Thankfully, she had calmed down with the soft rock playing in her ears. He would be more careful from here on out.

She slept most of the flight. Waking up, he looked down and searched the eyes hidden behind the glasses.

"The sun hurts my eyes," she muttered, while yawning.

Watching as she stretched, her shirt grew taut across her chest. He could not help but notice her ample breasts. She had always been beautiful. It surprised him at how much more beautiful she had grown.

Smiling and nodding at her. She was used to living in the night. He would have to get better at taking care of her needs.

He had been focused on the mission; had not noticed what she had been going through. Unsure what to expect, he knew she ate actual food, but was unsure how often she needed to quench her thirst for blood. Wanting to ask her so many questions, but knew she would not answer them. Worse yet, would she get upset by the questions. Plus, that so many humans were around would make it even harder to talk to her about this.

"Hungry?" he said, offering her the dinner plate he had the stewardess leave behind.

She nodded, pulling her hand from his before diving into the sandwich and chips.

He could see she was less tense now. Watching quietly as she ate, he studied her mannerisms. Watched as her teeth gently sunk into the sandwich. How her tongue swept out, licking crumbs off her lip. The way she kept side eyeing him. Smiling at her every time he caught her looking at him, her frown would intensify. She did not want him to know she was watching him back, he mused as his own smile grew.

After she was done eating, he reached up and brushed her hair off her cheek. She jumped, surprised. He chuckled at her nervousness. It boosted his ego, knowing that he caused it.

"Full?" he asked, grinning.

She glared at him for a moment, before nodding her head.

He tried to get her talking again, but she would not respond. Just kept listening to music for the rest of the flight. Feeling a little disappointed, he decided to back off, for now. Grabbing a book he had brought, he opened it up

Chapter 8

rriving in England, the cab dropped them off about half a mile from the vale in the countryside. The cabby was suspicious about dropping them in the middle of nowhere, but he did as they requested. Some humans were overly curious. Feya knew if you tipped too high, they would brag to others about dropping them off here. If you tipped too low, they would complain to others about dropping them off here. So you just had to find that average middle ground and hope the human wouldn't talk. With social media, it made it harder to hide these days. So many cab companies wanted to record their clients.

Sighing, she looked around before they entered the forest. Wistfully, she smelled the forest scents, moss, leaves, moist earth, and so much more filled her nostrils. Flashes of childhood memories came to her, running with Elwyn, her birth father's hand giving her candy, her mother walking in front of her in the forest that surrounded their village. She tried to remember her birth parents' faces, but those memories faded long ago. She would get glimpses of them, but nothing solid. It made her sad she had forgotten so much about them.

She felt her insides twisting as they got closer to the vale. Not knowing what was coming scared her a bit. She had never entered a vale before. Their small village had lived outside a vale when she was a small fae.

What if they realized what I am? She thought. *I am risking my life to prove I am capable and to get this man out of her head.*

Was paying back a debt worth risking her whole life?

Glancing at Elwyn as he dragged both their suitcases through the woods, she felt the flutter in her heart. The more she was with him, the more she felt it. She hoped the emotions would disappear, but she knew they were not. They were growing. Even knowing what she was, he did not fear her. Most magicals or humans when they found out, feared or were disgusted by her. She had very few friends and relationships because of this. She only had one constant in her life, her found family.

The air felt charged as they got close to the portal of the vale. It crackled with unseen sparks of electrical currents that she felt prickling her skin. The wind no longer blew the closer they got to the portal. A musty smell filled the air as if she was in a room that had sealed off for a long time. Everything was still. The leaves in the trees did not rustle, no animals or bugs made a sound. She saw the ring of oak trees in front of them. Surrounding a ring of grass with mushrooms in their center.

The nerves clutched tighter as they approached. She stopped walking, remembering the horrors of a fairy condemned to death for being turned by a vampire. She closed her eyes, remembering the night so vividly. Trying to block the nightmare, she took a deep breath.

They had gone to the small fairy village looking for someone to train her. A vampire attack recently devastated the faes of the town. Her father had stayed outside of town, letting her and Aguya enter the town. Uncle Leo and Brady had not been a part of the family then. It was just the three of them.

In the center of town, a stone table sat. Magical runes glowed on it. She did not recognize the runes at that time. Now she knew too well. A man laid on the table, crying in agony, begging for mercy and asking anyone to release him. His hands and legs bound with magical ropes to each corner of the table. She then noticed the bite mark on his neck. His blood slowly dripped out of his unattended wounds. Smelling his blood, she knew he had not gotten vampire blood in him. He would not be transitioning.

A village elder walked up to him, carrying a small knife.

Holding the knife, she started carving the first of many runes into his flesh. With each rune carved in his flesh, the man screamed in agony. As the magic spell took hold and burned his flesh, the smell of sulfur and blood filled the air. As she carved the 27th rune on him, his screams had become whimpers, his voice raw. A pool of blood lay under him on the table, as drips slid over the edges of the table to pool in the dirt.

As he still begged and pleaded for release, his tears and appeals fell on deaf ears. She dug the knife into his chest, breaking the ribs and cutting his still beating heart out. One last scream escaped his raw throat before he finally became silent. A bowl was brought over as she put the heart in it. Sprinkling a concoction of various herbs, she then set it on fire. The fetid scent filled the area, making Feya gag. She clutched onto Aguya's arm in fear and revulsion.

Soon after, they untied him and threw his body into a funeral pyre. No words honoring his life were spoken. They just left his body there to burn. She had been so sad knowing that no one would even honor his life because of the vampire bite. Aguya had her watch the whole thing. She was only fifteen years old.

She remembered the words Aguya whispered to her vividly. "That is why you never tell them what you are. They will never listen to you, to know what you have become."

Feya was drawn back to the present when Elwyn ran a finger down her cheek. Startled, she looked at him.

"Are you sure you want to do this?" he whispered.

Fear would not conquer her this day, or any. It was now or never. Taking a deep breath, she nodded. Walking past him to the circle. For a moment, she felt herself falling as she passed through the vale. Her stomach felt like it dropped to her knees. A wave of nausea hit her.

"I got you." Elwyn whispered, grabbing her elbow. She leaned on him for a moment, waiting for her senses to return to normal.

Her head was spinning, as if she had been spinning on a merry-go-round for too long. After a bit, her stomach settled, and she felt herself returning to normal. She stood another moment,

leaning on Elwyn for support before she gently pushed away.

A warmth flooded her from where he had touched her. Turning away, she paused in awe as she saw the kingdom for the first time. The imposing white battlement walls surrounded the castle. The drawbridge stood open, falsely inviting. Her nerves came back as she surveyed the castle as they approached.

Could they tell what I am from a glance? She thought. *Are there spells designed to keep my kind out? A million thoughts raced through her mind as she stared in wonder at the guard's gate.*

Two fae stood on both sides of the gate, holding lances. It was like they walked out of the middle ages. Their gray uniforms were the only nod to modern soldier garb. The tree of life sitting on their left breast. Bars on their shoulders must have stood for their ranking. Black shiny patent leather shoes sparkled in the sunlight.

They walked forward, Elwyn dragging their luggage behind him. She schooled her face up to hide her racing thoughts. Fear had settled like a lump in her stomach that someone would know what she was. Waiting to hear the guards shout at them, it surprised her when they entered without a single comment from them.

Once inside the walls, she could see fae folk walking around the stone lined path. No cars or motor vehicles of any kind were inside. She felt like she was in another world, another time. Stalls and stores lined the streets just inside, faes hawking their wares. Foods of every type filled her senses. The vendor signs were not lit up by neon or electricity. Street lamps filled with oils and herbs lined the roads. Clothing shimmered in the light, drawing her eye from one fae to another. More faes walked in this town square than any she had ever seen before.

Fear that someone would see what she was, made her step cautious.

She felt Elwyn's hand slide to the small of her back protectively as they stopped for a moment. She leaned into his hand for comfort. The fear in her was eating at her soul. All she wanted was to go somewhere to hide, to be alone.

"You good?" he whispered into her ear.

Nodding, she looked around at the people running around. The bright cheery clothes. Most had their wings tucked away, a few had them out on display. She admired the gossamer wings as they shined in the light. So delicate and beautiful, unlike hers. Feeling that sense of not belonging hit her hard. She pulled her sun hat down to keep more of the sunlight out of her eyes. Trying to hide her face from the others.

Biting her lip, she glanced down at her feet. Noticing her shoes were dusty from the walk to the vale. Just another thing that made her self-conscious. She thought about bending down to clean them, but figured it was pointless.

"Ready?" he said, softly.

She nodded, keeping her eyes averted.

"Alright." he said. He grabbed their luggage and started walking again. "I have a small wing in the castle we will stay in."

"Ok." she said, following behind him.

As they walked past the vendors, the buildings cleared up and the castle loomed in front of them. Her breath caught at the beauty of it. The exterior walls of the castle were ivory and gray marble, with hints of mauve. Stretching as far as the eye could see. Gingerbread style trim surrounded the windows. Glass so clean you could see the skies reflected in them. The azure tiled roof almost blended in with the blue skies hovering behind it.

A statue cast in copper of King Buer, the deceased husband of Queen Cassada, stood towering in front of the castle. His hand extended out in a gesture of welcome.

Inhaling, she smelled the roses that lined the walkway of the castle. White roses perfectly trimmed. White pebbles surrounded the beds of the roses as they created a hallway leading to the castle door. An intricately arched wooden door stood with the tree of life carved into it. The capstone above the arched door had a spell written on it.

Bless all who dwell within, bless the door, bless the walls, bless the windows and the roof. Only good may enter these

hallowed halls.

Next to the door stood two more fae guards in gray uniforms. They opened the door as they approached. As the doors opened, she got a peek inside the castle. The grand hall was opulent with splashes of color everywhere from paintings. A cream color painted the walls, making the artwork stand out. Paintings of hunting scenes, of battles long gone, of monarchs who had come before, and many others scattered the walls. A double staircase flanked a grand fireplace. Above the mantel was a painting of Queen Cassada and King Buer. A small, welcoming fire glowed from inside it. Looking down at the white marble floors, a red carpet runner would lead people up the stairs.

A doorman walked up to take their luggage as they headed up the stairs. The doorman trailed behind them. They walked down the hall on the second floor, before going up another flight of stairs. More paintings scattered the hallway. Some of the artwork looked centuries old.

At the top of the stairs stood a woman, her long chestnut hair lay in gentle waves down her back. She folded her perfectly manicured hands in front of her white sundress. The pink nail polish glinted in the light streaming through the windows. Her eyes twinkled with love as she looked at Elwyn. Blue eyes that matched his.

"Mom." Elwyn said, smiling at Olette.

"I was worried about you," she said, her smile broadening. "You were gone for so long this time, it seemed. With the attack the other night, I worried so. You have brought a guest. Who is this, may I ask?"

Her gaze fell onto Feya.

"This is Feya," Elwyn said, resting his arm on her shoulders. He pulled her close to him. Feeling the warmth that spread from Elwyn's touch, a blush spread across her face. "Feya, this is my mother, Olette."

Feya watched, waiting to see if there was any light of recognition lit on her face, but there was none.

"It's nice to meet you," Feya said, extending her hand out.

"She grew up in the village with me," he said.

"Oh," Olette said, ignoring Feya's hand. Still, no recognition lit her eyes. It was probably for the best. "It is so nice to see you again."

Feya nodded and stubbornly held her hand out still. "It is good to see you again."

Feya tried to draw from memories of Olette, but could not think of any. She had a vague sense she was Elwyn's mother, but that was it. If they had been walking on the street, it was doubtful either would have recognized each other.

Olette paused for a moment before taking her hand finally. Her smile faded and her eyes darkened for a second, then came back. Feya speculated about what that had been about.

"You look beautiful, darling," Olette said, her smile bright and friendly once again.

"We have some business to attend to, mom," Elwyn said. "Feya is going to help us figure out what is going on. You know, the queen's business."

Feya watched as shadows crossed through Olette's eyes. Feya wondered if she knew something. Feya purposely gentled her smile. She would bide her time and find out if Olette was hiding something.

"Come with me," Elwyn said, extending his hand out to Feya. She grabbed his hand and followed, watching Olette out of the corner of her eye. She saw the frown she gave Feya.

He guided her into a room decorated in blue. The bed was a giant white four-poster bed with sheer baby blue curtains surrounding it. A dark blue bedspread with streaks of gold covered the bed. The walls were covered in soft blue and gold striped wallpaper. White armoire stood between two windows. The windows were open, with sheer curtains blowing in the breeze. It had intricate carvings of a forest scene on it. She could smell the roses wafting in from the gentle gust. A white vanity with gold trim sat across from the bed.

"This will be your room." Elwyn said, his arm sweeped the

room.

"Thank you." she said, laughing.

He placed her suitcase and toiletry bag on the bed.

"I'll let you get some rest," he said, smiling down at her. "Unless you need some help unpacking?"

She paused as he was standing so close, she could practically feel his heartbeat in her own chest. She smelled the citrusy smell of the cologne he wore. She shook her head, absentmindedly.

"I'll be in the room on your right." he said, his voice husky. He pointed towards his room. "If you need anything just let me know. I am available anytime."

He reached up and brushed a strand of hair out of her face. A jolt of electricity shot through her. His smile broadened.

She nodded, nerves blocking her mouth from opening. Taking a step back to put distance between them, her legs bumped into the bed.

He chuckled, stepped closer for a moment. Leaning down close to her, for a moment she thought he would kiss her. Looking into his eyes she saw the different flecks of blue in his eyes. He stood up, and left the room

Confused, she took a steadying breath to calm herself. Running her hands over her face, she needed to stop letting him get to her. She was a grown ass woman, not some childish twit whose heart fluttered over a pretty face. Closing her eyes, she tried to think of all of his flaws. He never listened to her, constantly invaded her space, and… Nothing else came to her mind.

Sighing, she turned to her luggage. Muttering to herself, "Time to unpack, I guess."

Chapter 9

Feya jolted awake when she heard a crash. She realized the noise was coming from the room to her right, Elwyn's room. The noise of a brawl continued, as she jumped out of bed running through the hall. Throwing open Elwyn's bedroom door as he threw another fae to the ground.

She smelt Elwyn's blood before she saw the cut across his arm. The sweet coppery scent of strawberries, jasmine and plums filled the air. Bracing herself, she tried to focus all her rage at the fae trying to jump up from the ground.

Grabbing him from behind, she sank her teeth into his neck. As her venom entered his body, he calmed down and stopped fighting. Taking a moment to get just a sip, she felt the nectar slide down her throat. The warmth created a euphoria that spread through her. She then used all her restraint to release him. He fell to the ground after she released him. Fresh blood dripping from the two small punctures in his neck. The taste of it still lingering on her tongue as she looked down at the fae. Closing her eyes, she relished the taste for a moment. It was like craving something sweet and sugary. You did not need to have it, but you wanted to taste it so bad. Though once you tasted it, the feeling changed. You wanted to drink your fill. Taking a deep breath to steady herself, she pushed the craving away.

A short, squat little fae. Quite mousy looking with his brown eyes and brown hair. His clothes hung loose on his body, fraying around the edges. His eyes glazed from the venom racing through his veins. He sat on his knees on the floor, staring at her vacantly.

"What's your name?" she whispered.

"I am Sen Jogah," he replied.

Grabbing his chin forcefully, she asked "Who sent you?"

"I don't know," he mumbled.

"I said, who hired you?" she growled. Jerking his face closer to hers. Her rage took over for a moment before she reeled it in. She saw him wince from the pain of her nails digging into his chin.

"I don't know. They dropped a letter with half the money. It said to hurt him, but don't kill him. It said more money would come when it was done." he mumbled.

She stared into his eyes, checking to see if he had any other details, but knew he did not. Once she tasted their blood, she could feel things and thoughts they had. It usually only lasted for a few days, depending on how much she drank.

"Go home and forget you ever came here," she muttered. Releasing him, he fell to the ground. He slowly got up and walked out the door, as if in a trance.

Glancing back at Elwyn, she noticed he was naked except for the blood dripping down his arm. He was just staring at her, not saying anything. Her eyes drifted down the length of him. Stopping at his hardening shaft. Self-consciously, her eyes drifted back up to his chest. She stood in place as he strolled towards her. Bracing herself, she waited for the disgust he must have for her, the words of revulsion to come. He stopped when he was about a foot away. Staring at his chest, she was too scared to look into his eyes to see his repugnance.

Flinching as he brought his hand to her face, it startled her when he just brushed a bit of blood off her chin. She stared at his hand as it went back to his side. Confused at why he was being so gentle with her.

"Do we need to worry about him turning?" he asked quietly.

"No," she whispered. "He did not taste my blood."

"Alright," he said.

She screwed up the nerve to look into his face. He was just smiling down at her. No anger, no disgust, just that stupid smirk he wore.

Their eyes locked. Her cheeks burned as if fire had touched them. She heard his heartbeat racing, remembering anew that he was naked. Her eyes trailed down his strong, lean physique. Stopping for a second at his manhood again. It stood full erect now. Her blush intensified. She pulled her eyes back up, catching sight of the wound on his arm. The blood gradually dripped down.

Without thinking, she brought her finger up and swiped at the blood on his arm. She brought the finger to her mouth, licking the tip, tasting his warmth. The sweet taste of his blood drifting through her mouth. Hints of strawberry and plums filled her with just a hint of jasmine. She closed her eyes, relishing the taste for a moment.

Pausing, she opened her eyes, realizing what she had done. His hand reached up, sliding around the back of her neck. Tilting her head back as he brought his mouth down to hers. His tongue drew hers out as his taste washed through her. She felt her knees go weak. Then his mouth was gone, taking it with it his warmth.

She stood shocked as he growled, "What do you want?"

His words confused her as she stared up at him..

"I heard a commotion and came to check on you, my love," Olette said from behind her.

Feya froze as realized what was going on. Standing there, she knew, was the only thing hiding his naked body from his mom. Frozen in embarrassment, she knew if Olette had not disliked her before, she would now. Though she had a feeling, Olette did not like her before. Resting her head on Elwyn's chest, she wondered how she would get herself out of this embarrassing situation.

"Everything is fine," he grumbled. "Go back to bed. We

were just… having a discussion."

Feya groaned. He had to add the dramatic pause. As if his mother was not already suspicious. Here she was, standing in her nightgown with Elwyn naked. Of course, his mother would know what he meant by his innuendo.

"Are you sure, my love?" Olette said tentatively.

"Yes," Elwyn uttered savagely. "Mom, go away."

Feya heard the door quietly close behind her before she pushed away. This was a mission for her to prove herself, and all she had proven was that she was a lovesick child who could not control herself at the first scent of blood.

"Well, he was pretty useless," she muttered, trying to change the subject. She needed to get her head on straight. Start acting like an adult. Taking a deep breath to steady her racing heart, but it did not help.

"We can talk about…" he started.

"Could you please tend to your wound?" she said, interrupting him. The smell of blood was bothering her right now. She felt self-conscious after how she had just behaved. "You need to get that taken care of."

She turned to look out the window. She did not want to talk about the kiss. Did not want to talk about her drinking of not one, two faes blood. Hoping he would not talk about it either. She just needed time to think. To screw her head back in place and get back on the mission. She was supposed to be a professional here, and she was not acting like it. It would disappoint her father if he saw her behavior. He was probably already disappointed in her for running off like she did. Sighing, she turned from the window.

"Shit," Elwyn muttered. Scrabbling over towards the closet. "Give me a moment. I am sorry I forgot about… Crap."

"I am going back to my room. We can talk in the morning." She said, turning back to the door.

"Wait," he said, using a shirt to soak up the blood dripping down his arm. "I just need…"

She opened and closed the door before he finished his sentence.

"Well, well," Olette said, stepping from the shadows.

Feya jumped, startled by her. She had been so distracted she lost focus. Years of training washed away in a blink of an eye. That was twice she had been so preoccupied she had not realized Olette was there.

Turning, she started at Olette. Her pale pink nightgown swirled around her feet. She looked so tiny and fragile till she saw her face. Olette's blue eyes darkened with hatred. Her mouth curled up into a sneer. Anger radiating from Olette. Hearing the fast pace of her heartbeat as she stared at Feya with such intense hatred.

"I am only going to say this once." Olette whispered. "You are to stay away from him, you baseborn mongrel of a fae. I should have known you were just another whore."

Feya stood in shock, not sure what to say. She watched as Olette turned and walked away. Her nightgown swirling fiercely around her as she stormed off.

She knew Olette did not like her, but she had not realized how much till now. Plus a baseborn mongrel? They were born of the same clan, the same class, so Olette could take that insult and shove it. Feya just wished she had said a witty comeback before Olette had left. Sighing, she walked back to her room.

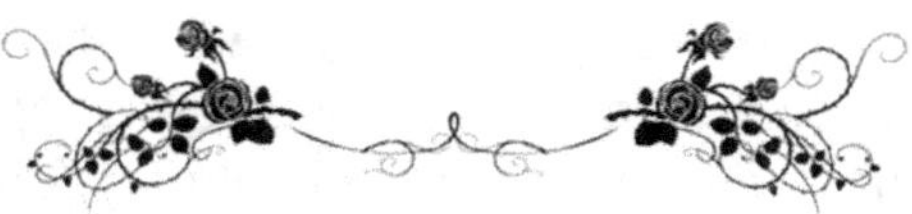

Feya stood in the mirror, surveying her outfit. Black slacks, button up black shirt, black flats. Feeling unsure, she turned away from the mirror. Nerves were getting to her and making her self-conscious. She walked to the closet and perused her clothing options, debating if she should change her outfit or not.

She dreaded seeing Olette this morning. Part of her hoped if she dallied around long enough, Olette would leave the wing. Walking away from the closet, she decided not to change her outfit.

Sighing, she dropped onto the bed. She did not want to face Elwyn or his mother this morning. What she needed to do was work on who was after Elwyn. That is what he hired her for. Taking a deep breath, she worked to clear the racing thoughts in her head. Counting her own heartbeats. Her father always had told her when you felt stressed or the thirst to coming, stop, take deep breaths and count your heartbeats. A silly trick she still did to this day. It usually helps, but not right now, not so much. Her thoughts were all jumbled up with her heart. She knew she needed to separate them, but did not know how.

A knock on the door startled her. She took a moment to listen for the heartbeat. She needed to get back to herself and stop acting like a ninny.

"Yes, Elwyn?" she asked, as she stood up to head to the door.

He walked in before she could even get to the door. Frowning, she realized she would have to lock that door.

"Good morning," He said, sounding cheery. His eyes sparkled with laughter, a dimple on one cheek, making him look adorable.

All she wanted to do was punch his other eye to give him a matching black eye. Instead, she just stared at him, not saying a word.

"Are you ready to go get breakfast?" he said, grinning from ear to ear. "Or are you full after that midnight snack?"

She squinted her eyes at him. She was pretty sure this pretty fool was going to be the death of her, or at least get her killed.

"Hungry it is," he grabbed her hand, dragging her from the room.

She followed him to the breakfast room a few doors down in their wing. Olette was already nibbling on some toast. She smiled brightly at Feya, jumping up and hugging her.

Feya stood confused. Unsure what to say or do. This was not the same Olette who had stood in the hall with her last night. Curious why Olette was acting like they were friends, especially after what she had said the night before.

"You look beautiful, Freda," Olette said, brushing a stray hair out of her face. Smiling a sweet smile that Feya could not return.

"Feya," Feya corrected. There she was, the Olette she had come to know and despise. She was trying to throw subtle shade while Elwyn was around. Feya now knew the game she was playing. "My name is Feya."

"Oh, yes," Olette said, waving her hand and laughing. "I am so sorry. I can be such a silly goose sometimes. Please sit and join us for breakfast."

Elwyn pulled out a chair for Feya to sit in. "Here you go, Feya."

She walked over, accepted the chair Elwyn held for her. Elwyn sat next to her and Olette across from her.

She glanced at the chafing dish in the center of the table. Grabbing some bacon and eggs, she started munching on her food. Hoping she could avoid conversation with them both by keeping her mouth full of food.

Olette and Elwyn discussed people they knew in the court. Olette was trying to catch Elwyn up on the latest gossip. Feya zoned out, happy to not talk at the moment. She stared down at her plate to avoid being dragged into the conversation.

The room went quiet without her realizing it.

Elwyn touched her arm. She glanced up at him. "Ready to get to work?" he asked.

She nodded.

"I'll join you," Olette chimed in.

"Don't you have a luncheon today?" Elwyn asked. "We got this. I know you have been looking forward to seeing your friends again. You have some fun."

Feya stood up and followed Elwyn out. Before she crossed the threshold, she glanced back and caught Olette's angry glance. There she was. The sneaky fae did not want her son to know that she despised Feya. She had to monitor Olette. Maybe if she explained she would not be here long, she would give Feya a break. She doubted it, but maybe. The bigger question was, did she want to talk to her about it to begin with? The answer was a resounding no.

She closed the door and followed Elwyn as he went down the stairs. Looking at the various paintings that lined the walls. Hundreds of years of paintings of scenery, various faes she did not recognize, fruit in a bowl, etc. They blurred together as they descended the stairs.

"We need to head to town and get you a ball gown for tonight," Elwyn said casually.

"Why?" she groaned.

He had never mentioned a ball before. She had never been to a fae ball before. A human one, yes, but that was eons ago. She did not even remember the fae etiquette for such things, let alone anything. It had been so long since she had been around a fae other than Brady. It scared her she would make a fool of herself. Her hope that she would be behind the scenes investigating people was dashed. He was going to throw her into the fire, whether or not she liked it.

"They are hosting a ball tonight," he stated. "I will introduce you to some players involved. At least two should be there. Plus, I get to show you off."

She stared at Elwyn, unsure how to respond to this last bit.

They went down a new set of stairs. This one dropped them off in the kitchen. She watched as the faes ran around prepping meals for the castle folk. The pots and pans clattering. The smell of dozens of different dishes being prepared. Spices, veggies, and meat simmering, baking and being prepared for the evening festivities.

They walked through the back door, Elwyn close behind. He rested his hand on the small of her back as he guided her along the path. An herb and vegetable garden surrounded the back door. Pulling her sunglasses over her eyes. She looked around at the pretty garden filled with vibrant colors and scents. Rosemary, Basil, and all sorts of herbs scented the air.

Chapter 10

Redd paced as he waited for the results of Aguya's current spell. He knew she had crossed the vale to a fairy realm. There was no way she had not by now. He just needed to know what portal, then he could worry about how to get in. His fear was that he would be too late. That fear was eating at his gut. He had worked so hard to keep her safe, to limit those who saw her. To teach her what she needed to avoid fae folk. All for her to run off and use those skills against him.

She was always such a stubborn chit, agreeing with him then heading off to do whatever she willed. Had he pushed her too far this time? He mused. He should have listened to her, heard her out. Instead, he had shut her down and refused to listen.

Memories of watching his clan, his own sires, brothers, sisters dying in battle. Having sworn he would sire no one after that bloody war that took everything from him. He was the last one left in his clan. A kindly priest had brought him in and healed his wounds. He had worked for the church ever since.

He had kept that promise until he met Feya, his daughter. He had been just another walking dead, one mission after another, until that little girl ran past him. Had not even seen him standing there in her haste. She had brought him back to life and he would bring hell down on anyone who hurt her.

"I think I have something," Aguya said.

Redd stopped pacing and looked at her. Excitement lit up Aguya's face. A moment of relief hit him, before a sense of panic hit him. What if it was too late? Shaking the thought away, he knew he could not let his mind go down that road.

They had tracked down the hotel she had spent that first night away with the boy in. The hotel had been registered to Elvis Smith. He assumed it might be an alias. After being alive for centuries, he learned some magicals kept the names close to what they were really called. They had searched the hotel from top to bottom, looking for clues. After checking out of the hotel, she went to the bank and withdrew money. That was where the trail went cold. She had not used her cards or her cell phone since the bank.

"I stopped trying to track her and started to track him," she said, triumphantly. "She did not think we would find him, so she put no spells to block him from our sight."

He could see how tired she was. There were dark circles under her eyes. They were all tired, having spent the last three days trying to figure out where Feya was. Everyone was working hard and doing all they could do. A thought of kicking Feya's ass ten ways to Sunday flitted through his mind.

"He went to England," she said, triumphantly. "A forest that is not too far from our home."

Redd smiled. "We shall head there and figure out how to get through the vale. I might have a friend who can help with that."

He tried to keep the smile in place to comfort everyone, but his eyes told another story.

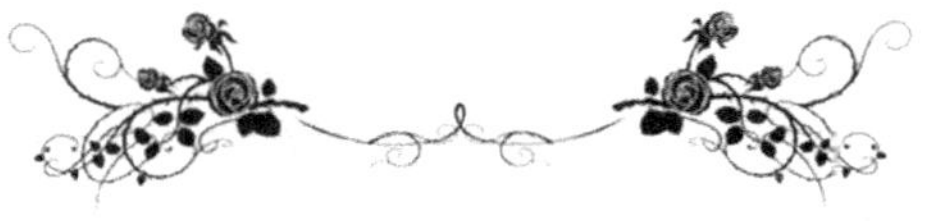

Elwyn sat in the chair waiting for Feya to come out in the seventh dress she had tried on. He had told her she looked beautiful in all of them, but she was not happy with any. He could tell she was self-conscious, but he did not know what words to say to make her feel better. No matter how many times or how

many words he used to describe how beautiful she looked in all the dresses, she found a reason to say no. The first dress was too revealing, the second dress looked too matronly, the next was the wrong shade of blue, and so forth the arguments came.

Tapping his fingers on the chair arm impatiently, he waited for her to come out in another dress. He enjoyed being with her, but he was tired of listening to her find flaws with each dress. He forgot how much he despised shopping. His mother dragged him on shopping trips occasionally and complained about everything.

He watched as Feya came out of the curtained dressing room. His breath caught as he gawked at her. The misty, wispy red dress seemed to float around her legs and cling to her torso.

"Turn around," he said in awe.

She complied. He saw the nerves in her eyes. She was going to complain about this one, too. He knew he had to stop her before she started, the dress was perfect.

The silky fabric floated as she turned. The dress was backless, so she could release her wings easier. Only two thin straps held the dress up. A high slit showed off one leg. The dark blood red color of the dress shone in contrast to her pale skin and jet black hair.

He watched her open her mouth and cut her off. Telling the attendant. "It's perfect. We will take it."

"Maybe..." Feya started.

"It's perfect." Elwyn said sternly, cutting her off. Walking over, he brushed his hand through her black hair. "You look gorgeous. This is the dress, trust me."

"I am just not sure, maybe I…" she mumbled. Her eyes were downcast.

"No," he whispered. He lifted her chin up. The knuckles of his other hand gently stroked her cheek. He watched as her eyes dilated. Lowering his mouth towards hers slowly.

The store attendant coughed, causing Feya to jump back. Elwyn turned to glare at the clerk.

"I'll go change back to my clothes," she said before running

to the dressing room.

Elwyn sighed. This was going to take longer than he thought. His problem was how much time he had. So far, the attacks had been minor inconveniences. He worried the attacks would become more violent. Maybe he should have just taken her to some tropical island instead of here. Then he could have focused all his time on her before returning, but he could not shirk his duties.

Looking at the attendant, he said. "Charge it to my account."

"Yes," the clerk said, walking away. Elwyn wondered why she could not walk away a moment ago.

A moment later, Feya came out. Her eyes would not meet his. He had hoped she would come around easier, but that would not happen. She had to make things difficult.

"Do you know where the guy from last night went?" He asked, changing the subject. Maybe if he refocused her attention, she would become more at ease again.

"Yes," she said, cautiously. "It won't matter, though. He knows nothing."

"But maybe someone around him does," he said, quietly. He knew if he pushed, she would spook. "We can go observe for a bit before we have to get ready for the ball tonight. Once I know where he is, I can also have someone watch him, just in case they reach out to him again."

"That could work," she muttered, shrugging. Her eyes stayed downcast, staring at his chest.

The clerk came back and took the dress. Wrapping it up in a box for them.

As they left the store, Elwyn followed Feya. She started walking ahead of him, guiding the way. It seemed like she was lost as she twisted and turned in what felt like a random direction through the streets and a few alleys. Turning right, then left. No destination seemed in mind. Following her, he wondered if she knew where to go.

"Where are we going?" he asked.

"This way," she said. Angrily glancing back at him like he was an idiot.

"I know that we're walking in this direction," he grumbled. "I meant, what is the destination we are going to?"

"I don't know that," she said, sighing. "I just know where to go. It's like something pulling me towards him. I just follow where it pulls me and just head that way."

"Alright," he said, reaching for her hand.

She stopped and stared daggers at him.

"I don't want to lose you," he said, offering her his most charming smile.

She turned and continued walking, holding his hand. She dragged him behind her as she twisted and turned through the city.

It was a minor battle he had won, but she was warming up to him. He knew she felt the same as he did. From the first day he had seen her when they were kids, he had been drawn to her. When he saw her again, the feeling hit him all over anew.

Elwyn followed Feya as they headed to where he did not know. Finally, she stopped in front of Ballybog's Tavern. It was a small ramshackle kind of building. The tavern was located in not one of the best areas of the vale. It was a wooden structure that had seen better days. The dirty white paint was peeling in spots. The front door hung askew, making it hard to close behind them. He could smell the smoke from Green Lust, a fae drug that was outlawed. The smell almost made him gag. He could not figure out how people got past the scent to smoke it.

Looking around, he found Sen at the bar, drinking. *A little early to be drinking,* Elwyn thought, chuckling. He took the lead, guiding Feya to a table in a corner. Just close enough to see and hear Sen, but not so close that he might notice.

A barmaid came up, her brown hair scraggly and unkept.

He ordered Alfheimr Ale for them both. The ale was named after the region they brewed in it, Sweden. Elves of the light brewed it.

As they waited for their drinks, he tried to figure out a safe topic to get Feya talking. Sen was just sitting and drinking, so might as well try to win her over again.

Looking at her, he said the first thing he thought was neutral enough for her. "Tell me about when you first met your family."

Listening to her, his eyes never left Sen. He realized nothing was going to happen here. She had been right, after all. Turning his eyes back to her, he saw the joy in her eyes as she told anecdotal stories about her family.

Sighing he texted one guard he worked with, Carden. Giving him the details of where to find Sen and to keep a close eye on him.

Chugging the last of his ale, he looked at Feya.

"Ready?" He said, holding his out to her.

Eyeing his hand, she slowly put her hand in his. Gently, he pulled her out of her chair and they left.

Chapter 11

Feya felt like a ball of nerves. It seemed she was doing most of the talking, nervous talking. She had shown Elwyn where to find the fae, Sen. Just another two bit hustler hanging out at a local tavern. They stayed, ordering a few drinks and talked. When he was ready to leave, Elwyn messaged one of his men to watch him. She had a sense it would do no good.

He had failed his mission. She mused. *Why would they use him again?*

He was a randomly hired henchman. What bothered her most was he was not supposed to hurt Elwyn. Who would want to kill the queen's right-hand man and her cousin, but only hurt Elwyn? She kept wondering what the bad guy was really after. Things just did not add up. The more she thought about it, the more frustrated she got. Her brain felt like the wheels were spinning, but she was going nowhere.

They got back to Elwyn's wing of the castle in time to get ready for the ball tonight. She had a pit in her stomach, thinking of the ball. Never having been surrounded by so many fae before, she felt apprehensive. So far, she had blended in when walking in the crowds, but she had not had to talk to them, etc. Would her social graces fail her? Could she remember all the etiquette that was required for these events? Too many things to remember. She wished she could just back out. Preferring to be behind the scenes, where she could observe and not deal with magicals. Maybe she was not cut out for this. Maybe her father had kept her behind the scenes all these years for a reason.

She flinched as the fae brushed her hair Olette had sent a handmaiden to prepare her for the ball. Which was probably for the best, since her go to style was either down or a messy bun. Her only issue was Deema, the handmaiden, was a bit rough.

Deema was shorter than her. A dour-looking fae. Her dirty blonde hair pulled back in a tight chignon. Not a single loose strand could be found. She wore no makeup except brown eyeshadow and brown eyeliner. Her black dress was loose and baggy, hiding her rail thin figure. Deema barely spoke to Feya, except to go over social graces. She had a feeling that Olette thought she was going to embarrass them, so sent this foul tempered fae to guide her. She felt her self-confidence waver as she listened more to Deema talk about etiquette.

"Not so tight." Feya groaned, as Deema tried to brush her hair to look like hers. "I think I just want my hair to be down tonight."

Feya sighed as her eyes met Deema's in the vanity mirror. She did not hide the disapproval of Feya at all. Obviously, leaving your hair loose was not proper etiquette, but the idea of having her hair glued to her head like Deema's was not her style.

"Turn so I can do your makeup," Deema said, dourly.

Feya looked at Deema's makeup and decided it was for the best she did not do her own. Maybe she should just get herself ready after all. "There is no need. I prefer to attend to that myself. Thank you."

Deema's frown deepened at Feya's words. "Fine." she huffed as she left the room.

Feya rolled her eyes and laughed. She had not meant to anger her. Maybe sticking with her relaxed style was for the best. She might be more comfortable if she just tried to be herself, instead of spending the night pretending to be someone else.

Turning back to the mirror, she started doing her own makeup. Since, she had told Deema she wanted her hair down, she guessed she would do that after all; less work anyway.

She slipped into her dress and debated the zipper on the

back as she eyed herself in the mirror. She liked the dress, but was not sure it was proper attire. When Deema saw the dress, she looked completely horrified. Maybe she should not have let Elwyn choose her dress. She could have fought harder, but she felt so out of place at the idea of a ball. It had made deciding what to wear feel insurmountable.

A knock on the door jarred her from her thoughts. She listened and heard Elwyn's heartbeat. He did not wait for an answer before walking in. She really needed to remember to lock that door. At home, no one ever just walked in. They always waited for a response. She glared at Elwyn for intruding. Maybe Deema needed to give him a refresher course on manners.

He paused, looking at her, his eyes sliding up and down her. She felt the heat rise in cheeks at his appraising gaze.

"Looks like I arrived just in time," he said, walking towards her. He slid behind her and zipped up the dress. His knuckles brushed her skin as he slowly took his time. A trail of heat was left from his touch. She closed her eyes, trying to get a grip on her emotions raging inside her.

"You look beautiful," he whispered in her ear.

She heard his heartbeat pounding faster. Her breath caught in her throat, as she felt his warm breath on her neck. She opened her eyes and met his gaze in the mirror.

She tried to step away, but his hand slipped around her. His palm pressed against her stomach as he pulled her towards him. She told herself to pull away, but her body would not listen.

She felt him pressed against her back. The full length of his body. His heart raced as fast as her own. A fire started to burn in her core as his hand pressed her closer.

His other hand came up, brushing her hair away from her neck before his mouth started nibbling on it. She inhaled deeply as an electric bolt shot through her. Her knees grew weak as she leaned back into him. Her head lolled to the side to rest on his shoulder, giving him better access to her neck. He groaned in response. She felt him harden against her backside. His mouth nibbled its way to her shoulder, while his hand roamed to cup her breasts.

"Ahem," Deema cleared her throat.

Feya jumped, startled to see that both Olette and Deema had walked into her room. Her face flushed with embarrassment. She started to pull away, but Elwyn pulled her back.

Does none of them have manners? She thought, *they all just walk in unannounced.*

"How can we help you?" He growled, with no pretense of trying to be civil.

"Deema told me that Feya said she wanted to do her own hair and makeup." Olette said, laughing. "I just wanted to know if she might need my help. This is for the Queen's ball, after all. We would not want her to look…"

"We don't need help, mother," Elwyn said, sighing.

Feya looked from Olette, who was fake laughing, to Deema, who looked revolted.

Did Elwyn really buy this act from his mother? Feya thought. *I will never understand these people.*

She tried pulling away from Elwyn again, but he just gripped her waist tighter. She felt his long, hard shaft against her backside and stopped fighting.

He probably did not want them to see his hard on, she mused. A giggle escaped from her.

"I am capable of attending to my own hair and makeup," Feya expressed with suppressed another giggle.

"Yes, of course you are, dear," Olette said sweetly. "You are a baseborn and have never had a lady's maid before, I am sure."

Feya bristled at the insult again, all laughter gone.

"I am born of the same station as yourself," Feya smiled her sweetest, most kind smile at Olette before reaching up to stroke Elwyn's cheek. This woman was going to continue to look down at her like she was garbage; she might as well have fun playing back.

Elwyn rested his check on her hand. Startled by his move, she did everything in her power to continue with her smile. Her eyes locked with Olette's. The disdain dripping from her stare.

She felt a moment of triumph as she gazed into Olette's eyes.

"We will be out in a few minutes," Elwyn said, gently. His fingers started tracing circles on her stomach. "Please shut the door behind you. I will attend to Feya's needs."

Feya inhaled as his fingers glided over the silk of her dress. She schooled her face as she continued to stare Olette down. Olette stood there, angry for a moment, before turning and leaving. Deema trailing hot on her heels.

Feya sighed after the door shut. Trying to pull away again.

"You think you will get away that easily," he whispered in her ear. Goosebumps trailed down her spine.

"I need to finish getting ready," she said, huskily.

"Alright," he said, as his teeth racked her neck.

"Elwyn," She gasped in exasperation.

Laughing, he released her. She turned to look at him, startled by the softness in his eyes.

"What do you need to do to get ready, Fe?" he said, trailing his thumb across her bottom lip. Her heart jumped at the use of her childhood nickname.

"I need to brush my hair," she mumbled, not sure what else to say. She had already done her makeup and her dress was on.

"Have a seat," he said, gesturing to the bench in front of the vanity.

Taking a deep breath, she did as he said. She closed her eyes for a moment to count her heartbeats. She felt the hairbrush glide gently through her hair. It felt nice to have someone be so gentle after how Deema had brushed her hair.

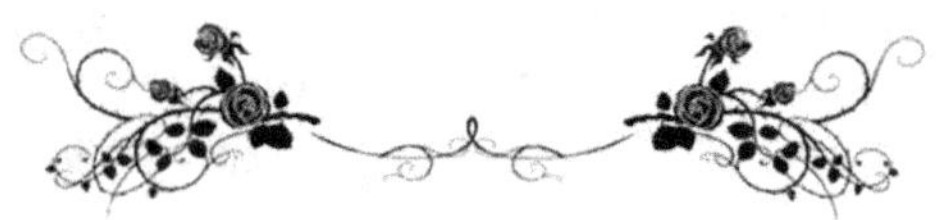

Feya clung onto Elwyn's right arm, his mother on the left, as they waited to enter the ballroom. There were a few other feas ahead of them waiting to be announced. She felt a knot in the pit of her stomach. She felt so out of place here. Plus, with Olette's constant backhanded compliments, she felt even more self-doubt. No matter how she tried to ignore the words, they still had taken hold. Two more couples were ahead of them to be announced.

She looked over at Elwyn. He was looking sharp in his gray tuxedo. The tuxedo was perfectly cut and fit him like a glove. Two slits in the back of the jacket were for him to release his wings with ease. The off white button-up shirt peeking out of his sleeves showing off his emerald cufflinks. Black patent leather shoes finished the outfit. Her heart fluttered looking at him. Every time she looked at him, he seemed to grow more handsome. Tonight, it was hard for her to take her eyes off of him.

One more couple.

Olette wore a pearlized white gown. It sparkled in the lights. The dress was very demure, especially compared to Feya's. She did not know how she did it, but Olette looked sweet and demure.

Feya turned back to the front. It was their time to be announced. She listened as the herald announced them. It was weird hearing them announce her by her birth name. Feya Elida Annwen of clan Talamh. She did not remember the last time someone had called her by that name. It did not seem like they were talking about her. They were talking about a stranger long dead. A seven-year-old who died on a cold dark night in the forest, the day Feya Ascelin was born.

Chapter 12

They entered the ballroom. Feya surveyed the ballroom, getting the lay of the land. Most of the faes ignored their entrance. Some others circled in a dance under the gilded chandelier in the center of the room. Red and gold jewels dripped from the chandelier. Some walking the perimeter drinking and talking. Dresses in a rainbow variety of colors swirled throughout the room. Males in a variety of more subdued colors mingled. The redwood flooring clattered from the shoes of those dancing in its center. Their dresses and suits were a blur as they circled the dance floor. A four string quartet played as a soprano fae sang an aria. Her voice was so soft and lilting it was surprising it carried so well over the din of the faes.

The queen sat on her throne on the dais behind the dance floor. A gold ornate throne with the tree of life carved into its back. Red pillows adorned the throne to make her more comfortable. Red velvet curtains were draped behind the throne, making the gold chair shine brighter. The queen was a pale, fragile looking beauty. Her dark brown eyes were enormous in her little Diamond shaped face. Her slanted eyes gave her an innocent, exotic look. Dark brown curls perfectly framed her face. Her eyes shrewdly surveying the crowd told a different story. Her white flowing ball gown draped down past her feet and pooled around the throne legs. As the queen moved, Feya could see a flash of silver. It was as if someone had delicately woven silver thread into the dress, only visible in certain lights.

Four guards flanking her in their gray uniforms. Two carried swords and two hand guns. Looking around the ballroom with decor that hailed from the Victorian era, two of the guards were rather incongruous with their modern weapons.

Feya looked over at Elwyn as he stopped to drop his mother off with her friends. Olette kissed his cheek before slyly sneaking Feya the stink eye. Sighing, Feya rolled her eyes at Olette. She did not want to keep up the pretense of ignoring Olette's rudeness anymore

"I see Eleazer over there," he said, gliding her across the room. "Let's go talk to him. I doubt he'll give us much here, but at least we can get a feel for him."

Eleazer stood by himself, glaring at everyone who came his way. His ash blonde hair hung to his shoulders. Light blue eyes were cold like ice. No emotion registered. A brutish man, looking ill at ease in his formal dour brown suit. He stood about 5'8". As they approached, his eyes looked them up and down disapprovingly.

"Hey, Eleazer," Elwyn said. "This is Feya of…"

Feya knew she could not let this slide. She had a few tricks up her sleeve as well. Taking a deep breath and exhaling, she focused all her energy on her words and on him hearing them.

"Yes, so nice to meet you," Feya breathed. Casting a charm spell with the words. An old vampire trick her father had taught her.

Eleazer turned to stare at her, dumbfounded. His eyes focused on her and nothing else. She felt a pull as he was trying to look away, trying to break the spell.

"Hello," he said, quietly.

"We just want to have a polite conversation with you," she said, staring deep into his icy eyes.

"Alright," he mumbled.

She could sense him trying to pull away harder from her spell. Taking a deep breath, she pushed a little bit more.

"Tell me your thoughts on the queen?" she whispered.

She felt him hesitate as he stared at her. Trying to figure out if he should answer her or not.

This would be so much easier if I could drink his blood, she mused. But she could not run around biting any fae suspected of treason. Especially in the middle of a ball. That was how she would get caught. Plus, she was not thirsty for the moment.

"I..." Eleazer stammered.

Releasing the spell, she laughed. She knew if she pushed too hard, he would suspect she was in his head. It was hard sometimes to decide when to keep pushing and when to pull back. So pull back for now until he let his guard down a bit.

"I mean, what do you think of her dress?" Feya improvised. Gesturing towards the queen on her dais.

He laughed with her, confused. He glanced over at the queen, confused. She could see the wheels turning in his eyes as he tried to figure out why he felt so strange.

"Such things do not concern me," he said coldly. Turning away to survey the room again.

"Are you enjoying the ball?" she asked him, looking over at Elwyn. He was staring at her curiously. She could tell he was trying to figure out what was going on, but did not have a clue. She smiled at him confidently.

"I am," Eleazer said, cautiously. Turning back to her, eyes locked with him once again.

Feya smiled at him sweetly. "I am sure you have been to hundreds of these things."

"I... I have," Eleazer stuttered.

Feya laughed flirtily. Her hand touched his arm as she smiled. She pushed the spell again. Her voice was husky as she whispered. "Tell me your thoughts on the royal court."

She stared into his eyes as she watched him melt and fall under the spell this time. It was so nice when they stopped fighting and gave in. She was not a fan of doing the spell in such a crowded spot. Hopefully, if they finished talking to the fae suspects, they could leave early.

"The queen is an imbecile," he mumbled. "She makes impetuous decisions that have negative effects. Her husband should have let their son rule or anyone else. Just not her. He was a fool if he thought she would keep the peace and rule well."

"Do you think she should die?" she whispered, her eyes focused on him. She watched as his eyes dilated as he fell deeper into her charm spell.

"No," he mumbled.

"What do you think should happen?" she whispered.

"The people will soon see," he muttered. "That she is not the right ruler. A new one will be appointed. Not a day too soon."

"Did you kill Bayard?" Feya said, breathlessly.

"No," he mumbled. "I do not have a death wish."

Feya paused, looking deep into Eleazer's eyes. Part of her hoped he would be the one. Then the mission would be done and over with so she could go on and head back to her family. Another part of her felt relieved he was not the one. That was an emotion she was not ready to explore.

"You are thirsty. Go get drunk and forget this conversation." She whispered. "Mingle with some of the other fae. You will remember this night fondly and enjoy yourself."

She watched as he turned and walked to the bar to get a drink.

"What was that?" Elwyn asked, frowning.

She looked up into his blue eyes filled with anger. Confused, she said, "I am doing what you hired me to do."

"I know that," he frowned, running a hand through his hair. "I mean, what was that thing you did?"

"An old vampire charm spell," she whispered, shrugging.

Looking away from him, she looked at the faes twirling on the dance floor. She had only been around those who approved of her spells, so his reaction confused her. He seemed upset that she had cast a charm spell. *Was this not what he hired me for?*

She wondered.

She thought back to her first fae tutor, and how she reacted to Feya's vampire side. There was always this fear of rejection that lingered inside her. No matter how she tried to get rid of it, it still persisted.

"Have you ever used it on me?" he growled in a low voice.

Shocked, she looked back at him. "Of course not."

"Promise me you will never do that to me," he retorted.

"What makes you think I would?" she said, anger and frustration rising in her.

How could he think I would do that to him? She thought angrily.

"Just promise, please," he said, lowering his tone.

"Fine," she muttered, trying to control the mix of anger and sadness in her. Turning away to hide her face. "I promise I won't use a charm spell on you."

She was reacting like a child with the range of emotions he brought out of her. Reacting this way was not something she was used to. All she wanted was to go up to the room and not be at the ball.

He grabbed her arm and spun her back around. He opened his mouth to speak, then stopped.

She stared for a moment, waiting for him to speak. Waiting for the words condemning her. She straightened her spine and stood up to her full height.

"Fuck." he said. "I am sorry. You caught me off guard and I did not handle that properly. Again I am sorry, Fe. Can I get a warning next time you pull a new magic trick out?"

"Alright," she mumbled.

"Please forgive me," He said, resting his forehead on hers. His thumb brushed a tear away from her eye.

She froze, wanting to forgive him and wanting to run all at the same time. Taking a deep breath, she weighed the options. She knew she would forgive him, but the sting was not going away. Sighing, she mumbled. "I forgive you."

"Thank you, Fe," he lifted his head up, staring down into her eyes. "You look beautiful tonight. The most beautiful fae here."

Rolling her eyes, she gave him a fake smile. "I'm only part fae. What are you trying to butter me up for?"

"A kiss," he said, tentatively. His eyes roving down to her lips.

Her heart quickened, her breath trembled from her lips. *How was it he could make me jump from one emotion to another so easily?* She pondered.

Feya shook her head. "We are here on a mission. We need to find out who is after you and nothing more."

He sighed, muttering. "Of course."

She surveyed the room, watching the faes dance, talk, and walk around the room. The vibrant gowns swirling around the dance floor.

"Over there," he said, pointing across the room. "That is Aelfric Tyronce. The shortest one in that group there."

"That narrows the search down," Feya muttered, trying to figure which group he was pointing at.

Rolling his eyes, Elwyn said. "See the lady in the gaudy purple dress? The one that looks like a dozen dragon hordes were hot glued to it?"

Feya laughed and spotted the dress. A short little tiny fae who looked like the dress was wearing her more than she looked like she was wearing it.

"He's the short guy there," Elwyn grumbled.

The band struck up a new song. She watched as Fae swarmed to the dance floor, laughing and getting in line. She lost sight of Aelfric as the crowd descended to the dance floor.

"Can we dance first?" Elwyn asked, his eyes gently enticing her. "Just one dance, pretty please."

She swallowed and nodded. Knowing she would regret

dancing with him, even as she put her hand in his.

Smiling, he guided her to the dance floor. They got in line with the others. She laughed and looked around, not sure what to do. Her family rarely went to dances, so she was not very good at these kinds of things. She watched as they swirled around in a line dance. Trying to follow the person in front of her, she twirled and laughed along.

Then she lost her smile as she watched the others release the charm mark that held their wings in place. They started to dance, using their wings to flow with the music.

Nausea hit her as she yanked her hand from Elwyn's. Without a second thought, she ran off the dance floor. Heading to the nearest door, she ran outside leading into a garden. Taking deep breaths to calm herself.

Chapter 13

lwyn watched as sheer fear hit Feya on the dance floor. It shocked him when she yanked her hand out of his and ran off. Just a second before, she was laughing and having fun. He stood there a moment, confused, before running after her. A feeling of panic washed over him that he may have done something wrong or she was thirsty. If she was hungry, he did not know what he would do to fix this.

He found her in the garden. She was sitting on a bench under a weeping willow, hiding. She looked so fragile and small. Her knuckles were white from gripping the bench edge so tightly. Her hair hiding her face as her head hung low.

He tentatively walked to her, kneeling down in front of her. Scared that she would run off again.

"What's wrong, Fe?" he said, quietly. His hand stroked her hair to the side so he could see her face.

She shook her head and brushed his hand away. "It's nothing."

"Then why run away?" he whispered. His hand came up, lifting her chin up.

He watched as fear, anger, sadness each crossed those green eyes. He kneeled there, confused at what could set off such a range of emotions.

She jerked her head, pulling her chin away. "I think you

forget I am not like you. I am not like them."

She pointed a finger back at the ballroom, derisively.

The emotion had left her eyes as she gazed back up at him. He felt sadness. He had thought they had made progress. Every time he took a step forward with her, she would jump two steps back.

"Then explain it to me," he whispered. He rested his hand on her knee, her slit having slid open, exposing it.

She was quiet for a moment, searching around the garden. Reaching up to her chest, she touched the rune that fairies are given to hide their wings at birth lit up. She broke the symbol by crossing her finger over it. The spellbinding her wings broke. He watched as her wings unfurled.

They were like no wings he had ever seen before. The sheer gray green membrane that stretched between elongated fingers reminded him of bat wings. With the fingers stretching the length of them. The arms were smooth and solid. With a claw at the end of the center top point. Stretching her wings out, he could see that her four wings had changed drastically since they were little.

He reached up a hand and gently touched one of her wings. The thin membrane was delicate under his fingers. He moved his fingers to trace one arm. The skin was so soft on them.

"They're beautiful," he whispered, looking into her eyes. He watched as shock lit up in her eyes.

"They are ugly," she murmured. Reaching up to tap her rune on her chest and retracting her wings. "No need to lie to me."

He moved his hand back as they vanished. Sorrow hit him, as he realized how deep her wounds for her vampire side must go.

Reaching up, he grabbed both her cheeks. She tried to pull away, but he would not let her. Forcing her to meet his gaze, he said. "They are the most beautiful and unique wings I have ever seen, Fe."

He released her cheeks, still staring into her eyes. He watched as she slowly leaned towards him. Her mouth tenderly brushed against his before pulling back.

He smiled at her. That was the first time she had initiated a kiss. He stood up, holding his hand out.

"Let's go back in. The dance will be over. They usually only do it once." He said, smugly.

She sighed and reached for his hand. He pulled her up and into his arms. Tilting her head back while cupping the back of her neck. He released her hand and brought it to the small of her back. He brought his mouth to hers as he gently nibbled her bottom lip. Before he slid his tongue in her mouth to duel with hers. He felt her melt in his arms. Tugging her closer as he devoured her mouth. The taste of her filled his senses. Her scent haunted his thoughts as he gently pulled back. He stared down into her eyes.

"We should head back in," he whispered, resting his forehead on hers. "We have been gone for a while."

He stroked her hair, then ran his knuckles down her cheek.

"Yes," she said, exhaling.

He breathed her in. Smelling the flowery scent of her perfume. Holding her for another moment, he relished the feel of her in his arms. Pulling back, he extended his hand out to her. Tentatively, she accepted his hand and let him guide her back to the ball. A new song was playing, and most fae had put their wings away.

Elwyn searched the crowd, trying to find Aelfric. He was nowhere in sight. He even looked for the fae with the hideous purple dress. She had also left. Thinking he tried to remember her name, Annabelle or Annalee or something like that.

"Shit! Aelfric must have left. I can't find him." He grumbled. Looking around the room again for good measure, he was still nowhere to be found.

"We will have to find a way to meet up with them all soon," Feya said, quietly.

He looked down at her flushed face as she looked around

the crowd. He squeezed her hand tight. She glanced up at him. Those misty green eyes were still dewy from her tears.

"I am sorry," she said, guiltily. "If I had not panicked, we would have run into him. Then one more person would have…"

"No, it is my fault," he said, cutting her off. He smiled gently at her to tamp the curtness of his words. "If I had not dragged you to the dance floor and took you to meet him this would not have happened."

"But…" she stuttered.

"Again, I wanted to dance with you and messed up the entire mission," he said, planting a kiss on her nose.

She looked down at the ground. He squeezed her hand again, trying to get her to look up at him.

"If they are gone…" she trailed off.

"Yes?" he said, leaning down closer.

She paused before speaking. "If the people we need to talk to are gone, do I need to stay here?"

"How about we go say hello to the queen and then we can leave?" he said, grinning. He knew his mother would stay all night, which meant he would get to be alone with Feya with no interruptions.

"You don't have to leave if you don't want to," she said, shyly.

"I want to leave with you," he whispered in her ear.

She blushed as it extended down her neck.

"Can I get just one dance with you before we talk to the queen?" he asked, brushing a kiss on her ear. "I would love to twirl around the dance floor with the most beautiful half fae here."

"Should we not focus on the mission?" she whispered. "Plus, are you sure it won't be like the last dance? Plus, I am sure I am the only one here."

"The mission is pretty done for the night so we can focus on us for now," he said, brushing his lips across her cheek. "Yes, I am sure that dance won't happen again. Fine, the most beautiful female here."

Rolling her eyes, she finally looked up at him. Sadness was gone, replaced by a shy smile.

"Pretty, pretty please," he whispered. "With sugar on top."

"Fine, just one dance," she sighed. He could see she was returning to her old self.

Laughing, he led her to the dance floor for a waltz. His one hand still holding her hand, the other cupping her lower back, pulling her close into him. They fell into step, the rhythm of the music guiding them as they twirled around the dance floor. His eyes locked with hers. She was all he could see.

His fingers tingled as he gently slid them back and forth on her lower back. Hearing her breath catch just before she leaned her head down on his shoulder, he felt elated. She relaxed into his arms, he pulled her in tighter as they made another lap around the dance floor. When the song came to an end, she lifted her head up and gazed into his eyes. He lost himself for a moment in the misty depths. She smiled before pulling away.

"Shall we go talk to the queen?" She said. He could see the panic from earlier was gone. She was calmer now, if a little shy.

He smiled and nodded. He held her hand as they walked to the queen. They were the only ones on the dais besides her guards.

The queen was still sitting on her throne, looking bored. She sat there with her white ball gown draping the floor in contrast with the gold chair and the red curtains. She looked so tiny in the big chair, a chair that had been designed for a king. Her brown eyes shined shrewdly as they walked up. Her dark brown surrounding her face with perfect curls. The white gold crown on top of her head was silver with opals sparkling around it. The tree of life, the royal family symbol, was front and center. Her angular face highlighted with a bit of blush and no other makeup. A sprinkling of freckles crossed her nose.

Elwyn bowed, with Feya following suit.

"Your highness," he humbled. Straightening up, he looked

down at Feya. "I would like to introduce you to Feya Elida Annwen of clan Talamh."

"Hello Feya," The queen greeted her. She looked Feya up and down.

"Hello, your highness," Feya said, tentatively.

The queen nodded, then returned her gaze back to Elwyn. "This is the person you hired to help you, I see. Come closer, so we may speak more privately. Do you have any updates?"

"I was attacked again," he said, laughing self-deprecatingly. As Feya and he stepped up higher on the dais. "He was a hired thug, but he never met who hired him. I have someone monitoring him just in case. We are searching other avenues as well. We have plans to meet with our other suspects casually. As per your wish, I am keeping everything on the quiet."

The queen nodded. "Find out who killed my dear cousin, please. Bayard did not deserve the fate they bestowed upon him. Continue to do it with the utmost discretion. We do not want the criminal to know we are onto them or to start any political battles by accusing the wrong person."

"Yes, your highness," he said, bowing again.

She waved her hand, dismissively.

Tugging Feya's hand, he led her away. He started to lead her out of the ballroom. Unfortunately, their escape was blocked.

"Elwyn," Tad said, smirking at Feya.

Elwyn rolled his eyes and laughed at Tad. They had gone to the military academy together. The blonde lothario was always at these events, looking for his next conquest. Elwyn put his arm around Feya's shoulders, pulling her close. He had to make sure Tad knew who she was with before he tried to run off with her.

"Tad," Elwyn said. "This is Feya. Feya, Tad. She is staying with me."

"Oh," Tad smirked. "It's nice to meet you."

Tad held his hand out palm up towards Feya. She glanced down at his hand, then his face.

Tad let his hand drop, startled by her response.

"And?" she asked with a sneer.

Laughing, Elwyn said. "I will have to catch up with you later. My date wants to leave. Nice seeing you again, Tad."

Elwyn did not wait for Tad to reply as he pulled Feya out of the room. He did not go to these events unless directed to. Most of the time, he could avoid mingling with the higher ups in the court ranks. Feya's frosty response to Tad made him feel better he had to admit to himself.

They walked back to their wing quietly, hand in hand. She tried to pull her hand from his once as he led her to his room, but he gripped her tighter.

"We should discuss what our next step is," he said, closing the door as he pulled her into his bedroom.

"Umm… alright." she mumbled. She walked to one of the wing chairs in front of the fireplace.

Frowning, he walked over to stand in front of the fireplace. He bent down, grabbing a few logs next to it and put them on the grate. Casting a spell, a flame lit up in his hand as he set the logs on fire. Turning, he sat across from her. He had not actually wanted to talk. It was just an excuse to spend time with her. He rested his elbows on his knees, leaning forward.

He debated where to start and what to say. He really did not have a plan at all. Usually, he just winged it. A fact that would piss his step-father off to no end.

"Tomorrow, we should go visit your mother's cousin in the morning," he said, rolling his shoulders.

He decided it was time to get out of his tux. It felt stifling to be in the stiff suit for too long. Standing up, removing the coat and tossing it on the back of the chair. He then removed his vest, realizing Feya was being quiet and had not responded to his comment. Glancing at her face, he noticed her eyes were quietly appraising him. A feral smile crossed his face. He started unbuttoning his shirt slowly. Watching her face as he did so. Slipping off his shirt, he tossed it on the chair behind him.

He paused, unsure how far he should push. She was still so tentative with him. She had been quiet and reserved since the incident with her wings. He stood there in his slacks and undershirt, watching her reaction.

"Are you taking everything off?" she asked breathlessly.

"Do you want me to?" he asked, looking down at her. His devious grin grew bigger.

Watching as she opened her mouth to speak, then closed it. Kneeling down, he reached up and brought her mouth close to his. His nose brushed her nose. Inhaling her breath as she exhaled deeply.

"We sh…should discuss this tomorrow," she stuttered.

Laughing, he pulled back and sat back in his chair. At least he knew she wanted him as much as he wanted her. He just needed to get past her hesitation and fear.

"Tomorrow then we shall visit your dear cousin after breakfast," he said, smugly.

"Alright," she said, looking at her hands.

Reaching over, he rested his hand on hers. She jumped, startled.

Her eyes met his, those green eyes shining bright with shyness and a bit of anxiousness. Squeezing her hands before releasing it. He did not want to press his luck with her. He was getting a little better at sensing when it was time to back off.

"You should get some rest," he said, standing up and extending his hand towards her.

She tentatively reached up and took his hand. He guided her to her room. Standing in front of the door for a moment, gazing down at those misty green eyes. They looked so wary once again. *One step forward, two steps back*, he thought, sighing. He opened her bedroom door for her.

"Goodnight, Fe," he said as he leaned down and brushed his mouth against hers. It took all his strength to walk away.

Chapter 14

Aethelredd stepped off the tarmac during the night. They had a few hours left until the sun came up. Just enough time to get to a hotel and get his room ready for the daylight. Being unable to go out at night made it ten times harder to get to Feya. It slowed them down by limiting the time they had to chase after her. He had thought about sending the others on without him. The problem was only Brady could get through the vale alone. Plus, they would need her to help them get through the vale.

The fear that something bad had happened to her was eating him alive. She had better stay safe, otherwise he was going to start a war. It did not matter if it was all the damn faes, he would hunt all down that hurt his daughter. He just prayed that all the years of training had prepared her for whatever she was facing.

Tomorrow they were meeting up with an old friend of his. Someone who would get them through the vale and find Feya. If she was unhurt and safe, he might just hurt her himself for putting them through this. He just had to be careful if Aguya found out who he was visiting all hell would break loose. Even after seventy-five years, she still held a grudge against Alvero.

They all hoped in the waiting limo. He looked at the faces of his chosen family. Everyone was tired and stressed out. He knew he should say some comforting words, but none came to mind. He had no words until his daughter was safe.

They drove in silence. Once at the hotel, everyone went to their rooms quietly. With the little energy Redd had left, he threw his blackout curtains over the curtains, shoved a towel under the door. He fell onto the bed, drained of energy. Trying to mentally prepare for what would come tomorrow.

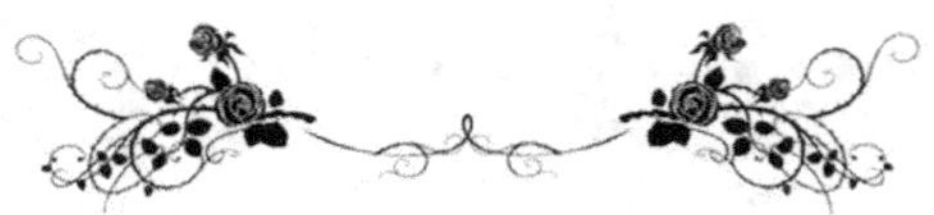

Feya woke up with both excitement and fear running through her. Last night was such a bizarre night. No matter what happened, Elwyn was always so patient and cheerful. It drove her nuts that he had never lost his temper or anything.

She sighed, climbing out of bed. She threw a light yellow sundress on. Looking critically at herself in the mirror, she tried to see if this was the right dress to wear to meet her long-lost cousin. Feeling restless, she knew she would never be happy with her outfit. Turning away, she knew if she spent too much time staring in the mirror, she would change her outfit dozens of times before giving up and wearing whatever. So she might as well just wear this outfit. She threw her hair in a loose bun to get it out of her face. Refusing to look in the mirror again, she left the room.

She walked to the breakfast room. Hearing Elwyn and Olette's heartbeat as she approached. Pausing, she took a deep breath. She had been hoping to have a restful breakfast without Olette's hatred of her. Mentally preparing herself, she counted her heartbeats.

With her head held high, she entered the room and sat at the table.

"Good morning," Olette said, cheerfully.

"Good morning, Fe," Elwyn said, reaching up and running his finger along her cheek.

"Fe?" Olette said, shocked. Feya knew she must have just realized who she was. Funny that it was a childhood nickname that jogged her memory. "You are dead!"

"Turns out I was not," Feya said, softly. She listened to Olette's heart pounding faster. Watched as her eyes searched

Feya's face.

"How?" Olette said, anger radiating in her eyes.

"Mom," Elwyn chided. "Give her a break.

Feya took a moment to decide what lie to say. She figured it was best to stick close to the truth. Keep it short and sweet.

"It's alright, Elwyn," Feya said, coolly. "My mother had me run and hide in the forest. A gentleman found me and raised me as his own."

Olette stared at her a moment, looking like she wanted to say more, but didn't. Something about her made Feya uneasy. It must be how much she hated her. She would be rid of her as soon as the mission was over. That should make Olette happy since she did not want her son with a baseborn fae. She pushed the thought away, not wanting to follow it down that rabbit hole. Knowing it would just make her angry. She was already feeling wonky, and did not need to make it worse.

"We ran into each other," Elwyn said, smiling at his mom. "The other week and I asked her to help me out. Plus, I get to catch up with her. Plus, she has not been to court before. I figured she might enjoy it."

Elwyn stood up, looked at Feya. "Finish your food so we can head out. Alright?"

Feya nodded as he bent down and kissed her mother's cheek. He left the room, quietly. Oblivious to the animosity between Feya and his mother. Staring at Olette across the table, she figured she might as well find out why Olette hated her so much.

"Why do you hate me?" She stated.

"Why do I hate you?" Olette said, cackling. "There is so much to hate about you, little Fe."

Hating the sound of her nickname coming out of Olette's mouth, she wanted to punch her in the face. Instead, Feya stared intently into her eyes blue. Eyes so much like Elwyn's,. Where his where gentle and kind, Olette's where cold and calculating. Refusing to back down, she met Olette's gaze dead on. It was now or never. She doubted they would ever be friends, but she needed to know what this fae was thinking about her. Did Feya remind Olette of where she came from and her snobby side was disapproving? Was it just her status in the fae community she hated or something else?

Olette stared back at her, folding her hands in her lap. Feya could tell she was trying to calm herself, but her heartbeat told Feya it was not working.

"My son deserves better than the likes of you," Olette sneered. "Nothing but a baseborn. A sad, pathetic ignoble. Just like your parents. I have worked hard to bring our station in court up. You will not come in and destroy that. Plus, once he's done playing trip down memory lane with you, he will realize what you are. He will tire of you soon."

Feya stared back, coldly. Keeping every emotion running through her head hidden. The urge to smack this fae and show her how much better than her she was, was hard to resist.

"Well?" Olette said, harshly.

"Your food is getting cold. You may want to eat up," Feya said, smiling coldly.

Feya picked up a piece of toast, taking a bit, her eyes never leaving Olette's.

Olette stared back before her temper snapped again, throwing her napkin on the table in a rage. She jumped up, knocking her chair over. Slamming the door behind her as she left

Feya dropped the toast, her appetite gone. If she only knew what Feya really was, she would have a genuine reason to hate her.

Feya walked next to Elwyn as they headed towards Nerine's estate. The walk was pleasant, the breeze gentle. She looked at the gardens in front of the estates. The gardens are in perfect bloom. She missed the mess of the outside world. The lack of symmetry created a beauty of its own. Everything in these houses was so perfectly cultivated. Cookie cutter houses with cookie cutter lawns.

Her mind was a mess right now. She tried to focus, but the anger at Olette clouded her mind. The words had stung more than she wanted. She had not thought of her childhood as being unworthy. What few memories she still had of Elwyn's family were of a happy family that did not worry about the finer things or status. Plus, since then, Feya's family had amassed quite a bit and were highly regarded in their communities. She was pretty sure she had more money sitting in her own checking account than Olette had in her entire portfolio. Feya had worked hard to earn her own way since she had not married for wealth and status.

"Here we are," Elwyn said.

Feya, jarred from her reverie, stopped and looked at the estate. They had all started to blend together. She could not tell one from the other. The white house, with the perfect garden. She started up the path, Elwyn striding up next to her.

She felt his hand grab hers. The thought of letting go crossed her mind, but felt she needed the support. Not sure why she should be nervous about meeting one of her mom's relatives. She had a family, she had a life, and there was nothing she needed here. A trip down memory lane was the last thing she needed. Just needed to focus on the mission and do her job. This was just another suspect and nothing more.

Elwyn lifted the door knocker and let it drop. The knock sounded so loud to her ears as they waited. A butler opened the door. A frail, lanky fae male with salt and pepper hair.

"How can I help you?" He said, bored. His eyes looked past them.

"Hello I am Elwyn Altalune," Elwyn said to the butler. "And this Feya Annwen, daughter of Elida, cousin of Nerine. We are here to request an audience with Nerine."

The butler nodded as he closed the door and walked away.

Feya stood waiting, hoping he would not take too much

time. She was ready to get this over with. A moment later, the door opened.

A woman answered with blonde curly hair that swirled around her face. A beautiful cherub face had eyes the same green as Feya's looked at them. Her ivory skin was a startling contrast to the red dress she wore. She was petite, at about 4 inches shorter than Feya's 5'8".

"Feya," she whispered. Grabbing her and pulling her into a hug.

Feya stood there, wrapping her hands around Nerine, awkwardly hugging her back.

"You look exactly like your mother," Nerine said, grabbing her hand. Her sweet smile produced two dimples. "She was always so beautiful and so are you. You have her eyes even. I remember spending summers playing with your mother. We would have so much fun together. She was very dear to me. Not a day goes by that I don't remember her fondly. I have some old paintings she had done here somewhere."

"Oh," Feya said, awkwardly. "My mother was a wonderful woman."

She dragged her into a drawing room, Elwyn close on their heels. A pink frilly room. Everything in the room was pink: the settee, the wingback chairs, the walls, even the end tables.

It looked like that pink stomach medicine humans drank exploded in there, Feya thought.

Nerine pulled Feya on to the settee next to her. Still holding tight onto Feya's hand. Feya peered into her face, searching for malice or what made people think she was after the queen. She could find nothing there to give her any sign. Either she was a talented actress or not the fae they thought she was.

"I was told you were dead," she said cheerily. "But they had not found your body. So I always held hope they would find you and now here you are!"

"My mother told me to run," Feya said, retelling the story she had said earlier. "That night. So I escaped into the forest. A gentleman rescued me and raised me like I was his own. I was very young and did not realize everyone thought I was dead. I apologize for any upset this may have caused you."

Nerine's face never changed from being cheerful, but her heart rate changed. Something about what she had said excited her. Feya realized she was looking at a talented actress. Disappointment washed over her. A small part of her had held out hope.

"I am so glad you were safe and loved," Nerine said, her smile sweet and serene. Her heart rate was erratic, the sign of a lie. "Tell me everything about your life. We will have to catch up. I am so excited to get to know you all over again. Do you remember when I met you as a child? You were always so precocious."

"Thank you so much for your concern," Feya said, smiling. *Two could play the act,* Feya mused. "When Elwyn told me you were here, I just could not wait to come meet you. Of course, we will have to catch up."

"You're welcome," Nerine said, seriously. "I cannot wait to catch up. You should have reached out to me sooner. I could have given you a proper introduction to court life."

"Of course," Feya said. Casting her charm spell, she was tired of playing the game and wanted to be done. "Please let me know what you have been up to lately."

She saw the hesitation in Nerine's eyes. Feya smiled, whispering. "Please."

Nerine started talking as she stared into Feya's eyes. "I have been looking for a new husband. My money is running out. When you showed up with an Altalune, I wondered how much money you had."

Nerine paused, startled, looking at Elwyn, then back at Feya.

"It's alright," Feya stated. She gently cupped her chin, guiding Nerine's eyes back to her own. Feya continued. "Tell me about the queen."

"She is a bitch," Nerine said, coldly. Their eyes locked. "She is jealous of my beauty and always tries to stop the marriages. Constantly warning people about me. Blocking my chances at a better life. She knows I am prettier than her and she can't stand it. I am sick of her getting in the way. I deserve a better life than this, and someone will give it to me."

Chapter 15

"What are you doing about it?" Feya asked, softly. Pushing further, and a bit harder. She was angry and done with Nerine.

"Nothing," Nerine muttered. "I can't do anything about it. She is too powerful. I don't have a death wish. I will find someone who will give me what I deserve. The queen can't stop everyone."

Feya smiled, finished with the conversation. "We had such a pleasant conversation, didn't we?"

Nerine stared at her blankly, nodding in agreement at the suggestion.

"You will think fondly of this, won't you?" Feya said. "You will remember me affectionately and never reach out to me or Elwyn again."

Nerine nodded again, blankly.

"Please show us out. You have a busy day ahead." Feya whispered. Nerine had been so easy to charm, a weak-minded narcissist. The disappointment faded a bit as she let go of the hope of the old Feya. Releasing the charm spell, as she released Nerine's chin.

Nerine laughed. "Let me show you both out. You would not believe the busy day I have ahead of me. I have enjoyed our chat. We will have to chat again."

"Of course," Feya said, back to her normal voice. She

knew they would never meet again. The twinge of sadness hit her again, but faded swiftly.

Elwin grabbed her hand as they walked back.

"You were quiet in there," Feya said tentatively.

"You had it," he said, quietly. "No need for me to interrupt. I am sorry."

"What do you have to be sorry for?" she said, shocked. Pausing in the street to look into his face.

"She is family," he said, stopping. "I know what family means to you. I am sorry that I did not prepare you more for her."

"It is not your fault," Feya said, smiling self-deprecatingly. "She is not the one who is after you. We will have to continue hunting."

"I know," he said, reaching up to cup her cheek. "And that is not my primary concern right now. You are. Plus, maybe I like the idea of spending more time with you."

Feya felt the nerves building up in her at his touch. The words coming out before she had a chance to think. "Your mother hates me."

Elwyn looked startled. "I would not say hate, maybe a strong dislike."

"I would say hate," she said, laughing. "She told me she hated a baseborn like me."

She debated telling him the rest, but decided against it.

"She will love you just like I…" he started.

"I doubt it," she interrupted. Not ready to hear whatever he was going to say. Pulling away, she started walking again.

Her emotions warring inside her. Churning like a storm. She needed a moment of quiet. They walked the rest of the way to the castle without saying another word. Even though they were a foot apart, it felt like miles. She knew she had upset Elwyn when she cut him off. That had not been her intention. Sighing, she bit her lip.

Breaking the silence, Elwyn said coolly. "For dinner tonight,

we are scheduled to eat with Raisa and Aelfric. I have invited them both over to the wing at 7."

Feya nodded, not sure what to say or do. So she stayed quiet.

They continued up the stairs to their rooms in silence. Knowing he was upset that she had interrupted him tore at her heart. She just could not hear what he was going to say. This was a job, nothing more. She could not spend her life with him at court. That would be miserable, plus always the chance of getting caught if she gets thirsty. He obviously wanted to be a part of the court. Even if she tried, it would not work out. They lived in two different worlds, worlds that were not compatible. Plus, she missed her family, especially after this morning's events.

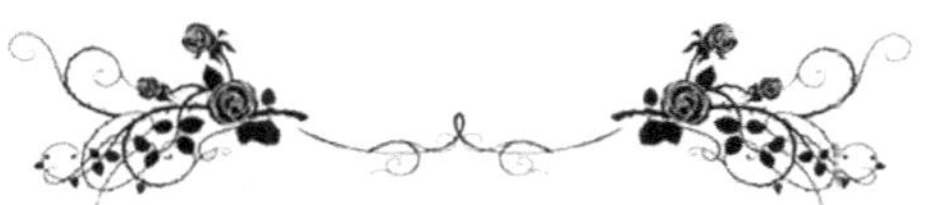

Elwyn paced his room restlessly. He had not meant to start to say those words. He knew he freaked her out. The expression she made when he opened his mouth said it all. Looks like he was back to square one with her. She would not even talk to him on the way back.

He punched a fist onto his desk, frustrated. Staring into her eyes, he had lost himself. Lost his fucking mind, obviously. Flinging himself into his chair, he taped his fingers onto his desk.

How was I supposed to win her trust? He mused.

Everything he did was wrong. He could not catch a break with her. His patience was running thin. Plus, his time was running out. He wasn't close to figuring out who was after him. At least they had knocked someone off the list.

Sighing, he leaned forward, putting his head in his hands. He needed to find patience and keep trying to win Feya over, all while finding out who is after the queen and himself. Nothing short of a miracle was what he needed today.

He heard Feya's bedroom door open. Looking at the clock, he realized it was lunchtime. He waited before heading to the dining room. Hoping that was where she had headed.

Standing outside the door, he paused, nerves eating at him.

When he opened the door, Feya was sitting quietly, eating a sandwich. She never looked up or acknowledged him. A pang of aching hit his heart.

"Feya," he stated, wanting to talk to her. Not sure what to say or how to say anything. "I just want you to know…"

He trailed off, at a loss for words. Restlessly, he stared down at his hands on the table.

"Yes?" Feya asked, warily.

"If something happens to me…" he started. Pausing as nerves made it hard to speak.

"Nothing will happen to you," she said fiercely.

"I don't want that to happen. I am just saying if it does…" he trailed off.

"Nothing will happen to you. Do you understand me?" she yelled.

Her temper startled him. He figured she might be happy to be rid of him at this point in time. Nodding, he stared down at his feet. He wasn't sure what he should say. He just wanted her to know what he was feeling. Which was a bad idea anyways.

He nodded. "I have no intention of getting hurt. I was trying to make plans, in case things went sideways. Especially since we are no closer to figuring things out."

"It won't," she muttered.

He laughed, smiled at her. She smiled back. His heart felt a little lighter. Maybe she cared more than he realized. He grabbed a sandwich from the center chafing dish. Every day, his mother chose the meals for the servants to leave. Today was brie with pistachio pesto sandwiches.

Leaning back, he was glad they were alone. He needed to get her talking. Get her to relax.

"We should discuss tonight," he said, between bites of his sandwich. "My mom will be out, so it will be us and them. Neither has invited a guest, but they will have their entourage in tow, meaning guards and such. We probably won't be alone with either at any time. I have already informed the wait staff of what the meal will be."

"Anyway, could we at least get the guards out of the room?" she mumbled, while stuffing her face. He had not seen her eat like this before.

"We will have to work on that," he said, taking the last bit of his sandwich.

He watched her patiently. Noticing a dab of mayo on her cheek, he grabbed his napkin to wipe it off. Their eyes locked. He felt his heart soar as he looked into her eyes. He saw the concern and happiness. She had been happy to see him, after all, and concerned for his wellbeing.

Maybe he did not have to be as patient as he thought he needed to be. His smile grew bigger.

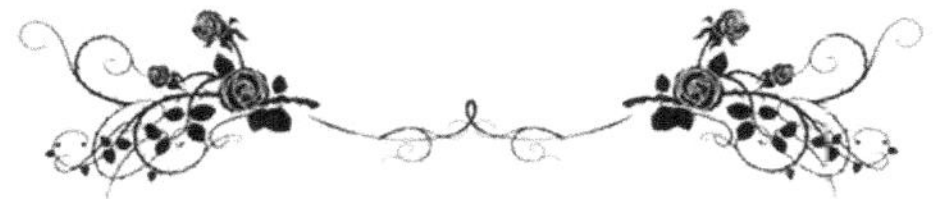

Aethelredd entered the clearing, having everyone stay behind at the trailhead. Aguya hated Alvero. There wasn't time for that drama. He made his way the last quarter mile to the ancient hut in the woods. The wooden roof was covered in moss. The wrap porch had a single rocking chair on it. Herbs hung from strings that dangled from the porch to dry.

He knocked on the door, knowing his friend already knew he was there. He probably knew the instant they entered his forest. Some mumbo jumbo about the forest creatures telling him.

"Old friend," Alvero said, laughing. Throwing the door wide open as soon as his knuckles hit the door. Redd was grabbed up into a big bear hug. "I don't get many guests these days. What brings you my way?"

Walking into the hut, Redd noticed Alvero had added no modern amenities to the hut he had for hundreds of years. Candles and a fireplace lit the room. No phones, no televisions. His only amenities were his books and sparse furniture. A rocking chair and wing-back chair in front of the fireplace. The small dining table sat in the center of the room, filled with bottles and books. A twin bed covered in quilts that looked like it was a hundred years old was on the opposite wall across from the fireplace. Bookshelves lining the walls filled with bottles of herbs and whatnot or a variety of books.

Redd stared at the old fairy. He still looked like he was in his 30s. His dark blonde hair and brown eyes twinkled in the light. His square jaw was covered in a scruffy beard. He was tall and lanky. His clan had long ago been killed off in a war, the same war that killed Redd's own clan. He had worked hand in hand with this fae on numerous missions. Now Alvero was mostly retired, living like a hermit in the forest.

"I need your help, old man," Redd said, stoically.

"Go ahead, tell me," Alvero said. He went and sat on the rocking chair in front of the fireplace. Pointing to the other chair.

Redd sat down, resting his elbows on his knees while staring into the fire. The fire warmed the room up nicely as the flames danced in the fireplace.

"My daughter ran off," Redd said, quietly. "She is in a fairy vale."

"I remember little Feya, always so rambunctious," Alvero said quietly. "But she is part Fae and an adult. If she wants to run off to visit her fae side is not something to worry about."

"She is not there on a vacation or to connect with a long-lost family," Redd grumbled, his eyes locked with his friends. "She took on a mission. What happens when they find out what the other part is?"

"Nothing good, that's for sure," Alvero nodded.

"They will execute her," Redd said. He took a deep breath before continuing. "I need you to help us get across the vale and stay in the vale unnoticed. It's not any vale, though.

"Oh?" Alvero said, curiously.

Redd sighed. "It is the vale. The one that holds Queen Cassada."

"Well, that creates a new set of problems," Alvero said, laughing. Shaking his head as he rocked in the chair.

"She took on a mission that she can't do on her own. If anything happens…" Redd said, his voice filled with despair.

"Are you sure she is there?" Alvero said, cautiously. "She has trained well and can handle herself."

"Very sure," Redd growled. "I know she needs help on this one. Can you help or not?"

"Have you ever been in a vale?" Alvero said tentatively. "It's not like how it is out here. Things are… different."

"Yes," Redd grumbled. Hoping Alvero would believe the lie. "Can you or can't you?"

"I can cast a rune spell," Alvero said. All laughter gone as he stared into the fire. "You will need to carry it with you at all times. Be extra vigilant when there. The weather is different, the sun is different in a vale."

"I will need one for Aguya too. Leo will stand guard at the entrance." Redd said.

Alvero nodded as he stood up to get to work. Redd watched as he carved a rune into two small pieces of wood. Then started creating a potion to dip them in. Grabbing bottles of herbs and tinctures off various shelves. Redd stared at his old friend while he worked, wondering how he kept track of what was what. None of the bottles had labels. So many looked like they had the same thing in them.

Redd's mind returned to Feya and about how he was going to drag Feya out of there faster than a cat on a mouse. She had just better be alright. He racked his hands down his face in frustration.

"If she," Alvero started, pausing for a moment. "Went on this mission alone. There would be a reason. Always was a level-headed girl. She will not appreciate you thundering in unannounced."

"I know that," Redd grumbled, turning away. If Alvero thought he could talk Redd into changing his plans, he was a fool.

"You may want to give her some space," Alvero finished. He lifted his charms up to admire his handy work. "You may want to just help her do her job. Or you may get in the way and cause

her to get hurt if they find out what you are. She was always pretty good about blending in."

Redd grunted, looking back into the fire. In his head, he knew he should heed Alvero's words, but his heart told a different story.

Chapter 16

Feya stood in the small dining room next to Elwyn. Her white silk dress skirted the floor. The V-neck front gave a glimpse of her ample cleavage. She wore a necklace that Elwyn gave her today, a silver chain with a little bat charm. It was a silver bat on top of a cameo style backing. He had thought it was funny; she thought it was cute.

She was ready to meet the next two people in the puzzle. The sooner they narrowed this down, the sooner she was with her family.

A tug at her heart pulled at her. She knew now that when she thought she just needed to be around him to get him out of her mind; she was wrong. The more she was with him, the more she knew it would be harder when she left. She glanced up at him. He was so handsome in this light. The candle light showed lighter highlights in his hair. His dark blue button-up shirt made his blue eyes look darker. His tight gray slacks looked snug, outlining his length. The bruise was fading and there was still a slight yellowish tint left behind.

She smiled up at him when he noticed her looking. Her cheeks burned brightly as she turned away. Looking at the dining table. The servants set the table with several choices of food. It all looked delicious. Braised beef, herbed mashed potatoes, roasted carrots and more lined the table.

The door opened up and Aelfric walked in. He was

beautiful. One of the most gorgeous faes she had ever seen. His dark-hair falling gently over half his face. He was trim and athletic looking. His face was delicate and angelic looking. What shook her most, though, were those dark black eyes. There was no emotion in those eyes, dead like a fallen, rotted tree. He lifted his chin up on his round cherub shaped face to stare down the best he could at them. He stood about two inches shorter than Elwyn.

His guards walked in behind him.

"I figured this would be an intimate dinner," Elwyn laughed. "Why don't you have your guards wait outside?"

Aelfric raised an eyebrow before waving his guards away.

Aelfric stood staring at Elwyn, then said. "To what do I owe the pleasure?"

"I thought it has been so long since we have talked," Elwyn said. He seemed so genuine when he laughed and smiled at him. "Plus, I would like you to meet Feya. This is her visit to the court, so I am introducing her to some of my friends."

Elwyn slid his arm around her waist. Feya felt the warmth spread from where his fingers toyed with the fabric around her waist. His fingers tracing circles on her hip.

The door opened and Raisa walked in. She threw her cloak at her manservant haphazardly. Her skintight black dress sparkled with rhinestones as they caught the candlelight. A slit went all the way up to her thigh. Her red hair, shining in the lights, looked like copper. When she saw her, her hazel eyes shined with annoyance. Her heart-shaped face screwed up into a scowl as she looked Feya up and down encircled in Elwyn's arm.

"Who is this, Elwyn?" she sneered, pointing her finger at Feya in disgust.

"Hello, my name is Feya," Feya said, walking over to Raisa and extending her hand towards her.

Raisa just sneered at her hand. Feya patiently continued to hold it out, waiting for her to take it. She did not know why Raisa was being hostile, but she was tired of rude female faes.

Raisa pushed her hand away, annoyed. She shoved past Feya. Feya heard her heart, wondering if she just bit her what

everyone would do. Would Elwyn be upset or congratulate her? She bet Raisa tasted yummy. The thought of saying fuck it and taste both their blood crossed her mind. Then she could be done with this dinner.

Sighing, she turned as Raisa walked over to Elwyn. She flung her arms around Elwyn as she reached up and planted her lips on Elwyn's.

Feya felt a rage burn in her core. She felt her fangs itching to dig into the flesh of Raisa's neck. She could almost taste her blood.

Elwyn laughed gently, pushing her away. His eyes locked with Feya's. She watched as the laughter left his eyes. She knew he read her anger, no matter how she tried to hide it. He looked sheepish as he stepped back as Raisa tried to reach for him again.

"Please have a seat," Elwyn said. He pointed to the chair next to Aelfric. Raisa sat down. "Raisa, why don't you send your manservant outside so we can have a quiet dinner without him watching us?"

"Fine," Raisa said, waving a dismissive hand at the fae. "Go away."

Elwyn pulled the chair out for Feya. Feya looked at Raisa as she sat in her chair. Elwyn sat next to her. Feya decided she wanted to play Raisa's game after all.

Reaching up, she brushed a stray lock of Elwyn's hair off his forehead. She watched as he paused and looked at her. Slowly, a smile spread across his face. Feya smiled back, not sure if she should regret playing with fire.

Elwyn put his hand on the back of her neck. Drawing circles with his fingertips. The warmth from his fingers made it hard to focus. She could see the anger in Raisa's eyes. She was not sure if she wanted to flirt to piss off Raisa, shrug off his caress, or...

Turning to Aelfric, she decided it was best to ignore the other two for now. Plus, looking at Raisa just made her angry. If only Elwyn would stop tracing those circles. She was having trouble concentrating with those fingers gently caressing her nape.

"So how do you know Elwyn?" Feya asked Aelfric.

"We have known each other for years," he answered. "I met him when he first came out of the academy. We have both worked for the queen for a while now. I, of course, have been in court longer, having worked with the king."

"Oh, interesting," Feya said. The tingling from Elwyn's fingers having spread. A shiver went down her spine as he traced the nape of her neck.

Aelfric took her words as encouragement to talk. "I used to work with the king on…."

Feya tried to focus on his words, but all she felt was Elwyn's fingers. A fire was simmering in her and she needed it to stop so she could focus. Reaching up, she grabbed Elwyn's hand. He stopped looking at Aelfric and looked at her. A mischievous grin spread across his face.

Feya sighed and turned back to the long winded Aelfric as he continued on with his monotonous voice and story.

"Upon the king's death, I offered my services to the queen. She, of course, accepted it." Aelfric said.

"Of course," Feya interrupted before he told his complete life story. She thought of charming him, but knew she was not strong enough to charm them both without drinking their blood. Her charm spells were not good in a crowd.

She knew she needed to talk to Raisa. She took a deep breath before turning to her.

Aelfric kept going with his story. "I have been indispensable to the queen, of course. On several occasions…"

Feya closed her eyes for a moment. Listening to Aelfric drone on about his accomplishments. He was going to put them to sleep with his vain ramblings.

Raisa knocked her glass over, spilling it onto Aelfric's lap. For a split second Feya thought maybe they could be friends, but Raisa opened her mouth.

"Oops," Raisa said. "I am sure Frida will be glad to show you where the bathroom is so you can clean up'

"You stupid twit," Aelfric growled, jumping up, outraged.

"My name is Feya," Feya retorted. Looking at Raisa's neck, she wondered if she would have time to drink the wench's blood. Maybe just a small taste or more. "I am sure Elwyn can show him the bathroom."

"I guess I will show you the restroom," Elwyn said, cautiously laughing. Standing up, he looked tentatively at Feya and Raisa. Feya knew he did not want to leave them alone.

Feya never took her eyes away from Raisa as Elwyn and Aelfric left the room. Raisa stared back defiantly. Feya, tired of playing, decided it was time to charm Raisa then send her on her way. She took a deep breath to steady her nerves. Closing her eyes, she counted her own heartbeats. She opened her eyes, meeting Raisa's.

"Raisa," she breathed the charm spell. She saw Raisa's eyes dilate as she fell under the charm easily. The simple fool was easier to charm than the others had been. "Tell me your feelings for the queen."

"She is a fool," Raisa said, her eyes never leaving Feya's. "An old rundown monument to the past. I hope she chokes on her own vileness."

"Have you been hiring people to kill people around the queen?" Feya asked.

"No," Raisa said.

"Do you know who is killing those around her?" Feya whispered.

"Why would I know that?" Raisa asked, confused.

"Do you know who might be hunting the queen?" Feya queried.

"No," Raisa said.

Pausing, Feya debated if she should continue to ask Raisa questions. She knew she should not bother to ask her next questions, but could not help herself. Knowing she should not, but

could not help herself. She should let Raisa have him that way. When the mission was over, she would go back to her own life, but the idea of Raisa and Elwyn made her sick to her stomach.

"Have you ever been intimate with Elwyn?" The question escaped from Feya's mouth before she could control herself.

"No," Raisa said. "Not for a lack of trying."

"What do you want with Elwyn?" Feya asked. Satisfaction at knowing he had not been intimate with Raisa made Feya smile.

"He is rich and handsome. Why would I not want him?" Raisa said.

Feya felt the anger boiling up in her. She tamped it down, trying to focus on her spell.

"It is time for you to go home," Feya whispered. "Never bother Elwyn again. Never try to seduce him again. Stay as far away from Elwyn as you can. You will forget our conversation. You will get up and leave quietly. If anyone asks, say you are bored."

Nodding, Raisa stood up and left the room without a word. The door quietly opening and closing behind her. Relief washed over Feya. She knew she should not have done the last part, but she could not help herself. Hopefully, Elwyn would not be too upset. Maybe she should not tell him the last part. What he did not know would not upset him. She knew the charm spell for her to fight her own emotions would not hold for long, but at least for a while, she knew Raisa would avoid Elwyn.

A moment later, the males returned. Feya looked back at them and smiled. Raisa did one good thing tonight. By spilling that drink, she created a distraction to separate everyone.

Elwyn looked around in confusion. Tentatively, his eyes met Feya's. "Where's Raisa?" He asked.

"She had to run," Feya said, flippantly. "Something came up she had to attend to."

Elwyn Looked at her strangely, like he was trying to read her mind to find out what had happened. Feya smiled at him sweetly, knowing he would not press her as long as they had an audience.

Turning, she looked at Aelfric. Using her charm spell, she said. "How do you feel about the queen?"

She was ready for this night to be over with. Emotionally drained after a long day of using her spells, being in the sun, and changing her sleep schedule. She wanted to end this dinner and go hide in her room.

Aelfric stared at her, confused, fighting the spell. Her spell was weak. She took a deep breath to steady herself. Once she felt centered, she opened her eyes and tried again. She locked eyes with him, compelling him with her eyes.

"How do you feel about the queen?" she said, more firmly.

He looked into her eyes, tilted his head, he stated. "I love her. One day, she will realize she loves me. She is so stubborn, always fighting her love for me"

Feya looked at him, realizing he was just an egomaniac. "Go home and remember what a wonderful time you had here tonight."

Aelfric stood up and left.

"I always worry if I speak, it will break your spell," Elwyn whispered.

"It is best if you don't," Feya said.

"Well, we might as well enjoy the meal, since all this food is here." He said, his charming smile back.

She nodded, glad that it was just the two of them. She would eat, discuss what they knew, and go hide from the world for a while.

"Tell me what happened with Raisa?" he said, while taking a bite of food.

"She is nothing," Feya said. "But a bitter fool. Jealous of the queen. Quite vain and annoying. She is not the one."

"I did not think so," he said, leaning back in his chair.

"Have you…" Feya stammered, then stopped. Why would she ask such a stupid question? It was none of her concern if he had feelings for Raisa. She was here to do a job and leave. She must remember that and quit acting like a jealous twit.

"Nope," he stated. "Never would I sleep with her. She is not my type."

"Alright," she said, quietly. Startled, that he had guessed wrong, but still answered her question.

"Were you jealous?" he teased.

"No." she said, flushing.

Laughing, he reached over and he cupped the back of her neck. Forcing her to turn her face towards his. She stared into those lecherous blue eyes.

"I am not interested in her at all," he said, bringing his face closer to hers. "You are the only one I am interested in."

Chapter 17

Aethelredd looked at the vale in front of them. A hazy field almost invisible to the eye. He could barely see it, almost did not sense it. No wonder it had remained hidden from humans for so long. When they first approached, dread filled his soul. It had taken everything he had to push past the spell and not walk away.

He had thought once they got closer and the spell was gone, he would feel different. The feeling remained. Every muscle in his body ached to turn and run. The knot in his stomach grew at the uncertainty about whether the rune spell would work. Aguya and he had little spell bags holding the rune spells around their necks. Looking at Aguya, he knew she was going through what he was also. Her hands trembled and shook as she clenched them into fists. Brady did not seem flustered at all. She was her happy, cheery self. The spell must only affect none faes.

They had come an hour before sunset. Brady had said they should not enter during the night. The guards would be more vigilant after sunset. So it had been decided to go as close to sunset as they could. They would enter the vale at 5 pm about an hour before sunset.

He adjusted his cloak to better hide himself from the occasional rays of sun that came peeking through the trees. Brady would blend in being a Fae herself. Aguya smelled like a fae, with a special perfume they had been given. Redd could smell the cloying scent on his own skin. It felt weird to not smell like yourself.

Plus, being tiny, Aguya could pass easier. Whereas Redd was tall, it would be harder for him to go unnoticed. Leo would stand out even more. There was no way he could pass as any kind of fae. Leo was going to stay behind, watching the vale, and keeping guard. He was already stationed just before where he started to get nauseous.

"What do we have to expect once we go through?" Redd asked Brady.

"I have told you several times," Brady grumbled.

"Tell us again," Redd stated.

Sighing, Brady grumbled. "We will enter the vale. You might get queasy, that is perfectly normal. The guards are usually posted by the gates once we enter. We will have to act normal. Do you know how to do that, Aguya?"

He felt the temperature around them rise as Aguya started to get angry.

"Now is not the time to start bickering." he scolded. Why Brady and Aguya had to keep making snide comments to each other was beyond him. Plus, it was driving him crazy. He wanted to focus on what was ahead of them, not their childish antics.

"No use in waiting," he growled. Taking a deep breath as he stepped forward through the vale.

The wave of nausea hit him like a ton of bricks. He stumbled as he felt himself falling. He hit the ground, dry heaving. His head reeled as he tried to stumble to his feet. He felt Brady's hand grip his arm, helping him steady himself. The nausea lingered as he leaned onto Brady.

Looking around, he tried to get his bearings as his stomach slowly settled down. He no longer felt the need to run, either. They were still in the forest, but the air smelled different. It smelled like spring. All the plants were in bloom. As his vision focused, he saw the pristine white walls of the castle's bailey a quarter mile in front of him. The afternoon sun was hurting his eyes and giving him a migraine. He tugged his cloak further over his face to stay in the shadows.

He shrugged Brady's hand off as he felt steadier. Looking

around, he spotted Aguya leaning on a tree. Her eyes were closed, as she looked like she was close to vomiting.

"Get yourself together," Redd told Aguya.

He knew if coddled her, she would lose her temper and now was not the time to piss her off. Their eyes locked, and she nodded. The fire burned in her eyes. He could tell she was as worried about Feya as he was.

He looked at the sunlight stained ground standing between him and the castle walls. Trying to remember the last time he had left a place during the day. It had been ions. Last time had not gone so well either. He just needed to remember to be careful and stay in his cloak. He steeled himself, then started forward.

He had never been inside a fairy vale before. It was such a strange sensation. The air felt weird around him, as if it was charged with a magical energy. It smelled different, as if spring was in perpetual bloom. Even the sun felt different, the rays were brighter; the warmth was just the perfect temperature. This must be what Alvero meant.

He hoped the sun would go down soon. On the other side of the vale, it went down at a little after six pm this time of year. The season was different here. It was not fall; it was spring inside the vale. He hoped it would not affect sundown. He was not sure how long he could hide under this cloak. Shaking his head, he pushed the thought away. They can control the weather in a vale, but the sun? Most likely not.

They approached the gates. Brady smiled and waved at the guards like they were old friends. They entered without the guards batting an eye. Peace had made them slack at their jobs, it seemed. They walked straight in and entered the town, sitting in front of the castle. He looked at the quant shops that filled the town square. Vendors and carts everywhere. Dozens of fae walking around shopping and talking. No other magicals were here. There were strict rules about other magical creatures entering the vale.

They walked through the town and tried to find a quiet spot. Finally, they found a secluded alley. No one was in it and it provided some privacy from the main thoroughfare. Turning into it, they walked behind the building. Luckily, it was hidden in the shadows. Redd's eyes needed a rest.

"Hurry," Brady said, anxiously to Aguya.

He watched as Aguya pulled out Feya's hair brush. Plucking a strand of black hair out, she held in her hand as she quietly whispered the spell.

I call upon the element of fire, guide me to what is lost. A lock of hair to track far and near. Track her spirit and direct me to what I seek. The fire flame, bright and strong, guide us, as will it so mote it be.

He watched as a spark lit up her golden eyes, as they seemed to glow from within. He knew she had found the path. A bit of relief hit him when he realized that meant Feya was alive, at least. They walked behind Aguya as she led the way towards the castle. No one seemed to pay them much attention, lost in their own world. They followed Aguya as she weaved her way through the crowds as if in a daze. They were heading straight to the castle.

He grabbed Aguya as she walked to the front entrance of the castle, his hand burning in the sun. He inhaled due to the pain, quickly jerking his hand back under the cloak.

Aguya turned to look at him. Blinking her eyes as she came out of her haze.

"You really think we will get past those guards at the front door?" he mumbled, as the pain shot through his arm. The sun had scorched his skin. It had only taken a split second, and the pain was intense.

It was not healing. Usually, that small amount of sun would heal within a few moments, but it was not healing. Extra precautions would need to be taken while here. He did not know what protection spells were here or how it would affect him. He knew now the sun here was more intense and would hurt a hell of a lot more.

Aguya shook her head. Pausing a moment, looking around, she surveyed the castle. He watched as she searched for another path to travel. The blisters boiling up on his hand sent stabbing pains through his arm. Taking a deep breath, he focused on his own heartbeats and the idea of how he was going to beat his daughter.

"I see another way," she said, turning to walk around the castle.

A few fae tended to the gardens surrouncing the castle. The gardens were perfect. Everything looked so pristine, as if everything was put in its perfect spot. Every flower petal, every branch, etc. Not a single dead leaf or flower.

He hated it. He had always found beauty in the imperfect. It was always so bland to watch perfection.

A twinge of pain shot through his arm, causing him to flinch. He would have to have Brady tend to his hand as soon as they found Feya.

A wave of fear washed through him. If she was in a prison cell, he would tear down every brick of this castle to free her. If they had hurt her, death would be a welcome reprieve for what he would do to them.

He watched as Aguya stopped a bit away from the back entrance. It smelled like it was a kitchen, fresh bread wafting in the air. He inhaled deeply as he smelled the rest of dinner cooking. At least the servants would be busy with dinner.

"How do we get past all the servants?" Aguya mumbled. Her face screwed up in frustration.

Brady sighed, giving them both dirty looks. "Just follow me and keep your mouth shut."

They followed behind Brady as she grabbed a basket and strolled through the herb garden. She filled it with various herbs. She waltzed through the kitchen door as they followed behind. Acting like she did this every day.

He heard Brady's soft lilt as she started humming a song he did not recognize. A moment later, he heard another fae start humming with her. Brady walked up to her and handed her the basket of herbs.

"Have a lovely day," Brady said, smiling. She continued her humming as the fae grabbed the basket in confusion.

Redd was not sure what had happened or if an alarm would be raised soon. Brady just confidently walked away, Aguya and he followed her. She stopped a bit down the hallway, then turned to Aguya. They paused for a moment in the hall.

"Should we wait till the sun goes down?" Brady asked tentatively.

Redd debated his answer. Looking at Aguya, he whispered. "Do you think she is in prison?"

Shaking her head Aguya, pointed up to the floors above them.

"Can you tell if she is hurt?" Redd asked, knowing she probably could not.

Aguya shrugged, biting her lip. "She is upstairs, whatever that means."

He stared at them, not sure how to proceed. For once, he did not have a plan. It surprised him they had made it this far. Knowing she was not in a dank cell below the castle, or worse, was a bit of relief. She was alive. That counted for something.

"I think," Brady spoke up, her voice firm and certain. "We should wait till after sundown. That way, we don't have to worry about the sun. We can find a closet or something to hide in for now."

Redd nodded.

Chapter 18

Elwyn's mouth crushed up against hers. She thought to fight for a moment, but then he thrust his torgue in her mouth. All thoughts of struggling vanished as soon as she tasted him. The warm, heady taste of the red wine lingered on his tongue as it explored her mouth. Her tongue tentatively tangled with his. Her head spun from the intoxication of his taste. She tentatively scraped her fangs on his tongue as it slid in and out of her mouth. A guttural sound escaped from his throat.

His right hand gentled on the back of her neck as his other hand reached up and cupped her check as he subdued the kiss. His fingers blazed a trail of fire down to her neck, over her shoulder, continuing its exploration to her breast. Her breath caught in her throat, her skin felt flush from his touch, as his fingers dug into the delicate flesh of her bosom. Arching her back so she could give him better access. Her breast swelled and molded to his hand.

She reached her hand up to touch him, knocking his glass of wine over onto his lap. He jumped up, shocked. She looked at the red wine that stained his lap. As the red stain spread across his gray slacks, a giggle escaped out before she could stop it.

She locked eyes with him, seeing the annoyance there before it faded to laughter. He shook his head and extended his hand out to her, palm up.

She gazed into his eyes, knowing the hand was more than

helping her up. She hesitated for a moment, fighting the lust that was raging a war inside her. Fighting the longing for his touch, his taste. Taking a deep breath, she knew there was no longer any use in fighting her feelings for him. Fighting them was exhausting, so lifting her hand up, gently rested it in his. She could take this time they had and cherish it before she left to return to her family.

Roughly, he yanked her up into his arms. His mouth came down, nibbling on her lower lip, before his tongue started tracing the outline of her lips. She gasped, her mouth opened as his tongue thrust into her mouth. Their tongues clashed. He filled her senses. His taste, the wine that still lingered on his tongue. His scent, that citrusy musk with hints of jasmine, strawberry, and plums. The scents mingled in the air that surrounded her. His touch, scorching her as his hands roamed her body. Hearing his heart thumping in his veins; a tempo her own pulse matched. Her hands wrapped around his neck, pulling him closer.

His hand cupped her buttocks, pressing her closer to him. She felt the cold, wet wine seeping into her dress and the hardness of him pressed against her. He pulled his head back. She grabbed a chunk of hair to push his mouth back towards her, but he did not budge. Opening her eyes, she glared at him.

He chuckled softly, his eyes looked vulnerable, "Fe, come with me, please."

Gazing into his eyes, she contemplated what to do. His voice sounded unsure of himself. She had never seen his eyes so vulnerable before. She knew he was worried she would reject him. Peering into his eyes, she bit her lip as she nodded her head.

He leaned down and brushed a soft kiss across her mouth. His nose nuzzled hers. The tenderness made her heart skip a beat as she nuzzled his nose back.

He pulled back, grabbing her hand, before pulling her out of the dining room and down the hall. He opened his bedroom door, kicking the door closed behind them. Grabbing her, he pressed her into his arms.

"We should," she started, as his lips nibbled her ear. The thought vanished as his tongue flicked her earlobe, sucking it in and she could not finish the sentence. She tried to catch the thought, but his teeth scraping her ear kept chasing them away.

"Should what?" he asked, pulling back. His blue eyes darkened with sexual desire.

Blankly, she stared back at him, trying to figure out. It took a few seconds before she could catch the thought again. "Lock the door."

Laughing, he nodded and walked to the door to lock it.

Coming back, he unceremoniously pulled her back into his arms. His hands roaming over her body. His mouth nibbled on her ear, leaving a path of heat as he moved to her neck. Tilting her head, she gave him better access to the delicate flesh of her throat. His teeth scraped across her neck before nibbling a trail down. A gasp escaped as he brought a hand up to cup her breast, then nipped the top of it that was exposed above her dress. Gently, he sucked the flesh in, leaving a small love mark.

His hands stopped roaming her body and went to the zipper of her dress. Slowly, the zipper slid down. His hands reached up, guiding the thin straps of the dress down her body. The dress caught on her nipples, causing them to harden before sliding down again. His knuckles scraped her skin as he slid them down her arms. The fabric caressed her skin, causing gooseflesh to pop up as it slowly slid down.

Elwyn stepped back, his smoldering gaze appraised her as it traveled up and down her body. Deciding to be bold, she hooked her thumbs into the sides of her panties, shoving them down. His gaze followed the panties as they slithered down her legs. Slowly, she stepped out of the pile of clothes naked except for her high heels. Nonchalantly, she kicked her heels aside.

He stood there, his eyes taking in every inch of her body, a warm flush touching each spot his eyes grazed. She had not felt beautiful much in her life, but the way he looked at her made her feel so.

Stepping forward, she reached up to unbutton his shirt. Her confidence wavered as her hands trembled. She clumsily unbuttoned his shirt.

"I can do that," he whispered, reaching his hands up. Gently, his one had covered both of hers.

"I want to do it," she whispered back. She brushed his hands away as she continued unbuttoning his shirt. Her hands became more confident as she worked her way down.

He smiled at her and let her fingers work their klutzy magic on his clothes. She slid the shirt down his arms as her fingers lingered on his muscular biceps. She hesitated just for a second at his slacks zipper, before unzipping them. Her hands slid to the waistband, sliding his pants and briefs down together.

She stood there, staring at Elwyn's handsome face. His chestnut brown hair was tousled and falling haphazardly over one blue eye. The other eye shining brightly with hunger. He stood still, letting her take her fill. Her eyes traveled down his broad shoulders, muscular chest. She brought a finger up and traced it down his torso. She heard him inhale and pulled her hand back. Her eyes met his.

"Don't stop," he whispered. Grabbing her hand and placing it on his chest again.

She ran her hand over to his arm, noticing the bandage covering up his wound. A slight smell of blood still lingered from the healing wound. Her hand continued its journey down him. Stopping just above the swollen flesh of his manhood.

She dragged her eyes back up, meeting his eyes again. She felt compelled to move closer to him. Her hand wrapped around his shaft, gently squeezing. Slowly, she slid her hand down the length of his shaft. Feeling it pulse in her hand. Her other hand traveled back up to wrap around his neck as their mouths met. She felt the urgency in the kiss. As her hand slid up and down his shaft, she felt a warm droplet slid from the tip. He crushed her to him. Her hand released his shaft as he cupped her ass and lifted her up. Wrapping her legs around his waist, she felt his hard shaft nestled between her legs.

Biting his lower lip, she gently scraped her fangs along it. Laughing, he softly bit her lip back before sucking into his mouth. His teeth scraped her lip as he released it. Carrying her to the bed, he laid her down on the bed. She felt the weight of him as he shifted on top of her. Her nerve-endings were on fire, feeling the length of him pressed against her as he nuzzled between her thighs. She tugged at his hair, dragging his mouth to hers. Thrusting her tongue into his mouth, she grew bolder. She was now the aggressor.

His mouth pulled away as he kissed her jaw, her neck. His tongue and lips blazing a trail across her collarbone before working its way down to her breasts. Her breath caught in her throat as he sucked a nipple into his mouth. As the pleasure washed through her, her fingers dug into his back. Her heart felt like it would burst from her chest. It was beating so hard. His other hand kneaded her breast.

When he pulled away, she inhaled deeply, his citrusy musk filling her nostrils. His eyes locked with hers as his tongue flicked across the other nipple before sucking it into his mouth. Showing the other breast the same devotion as he suckled on it. Her legs clenched tighter around him as he loved on her breasts. He lashed the tip of her nipple with his tongue before scraping his teeth across it.

Pulling up, he grabbed her legs and unwrapped them from his waist. A cocky grin spread across his face as he stared down at her. His tongue tracing down stomach, stopping for a moment at her navel, his tongue dipping in.

The emotions raging through her body were something she had never felt before. There was such a pull to him, she felt she could not get enough of his touch, his mouth, his scent, just him was all she wanted. Her nails digging into his shoulders, breaking the flesh, leaving crescent shaped marks. The smell of fresh blood filled her nostrils as she inhaled deep.

His mouth trailed kisses and bites down her abdomen. Flicking her clit with his tongue a fire spread throughout her. He scraped his teeth across her clit before tenderly sucked it into his mouth. The roaring flames built inside her as he nibbled and sucked on her. His finger delving into the soft folds of her womanhood, sliding in and out. Her back arched up to meet his mouth and fingers, thrust for thrust. Her fingers dug into the taut flesh of his shoulders. Right before she thought she would explode, he pulled away. He leaned over her, smiling at her as his mouth descended to hers.

His tongue dueled with hers as he was poised above her. Feeling his weight slowly shift above her, he slowly penetrated her. He filled her up with his size. The fire continued to lick at her as he started moving. She matched his tempo as their hips and tongues beat to the same drum. The fire felt like it would consume her as it grew hotter and hotter. As his shaft nestled between her loins, the thrusts became faster and more frenzied.

He leaned on to one arm as he brought his other hand down to caress her clit. The fire raged brighter as it consumed her. Her teeth sunk into the flesh of his shoulder as the sweet nectar filled her mouth. The taste of lavender permeated her senses as his blood slid down her throat. A power surged through her veins as the euphoria of drinking his blood hit her. With his blood filling her senses, his emotions hit her, too. She felt the fire that burned deep down in him for her. Releasing his shoulder then her body trembled, and she shook as the explosion of ecstasy rocked her. She felt the pulsing of his release a moment after.

Sitting there, his forehead resting on hers. She breathed him in. Then he rolled over, pulling her with him so she was on top of him. Her head rested on his chest. She listened to his heart as it went from thundering under her ear before slowly going back to normal.

"Sorry," Feya muttered as the smell of blood still lingered in the air. "For biting you."

"It wasn't so bad," he laughed.

A moment passed in silence as they sat nestled in each other's arms.

"Feya," Elwyn whispered. His fingers drawing lazy circles on her back. "You are mine."

Feya smiled and snuggled deeper in his arms. Elwyn bent down and kissed the top of her head.

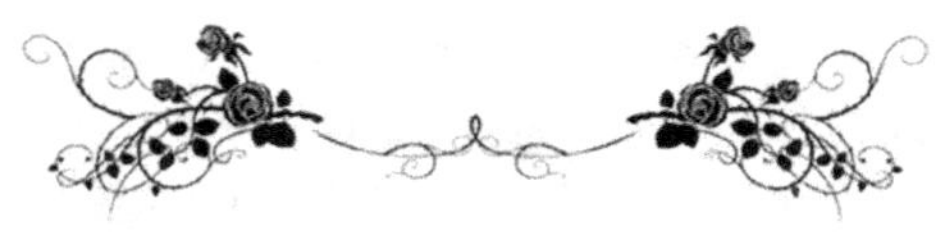

Redd stood in the dark linen closet for the last two hours, waiting for it to be safe. They had intended to leave as soon as the sun went down, but it being the dinner hour, faes were running up and down the hallways. He wished he had not chosen to listen to Brady after all. If they had just gone up to Feya, they could have been on their way home by now. He leaned his head back on the wall, listening for footsteps outside the closet. It has been a while since he heard heartbeats or footsteps.

"Can we leave yet?" Aguya grumbled, waving a hand towards Brady. "I am tired of being squished up next to her."

Since it had been a while, it should be safe, he mused. Plus, he was ready to go find Feya and get the hell out of this vale. The veiled hostility between Aguya and Brady was getting on his last nerve. They usually were not this bad, having long ago come to some kind of understanding.

"Yes," Redd breathed. Sighing, Redd stood up and stretched. As he opened the door, he listened again. The hallway was still empty, luckily.

"Where now?" Brady whispered.

"Up," Aguya whispered back. Pointing to the ceiling, as if that explained it all.

They followed Aguya as she walked to the stairs. Heading up the stairs up and wandered through halls to another set of stairs. Redd wondered if Aguya really knew where they were going. His arm still ached from the wound. He did not want the others to know that he had not healed. While they waited in the closet, he should have asked Brady to heal it. He had hoped they would not be in the closet as long as they were.

They finally came to a landing, and he could smell Feya. A wave of relief hit him.

There, Aguya pointed to a room halfway down the hall. Redd looked out the window. The sun had finally gone down, and it was night. With his good hand, he pushed his cloak off his head.

He stood in front of the door, listening for Feya's heart. He could hear it, and it was calm. Relief washed over him. He lifted his hand and knocked on the door.

Chapter 19

Feya and Elwyn laid there cuddling in bed. A warmth spread through her from being in Elwyn's arms. Her head rested in the crook of his shoulder. She had tried to fight the emotions she had for him so hard, now she did not know why she had fought them at all. She traced swirls with a finger on his chest as she listened to his heartbeat next to her ear. The drumming helped her relax. His skin felt so warm next to her skin.

A knock on the door startled her out of her reverie. Feya froze as she realized whose heart was beating on the other side of the door. Every fiber of her being chilled as a million questions raced through her mind.

"Holy shit," she muttered, sitting up in bed.

"It's probably just my mother," he whispered in her ear. He pulled her back down as he started nibbling on her ear. "Ignore it. She will probably go away soon. The door's locked, remember? She can't just walk in."

"It's not your mother," she groaned. Grabbing one blanket on top of the bed, she jumped up and walked to the door.

Pausing, her hand hovering over the doorknob, wishing she could just vanish. Her brain tried to process how they had gotten this far into the vale? How had they tracked her down? How had they gotten through the vale undetected? Thoughts collided and flashed through her mind as she listened to the heartbeats outside the door. Her father, Aguya, and Brady's hearts.

"Put something on," Feya muttered over her shoulder. As she worked the nerve up to twist the doorknob.

"Open the door, little one," Redd growled. His fingers tapped on the door impatiently.

A groan came from behind her. She turned to see Elwyn rubbing his hands across his face. "Is that your father?"

"Yes," she sighed.

Sighing, she cautiously opened the door. So much for proving herself. Here she was looking like an ashamed teenager, a bedspread her only cover staring at her dad. Lifting her chin up, she stared at him defiantly, trying to hide her feelings of inadequacy.

"I told you I was on vacation," she growled. Deciding sarcasm was the only route she had to take.

Brady gasped, covering her mouth with her hand. Aguya started howling with laughter.

Her father glared down at her. She watched as his eyes surveyed her. Noticing the concern in his eyes, guilt washed over her. Then she watched as concern turned to anger. Mentally steeling herself for the lecture she was about to get.

"You're not hurt?" he accused harshly.

"Obviously not," she grumbled. "I know how to take care of myself. You were told what I was doing. I am a grownup and can take a trip when I feel like it. Plus, you sound a little disappointed that I'm not hurt."

She heard Elwyn getting out of bed behind her, but was too embarrassed to turn around. Hearing the rustle of fabric, she assumed he was wrapping himself in a blanket, too.

She saw the look of disdain cross her father's face. "Boy, you could put some clothes on. Show some dignity"

She turned and watched as Elwyn stood there naked with no shame or attempt to hide. Her skin felt like it was on fire as she flushed. He smiled and winked at her. Feya debated about running over and punching Elwyn for acting like a twat.

"I am," Elwyn laughed. Reaching down, he picked up his wine stained slacks. Casually, putting them on without a care in the world. "My dignity is hanging out front and center. Plus, you barged into my room in the middle of the night. You had to have expected something like this."

Feya groaned as her cheeks burned brighter. Turning, she looked back at her father. Pulling the blanket tighter around herself. Her fleeting moment of self defiance vanished as embarrassment washed over her.

Elwyn walked up smiling at Redd. Could he not be serious even once, she thought. As he cockily wrapped his arm around Feya's shoulders. Elbowing Elwyn in the gut, she felt a slight flash of satisfaction when he grunted.

A scream broke the tension. Turning to see Olette, fear and panic in her eyes as her face drained of all color. Backing up against the wall, as she glanced from the vampire to the fire witch standing between her and the safety of escape.

Great, just another reason for Olette to hate her. If she was keeping track of which, she was not. Or at least not that she wanted to admit to herself.

Feya stepped into the hall, about to cast a spell, but Redd stepped forward to handle it. His hand reached out, lifting Olette's chin up.

"Calm," he whispered as Olette stopped screaming instantly. Her eyes glazed over as she stared, transfixed. "Everything is alright."

Smiling up at Redd, Olette said. "Everything is alright."

"You want to rest up? You have had such a long day." Redd said, his hand stroking her cheek.

"I have had such a long day," Olette said, sighing. "I need to go get some rest."

Olette turned and calmly walked away. Entering her bedroom as if nothing was wrong.

Deema was the only fae who came running at the scream. Being the only other fae in the wing besides the three of them. Deema leaned against the wall, a mask of terror on her face as a whimper escaped. She cowered down as Feya came closer.

"Deema," Feya said, using her charm spell. "You are having a dream. Go back to bed."

Deema fought the spell for a second as fear consumed her. Feya stepped closer as she bent down. Feya's eyes captured hers as she got lost in the spell.

"Deema," Feya whispered. "This is just a nightmare. Go back to bed."

Deema conceded. Turning, she stood up and in a daze to head back to her room.

Feya wished her spell was as strong as her father's. She had never been able to charm even half as well as he could. It annoyed Feya that she felt she had to work harder to get half the effect her father did. No matter how hard she worked, her vampire magic was just not as strong as his.

"Well," Elwyn said, grinning like a fool. "Isn't this just an interesting night? We will get you guys a room to rest in. I suggest you not leave this wing for the duration of your stay. Would hate to hear about the drama of you guys getting busted. We will have to find a way to explain this to my mom and Deema. Since we were not expecting guests, we have little set up. Aguya and Brady can have your old room, Fe. You want to grab your belongings and throw them in our room? Hmm, where to put you, Redd?"

"It's Mr. Ascelin to you, boy," Redd growled.

Elwyn laughed and walked down the hall to another room. "It's nice to meet you, Redd. My name is Elwyn. Feya has told me so many nice things about you."

Feya hoped Elwyn would stop with the slight taunting he was doing, but she knew he would not. He was like a man-child sometimes.

Elwyn threw the door open and turned the light on. "We will throw you in here, Redd. You'll love it. Let me find you bedding."

Feya groaned. Obviously, Elwyn was going to keep it up until a fight happened. The room was a sunny yellow decorated room. There were three other rooms, and obviously Elwyn chose the sunniest of rooms. Why Elwyn had to choose now to be an ass to her father was beyond her comprehension. How was she going to explain this to Olette? A vampire and a witch inside the vale. Plus, she was pretty sure her dad would not let her stay a moment longer. So she would not even have a chance to explain to Olette the only silver lining of leaving.

"Feya," Redd said, sternly. "We are leaving now."

Sometimes she thought he could read her mind. Looking into his face, she tried to decide if he would listen to her or not. The look on his face said it all. He was not in the mood to listen to her. Her mission was not completed, and she wanted more time with Elwyn. She could deny it till she was pushing up daisies, but she wanted to be with him for as long as she could be.

"I think we should stay," Brady said, giggling. Feya looked at Brady, astonished. She did not think she would find an ally in her.

"For once, I agree with her," Aguya said, pointing a derisive finger towards Brady. Feya stood with her mouth agape. Two allies that was something she never saw coming.

"Then it is settled," Elwyn said, his grin grew bigger.

Feya sighed. Elwyn was starting a battle with her father and was being purposefully obtuse about it. Maybe she should take a page from his book and stand up to her father.

"We are not staying," Redd growled, louder.

Feya took a deep breath. She exhaled and looked at her dad. "I am not leaving. I am staying here for the time being. You can choose to sneak out the same way you came in or help. I am going to finish what I started."

"You mean sleeping with the client like a common whore?" he growled as he got in her face.

Feya inhaled at the insult her father hurled at her. She knew he did not mean it. He was just angry, but the words still stung. Redd's temper was notorious for saying things he did not mean when angry. He usually apologized later.

She felt Elwyn's hand grab her and shove her behind him. Startled, she stood frozen in place as she watched Elwyn get in her father's face.

"You will not talk to her like that," Elwyn said, with cool disdain.

"Well, well," Redd said. "The boy has a backbone."

"Father," Feya said, cautiously. Hurt at his words, she just wanted to end the fight before it got out of hand. Elwyn did not know her father and his temper. "Please, let it go."

"No," Redd said, shaking his head. "Can't do. Boy wants to stand up like a man, so I…"

"You are under the impression," Elwyn said, laughing coldly. "That calling me a boy makes me less of a man. That you are magically hurting my feelings with your childish insult. Trust me, when I say I don't need to prove anything to you, but you will not insult Fe again. Do we understand one another?"

Redd stood there staring at Elwyn. His eyes squinted as he turned his head to the side. Feya tried to push her way between them, but Brady pulled her away.

Redd laughed suddenly. Feya stared in confusion. A grin spread across his face. Redd reached up and tousled Elwyn's hair.

"Show me where I am staying," Redd chuckled. "We will get settled, then go over details of the mission."

"We can do that in the morning," Elwyn stated, pushing Redd's hand away. "Feya, get your stuff and move it to our room."

Feya let Brady drag her into the room. Aguya shut the door behind them. Feya walked to the closet, dropping the blanket. Grabbing a shirt and leggings, pulling them on. She noted Aguya's silence behind her.

"I will help you," Brady whispered. "Just let it go."

Feya went into the room. Aguya shut the door behind them. Feya walked to the closet, dropping the blanket. Grabbing a shirt and leggings, pulling them on.

Brady went to the closet and started folding her clothes and putting it in her luggage that had been on the floor of the closet.

"Are you going to tell us?" Aguya said, breaking the silence. Turning, she looked at Aguya. Her arms were crossed in front of her chest and her foot was taping on the floor.

"Tell you what?" Feya sighed, being purposefully obtuse.

"Leave her alone," Brady scolded. As she finished packing the clothes up.

Aguya snorted. Feya felt her eyes on her as she tried her best to ignore it. She paced around, listening to Brady pack up her toiletries. Her mind kept roaming to Elwyn and her dad. She worried they would get into a fight. So far, things had been quiet outside the room. Finally, she stopped and looked at Aguya. She might as well get this over with.

"I am dating Elwyn," she said, rolling her eyes. She waited for the lecture, but it did not come.

Aguya nodded. "Do you like him?"

Taken aback, Feya debated the answer. Before just nodding.

"Alright then," Aguya said. She looked around. "I am not sharing a room with her."

"Please," Feya sighed. "Can we not fight tonight?"

Aguya stared at her for a moment. "We will share a room for tonight only then."

"Thank you," Feya mumbled.

"We were worried about you," Brady said, her voice trembling. "You are never to do this to us again. Do you understand me?'

"Yes," Feya whispered. She felt the guilt of not even having thought about how they would feel these last days. She had been so wrapped up in her feelings and trying to figure out what was going on here that she had not thought about them.

"Everything is ready," Brady said.

"I'm sorry," Feya said, quietly. Brady's calm demeanor made the sting of guilt hurt ten times more. She looked down at her feet as she shuffled back and forth.

Brady walked over to her, putting a hand on her shoulder, and said. "It's alright. I understand why you did it."

Feya looked up and smiled sadly. Even knowing she understood, it did not dull the sting.

"Ugh," Aguya groaned, rolling her eyes. "Can we please stop with the hallmark moment?"

Feya giggled. It was no surprise that Aguya changed the subject. She was not big on showing emotions. Except maybe anger. That was Aguya's go to mode.

"Alright," Feya said. She picked up her bags. "I will let you guys get settled. Goodnight."

"Goodnight," Brady replied.

She left the room, closing the door softly behind her. Elwyn was leaning on the bedroom door, waiting for her. He came forward, grabbing her luggage from her. Quietly, they walked to the room. Setting the luggage down, he turned to look at her.

"You alright?" he whispered, his hand coming up to stroke her cheek.

"Yes," she nodded. "Why do you have to pick fights with my father?"

"What do you mean?" Elwyn asked. His lips came down and brushed across her forehead. "I was perfectly nice."

"You were being an ass," Feya said, rolling her eyes. "You probably chose the girliest bright cheery room on purpose."

"That happened to be a perk," Elwyn laughed. "It's also the room without windows, so less sunlight."

Sighing, she leaned into him. "Thank you."

She was not sure how this was going to work with her father here now. Not even sure if he would take over and not let her do anything as per every other mission they had done. She was to stay in the background and run at the smallest hint of danger. For all the centuries, she would be alive, it seemed.

She felt Elwyn's arm wrap around her. Snuggling into his arms, she felt safe. Even knowing that it would not work. She would eventually leave with her family and he would stay here where he belonged. Closing her eyes, she tried to push the thought away. It filled her with sorrow, thinking they might never see each other again. Taking a deep breath, she focused on the mission and the time being. Enjoy the moment and do not stress on the inevitable.

Pulling away, she looked up into Elwyn's eyes. Getting lost for a moment in the blue depths.

"You're tired," he stated. His lips coming down to brush against hers.

"It will have to wait," she mumbled. "My father will want to talk to me."

"He can wait till the morning," Elwyn said, quietly his mouth hovering over hers. "Get in bed."

His demand caught her off guard. She shook her head and pulled away.

"That wasn't a question," he said, grinning.

Rolling her eyes, she turned to leave the room. His hand reached out, wrapping around her waist from behind, pulling her close.

"I meant what I said," he said. His other hand came up and tilted her head to the side. He nibbled on her neck, leaving a trail of heat.

Sighing, she wished she could do as he said. "My father will not allow that."

"I told him we would talk in the morning," he whispered in her ear as he nibbled on her earlobe.

"I should go talk to my father anyways," she grumbled. Using the last of her willpower, she pushed away.

Elwyn laughed as she walked away. She went to her father's bedroom door, hesitating before she knocked.

"Go to bed Feya," Redd grumbled.

Shocked, Feya stood there in silence. What no lecture? She thought. Staring at the door, she wondered if her father was truly that upset with her or if he was understanding like Brady was. Sighing, she turned and walked to Elwyn's room. Her room now, she guessed, at least for the time being.

Chapter 20

Feya walked into the dining room hungry yet dreading the morning to come. She was not sure when she would have to have the talk with her father, but she knew it was coming. Plus, then having to deal with Olette was another stressful thought.

Luckily, she was the first one up. The servants had already dropped the breakfast tray off so she could start eating in peace. Grabbing scrambled eggs and toast. Chowing down, she heard the door open behind her. Brady's heartbeat approaching her.

"That looks yummy," Brady said, sitting next to her. She started making a plate for herself.

Then the other shoe dropped, she could hear Olette's heartbeat heading towards her. Leaning back in the chair, her appetite gone, she waited for the door to open.

As soon as the door opened, Olette paused.

"Who is this?" Olette said with cool disdain.

"Brady, Olette. Olette, Brady," Feya stated. She really was not up to this after all. At least her father's charm had worked at least.

"It's so nice to meet you," Brady said cheerfully. Standing up she approached Olette, holding her hand out.

Feya turned in time to see the sneer cross Olette's face. If she was not Elwyn's mother, she would have slapped that sneer off her face.

"Brady," Feya started. "Will be staying for a few days. We have two other guests as well."

Glaring at Olette, she tried to think of a good reason for the guests. Her mind came up blank.

Elwyn breezed in, walking straight to the windows.

"Let's close these," he muttered.

Feya turned an ear, hearing two more heartbeats standing outside the dining room.

"Whatever for?" Olette asked, her demeanor changing to the sweet, loving mother. As she walked over and smoothed Elwyn's hair down.

Standing there shocked, Feya wondered how she could do such a dramatic shift.

"Come on, mom," Elwyn said, swatting her hands away playfully. "We have company, and I don't want you to freak out."

"Whatever do you mean, my love?" Olette asked, startled. Taking a step back to survey the room. "You have invited more faes to stay with us?"

"Not quite," Elwyn winced.

The door opened, and Redd and Aguya entered. Olette's screams reverberated throughout the room, as Deema came running down the hall. She stormed into the dining room, took one look, and started running back down the hall. It took Redd two steps to grab Deema by the back of her collar.

"Calm," Redd whispered. "Sit."

Deema sat down on the floor in the hall obediently.

Walking over to Olette, Redd kneeled down, whose screams turned to whimpers as she leaned against the wall. Feya knew she should feel bad, but her secret inner evil self found it funny.

"Shhh," Redd breathed. "You need to spend the day shopping. You have so much you need to buy and will have trouble finding it. Take her shopping with you to help you carry your purchases. Forget you met us."

Turning to Deema, Redd whispered. "Forget this morning and go shopping with your mistress."

Dazed, Olette and Deema walked out of the room.

"Feya," Redd growled, turning to Feya. "Start talking."

Feya sighed as she started spilling the details.

Elwyn rolled his shoulders as they walked to the path to visit Reece Pellings. They had spent the morning going over and over everything with Aethelredd. He was trying his best to get along with Feya's adopted father, but the man was driving him nuts. He still did not know how they got through the vale undetected. Asking Redd had just led him in circles. He would not tell him the truth either way, but it would be helpful to know how it had happened.

Sighing, he looked down at Feya. Her black hair shone in the light. No matter how many times he looked at her, his eyes still could not get enough. He had spent many years looking for her, and now she was there next to him.

Reaching over, he gently grabbed her hand. She glanced up at him in shock. He smiled at her before looking away. He felt happy that she was no longer pulling away from him.

Redd, on the other hand, would put him down at every opportunity. He was happy that he could not go out during the day. Otherwise, he would never be rid of him.

Taking the long route, so he could spend some more time with Feya, they walked through the streets of the village surrounding the castle. He knew she was not familiar with the land, so she would not realize it.

The tiny houses that were splashes of colors with their pretty little gardens lined the streets. Daffodils and petunias scented the air as they walked. The cobblestone road with its hints of grays and tans lined their path.

He listened as her shoes clicked on the stones as they

walked. Glancing over a breeze caught the strands of her black hair as it flew around her. She looked up at him, her green eyes shining. His heart swelled, and he knew how he felt about her. He had tried to keep it to himself, knowing how she would react. Maybe he had always known, and that is why he had told her to run that day. Even when they were kids, he had been drawn to her.

Leaning over, he brushed his lips against hers.

"We're in public," she mumbled, her green eyes darting around.

He laughed at the blush spreading across her cheeks.

"No one," he stated. "Cares about what we are doing right now. They are all lost in their own world, just as we should be."

Huffing, she glared at him. He smiled back at her, bending down to put a peck on the tip of her nose. Rolling her eyes, she turned forward.

"How much longer till we get there?" she grumbled.

"We are almost there," he said, grinning.

He knew he would win her over. He just needed to solve this case and then put his full attention on her. Plus, she was warming up to him. Even if she did not want to admit it. She was a stubborn little thing, fighting every advance he made. Till last night, he wanted to ask what had made her change her mind, but knew she would not answer. He knew she had been jealous of Raisa last night. For a moment, he thought he would have to break up a fight. He was pretty sure Feya had cebated biting Raisa and drinking her blood. He had been nervous about leaving them alone. It had surprised him when he saw Raisa leaving without a word.

He turned to the street that Reece's summer home was on. He knew he could not keep putting off going there. Time to get back to work.

He had checked in earlier with his contact, watching the hired thug. Nothing new. He had not received another payoff at all. He had known it would be a dead end, but better safe than sorry.

The yards got bigger, and the houses got bigger as they walked further down the street. They walked up to a baby blue house. Pretty pink tulips lined the walkway to the front door. He never understood how such a bear of a man lived in such a frilly house.

They knocked on the door. A few minutes passed and still no one came to answer.

"Maybe they are not home," he muttered.

Wondering if he could remember the exact path they took to get here so she would not be suspicious. Doubted it, he had been wandering aimlessly. He would just have to wander aimlessly on the way back. He had a feeling that Reece was a dead end, too. His thoughts were that an unknown player was behind this. None of the people on the list seemed to add up. He felt like he was just chasing his tale, pursuing these ends. Plus, there was no connection between the queen's cousin, his step-father, and himself.

"Someone," Feya said, quietly. "Is in there."

Nodding, he knocked again, but louder.

Finally, he heard someone coming to the door. The steps slowly got closer. The door creaked open and the oldest fairy he had ever seen stood before them. His shoulders were hunched over. Thinning gray hair combed over to hide his bald spot. His gray eyes twinkled at them kindly.

"How can I help you?" he said, with his raspy voice.

"We wanted to request an audience with Reece," Elwyn said. "I am Elwyn Altalune, and this is Feya Annwen."

The old fairy stared at them for a while, making Elwyn wonder if he understood him. Then after a while the fairy nodded and walked away, leaving the door partially open.

"Do we follow him?" Feya asked, confused.

"Etiquette says no," Elwyn said, wondering if they were supposed to follow him. Just when he thought the old fae would not return he did.

"The master is not home today," he rasped. "You may come

back tomorrow at teatime."

Without waiting for a response, he shut the door on them. Elwyn knew he was lying, but did not press it.

"That was weird," Feya muttered.

"To say the least," Elwyn laughed. "Guess we will come back tomorrow, then. Why don't we go into town and have lunch? Just the two of us."

He watched as her eyes wavered back and forth on the decision.

"Please," he whispered. Bringing his hand up to stroke her cheek.

"Fine," she said, rolling her eyes.

Laughing, he guided her hand through the streets till they got to the market square. He looked around at the vendors, trying to decide which one he would take her to.

"Is that honey cake I smell?" she asked, her eyes open wide. Glancing down, he saw the childish delight in her eyes.

"Yes," he said, smiling. "It is. Is that what you want to eat?"

"Yes!" she exclaimed. "I have not had honey cake since I was a child. That was my favorite. I used to love when my mother would make it. I wonder if it will be as good as I remember my mother's being."

Tugging on her hand, he guided her into the cafe. Pastel frosted treats filled the display case. The sugary concoctions filled the surrounding air. He had to admit; they smelled good. Little wooden tables and chairs painted light blues and pinks scattered around the room. The walls were filled with paintings and various pictures from around the castle.

They walked to a table by the stained glass picture window in front. The warm stream of lights dancing across the table.

A sweet little red headed freckled faced fae came up offering them menus. Glancing down, he surveyed the menu, perusing what the offerings they had. He had never been to this cafe before, so he did not know what would be good.

"What can I get you?" the redhead asked.

"I would like a honey cake and everpeach to drink," Feya said.

The warmth from the smile Feya gave him made him feel at peace. He had been worried that it would take longer to win her over.

"I will have the same," he said. "But add in a ham and cheese sandwich, too."

"Do you think it will be as good as I remember?" Feya mused.

"I guess we will find out," Elwyn said, laughing. "I am glad we got to spend some time together alone."

"We spent last night together," Feya laughed.

"You're right," he said, winking.

Sitting and talking, he watched her face as she told him anecdotal stories of missions they had gone on. The way her face lit up as she talked about her family. The way the different colors from the stained glass danced across her face with the shifting light.

Chapter 21

Feya and Elwyn made the trek back to their suite in the castle. Elwyn felt relaxed, but the closer he got to the castle, the more anxious he felt at the thought of dealing with Redd. Knowing that when they explained they did not get a spontaneous audience; Redd was going to be upset. He tried to think of a way to word it to soften the blow, but no ideas came to mind. So, he would just have to gear up for a fight with Redd again. Never would he get used to dealing with that vampire. The night before his temper snapped, he seriously thought he was going to have to fight the bastard. It stung a little that Feya did not have confidence in his fighting and magic, but she had never seen what he could do. For some reason, standing up to Redd had made Redd respect him, but only a bit. He still kept calling him boy.

Plus, he was worried about his mother. Redd kept doing that charm spell on her and Deema. He did not know if constantly changing their memory would have side effects. Especially since he had done it twice in less than twelve hours.

He started dragging his step as they got closer. He really did not feel like being lectured by Feya's father again. Diplomacy was not a mood he was in right now. Plus, he wanted to drag out the time alone with her. Even though they were not talking, he just enjoyed being with her.

"Why are you slowing down?" Feya said, breaking the silence.

Laughed, he said. "I really don't feel like explaining to your dad that we did not succeed at talking to Reece."

"Ditto," Feya said, sighing. "He does not like it when missions don't go smoothly."

"How do I keep him from using a charm spell on me?" he asked curiously.

"I can give you a rune," Feya shrugged.

Laughing, Feya shook her head. Watching as she pulled a marker out of her bag. It was the same one he had watched her draw a rune on her own arm while they were in New York. Grabbing his wrist, her hand felt warm as she drew a rune on him. It was not a rune he recognized. He thought he knew them all. In school knowing the runes and what they meant was very important. A lot of beginner magicals started out using rune to help focus their magical energy. It had been a long time since he had used runes in his own magic.

"This will make sure he can't charm me?" Elwyn asked, raising a skeptical eyebrow.

"Yes," Feya laughed.

He could not help but laugh back. She was in a good mood. They were close to the castle and would not have alone time again until tonight. He grabbed her around the waist and dragged her to him.

"Elwyn!" she exclaimed with mock exasperation. "We are in public! What will the staunch old faes think?"

"They'll be jealous," he whispered as his mouth descended to hers.

He used his tongue to gently nudge her mouth open. His tongue delving into the depths of her mouth, tasting every bit of her. The lingering taste of honey cake and Everpeach was on her tongue. He savored the taste of her. Her hands slid up his arms and wrapped around him. She melted into his arms. He slid his hands down to her ass, cupping it as he pressed her up against his dick. He wanted to take her now, but knew it was the wrong place for that. Pulling back, he looked down into her green eyes.

Since she had bitten him, he felt more connected to her. A

weird sensation of knowing what emotion was going through her. Every once in a while, he would feel she was looking at him or sense a feeling she was feeling. He could sense she wanted him as bad as he wanted her.

"My sweet Fe," he said, smiling at her.

Rolling her eyes she pulled back. "Sweet is not a word most people use for me."

"That's because they don't know you," he said, brushing a kiss across her forehead. "I have a question for you."

"Ok," she said tentatively.

"So," he started, pausing to figure out how to phrase it. "Since you bit me, I keep getting a sense of what you're feeling. Ummm… Did Sen feel what you felt?"

Laughing, she shook her head. "I did not connect with him like I connected with you. It was different. I feel him, but he does not feel me. Does that make sense?"

"What you're telling me," Elwyn stated, cockily. "Is that because we were fucking it built a connection between us when you drank me?"

"Oh," Feya said, rolling her eyes. "My goddess, Arianrhod."

Feya pushed him away, laughing. He grabbed her hand and finished making the trek to the castle for the dreaded conversation. His heart felt less bogged down now.

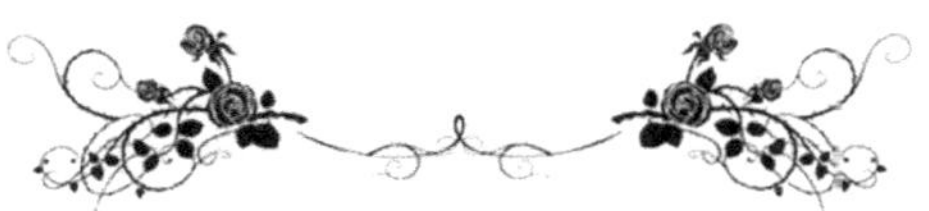

Feya rolled her eyes at her father. He was upset that they had been gone so long and accomplished nothing. She knew he was restless since he had to stay in a room with Aguya and Brady to avoid seeing Olette and Deema as much as possible. This morning's charm spells were working well since they were both still shopping. Doing the charm spells too many times would cause blank spots in their memories, which could cause trouble. So they had to be careful. Plus, that was something she did not want to explain to Elwyn. At least he had used a believable charm on them. Olette seemed like the person who would enjoy shopping all day.

Watching as Elwyn defended their time away made her want to hug him. It was rare that someone other than herself was on the receiving end of her father's temper.

"Maybe," Elwyn exclaimed. "Just maybe, we needed a break from your incessant belittlement. Neither of us are children, so you should quit treating us like one."

"Boy," Redd insisted. "You may think you are, but you're rather cute. Like a dog chasing its own tail. Plus, Feya, don't think I didn't notice you rolling your eyes over there. Keep rolling those eyes to the back of your head, you might just find your brain."

"Remember," Elwyn stated. "That time you said that thing I didn't care about? Well, that time is now and every other time I have and to converse with you."

"Well, well, well Boy," Redd sighed. "A sharp tongue is not an indication of a sharp mind."

Feya sighed and sunk deeper in her chair. She had grown bored with listening to them insult each other. Brady sat in a chair across from her in Redd's room. The yellow wallpaper littered with bright yellow flowers was driving Feya nuts. Too bright for her taste. Aguya stood in the corner leaning against the wall, a smirk on her face as she intently watched the males.

"Children," Brady exclaimed. Apparently, Feya was not the only one over the drama. Sighing, she hoped Brady could get them to stop. "You are both grown men. Act like it. It cannot be helped that they could not talk to him. They will go back tomorrow. That is the end of it."

"The boy there," Redd grunted, pointing at Elwyn. "Should have pushed past the puny little old fae. Was he not male enough to take a little weak fae?"

"You are right, Redd," Elwyn sighed. "I should have knocked the little old male over and stormed the house. Demanded answers, but alas, I did not. Maybe if I was more of an ass like you, I could have picked a fight with an innocent little ole fae."

Feya sat up in her chair. She knew she was going to have to break up the fight soon. It startled her when Redd just laughed.

"Get out of my sight, Boy," Redd said, still laughing.

Feya stared in confusion, not sure how to proceed. She watched her father carefully, trying to figure out what Redd was up to. Out of the corner of her eye, she watched as Elwyn stood up and walked to her.

"Feya," Elwyn said, holding his hand out to her. She tentatively took it, her eyes never leaving her father. Her father's eyes watched Elwyn bemused. Elwyn pulled her out of the room to their shared room.

As soon as the door closed behind her, Feya whispered. "Please, stop instigating fights with my father."

"Eh," Elwyn shrugged. "It's our thing. We insult each other. Plus, he starts it. Why don't you go tell him not to instigate fights with me?"

Rolling her eyes, Feya thought about what to say. She knew her father was instigating fights with Elwyn, but she did not want to deal with her father over it. Elwyn, on the other hand, she could at least try to get him to stop. He was more likely to listen to her, anyways.

"I understand," Feya said, changing tactics. Maybe she could try cajoling him. She lifted her gaze to meet his. She put a hand on his chest. "He is starting this little childish fights with you. I want you to brush off what he says and walk away. Be the bigger male."

He smiled down at her. "There's the Fe I remember from childhood. You think batting those lashes at me ever worked?"

Sighing, she shoved him away and walked to sit on the edge of the bed. "Asshole," she muttered.

Laughing, he walked to the bed and pushed her down. He climbed onto the bed, straddling her. He bent down, nuzzling her neck with his nose.

"You really think I am an asshole?" he whispered.

Goosebumps ran down her spine. She closed her eyes,

trying to focus on her words as he nibbled on her neck.

"Yes," she breathed.

"Really?" he whispered, as he lifted her shirt up. His teeth scraped the top of her breasts above the cups of her bra. She arched her back to get closer to him. "Are you going to answer my question?"

"What question?" she muttered, all her thoughts centered on his mouth and hands. He pulled the cup down on her bra, slowly circling her nipple with his tongue.

"Do you really think I am an asshole?" he whispered, before sucking her nipple into his mouth.

She tried to focus on his question so she could answer it, but a fire was building inside her.

A knock on the door startled them both.

Groaning, Elwyn exclaimed. "What the fuck do you want?"

Feya paused, realizing it was her father's heart she heard outside the door.

"I just wanted to make sure everything is alright," he said. "I didn't hurt your little fae feelings, did I?"

"Yes," Elwyn shouted. "Everything is fine. No, you didn't hurt my manly feelings. Go away. We are talking here."

Feya punched Elwyn in the gut, feeling satisfied by his grunt. Whispering, "You are an asshole and you are completely acting like one."

"We are fine, daddy," she said, louder. "Just talking."

"Why don't you come out here Feya?" Redd said, sternly. "We can discuss strategy."

She knew he knew what they had been up to. He must have heard her heartbeat speed up. How was she to enjoy what little time she had with Elwyn when her father was going to do his damndest to stop them? She sighed, debating what her choices were.

"Give me fifteen minutes?" she muttered.

"What did you say? I couldn't hear you." Redd said.

Elwyn dropped his head onto her shoulder, muttering, "Bullshit."

She knew her father's hearing was excellent and had heard every word they had said. Most likely, even heard the whispers.

Raising her voice, she growled, "Give me fifteen minutes."

Closing her eyes, she tried to figure out how this was going to work out. She knew as soon as they solved the case, she would be leaving. The longer she was here, the more likely her secret was found out. Her father would not leave until she did. This also put him in danger, as well. How was she to solve this case, keep Elwyn and her father from fighting, spend time with Elwyn, and not punch Olette in her face? Suddenly, she felt so overwhelmed. She loved her father, but she wished he would let her have some space.

Elwyn shifted his weight on her as he lifted his head up. She opened her eyes, staring into those blue eyes.

"We will find the time," he whispered. "Plus we still have 14 minutes left."

Laughing, she wrapped her arms around him. He was such a dolt. She smacked a kiss on his lips.

"What am I to do with you?" she muttered.

"I can think of a few things," he winked, rolling them over so she was on top.

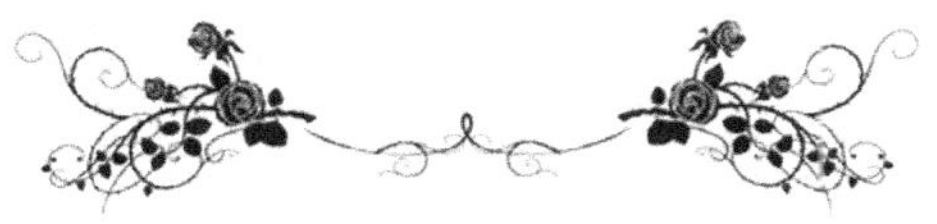

Feya had watched as her father charmed Deema and Olette again. Her inner demon was still getting a kick out of this. He charmed them to go straight to sleep after shopping all day. Elwyn had looked dismayed by the amount of bags they had drug back and by the charm spell. She knew he was worried about his mother and the effects of the charm spell. So far, with it just being missing minutes in both of their memories, it should not be a concern. Deema, he did not seem to mind though, which Feya found funny.

What was truly bothering her, though, was that her father was sitting in her and Elwyn's bedroom, making Elwyn go over everything for the second time tonight. They sat in the armchairs in front of the fireplace. Elwyn had his head in his hands as mumbled the story over again. Her father interrupted often with inane comments that he knew would annoy Elwyn.

All he wanted to do was go to sleep at this point. All hope of getting laid was blown out the window. Since her father was going to do his damndest to disrupt their alone time and ruin the mood.

Sighing, she flung herself back on the bed, throwing the blanket over her head. If only her father would take the massive hint she was giving him. Which he obviously was not. So she was going to be louder.

Flinging the blanket aside, she stood up on the bed. Deciding Shakespeare was the most dramatic thing she could think of, she said. "To sleep, perchance to dream."

Flung herself back down on the bed, she grabbed the covers and threw them over her head.

"Feya," Redd scolded. "I thought I taught you better manners than that. Sorry, my daughter gets grumpy when she is tired."

"Then, maybe," she growled. "You should leave so I can sleep and be less grumpy."

"In just a minute," Redd stated. "One more question."

Groaning, she listened as her father started his questioning all over again.

Chapter 22

Feya stood next to Elwyn as they waited for the old fae to return. He had been gone for about quite a while now. She was tired and grumpy. Her father had come to their room to talk until the wee hours. He was doing everything to make sure they had no time together. It was driving her nuts. Now she was standing in front of this door. She had forgotten her glasses, her head was throbbing, and she wanted to bite someone's head off, literally. A tall glass of someone's open vein sounded so good right now.

Elwyn squeezed her hand and whispered. "Relax, you're too tense."

"I forgot," she muttered. "My sunglasses. Plus, I am tired. My father did not give us much peace last night."

"The good news," he whispered into her ear. "Is we can sneak off somewhere after this meeting. Just you and me."

Laughing, she shook her head. She did not understand how he was in such a cheery mood. If this was the person they were searching for, she would probably be gone in a day or so. Maybe he would be happy to see her go, and that is why he was acting this way. She side eyed him, trying to gauge his feelings for her. He saw her look at him and bent down and kissed her on the mouth. The warmth of his mouth spread throughout her, making her feel tingly. She could still feel his blood running through her veins. Feel the lust that was coming from him, hear his racing heart, smell his blood lingering from his still healing wounds.

The door opened up and the old fae stood there, staring at them as if they had grown a griffin head. What great timing they seemed to have, she thought, sighing.

"Is he ready to see us?" she said, trying to smile cheerfully. She knew the smile did not reach her eyes.

They followed the old fae male into a dowdy drawing room. Watching him lead the way, she noticed the fraying of the cuffs of his jacket and the hem of his pants. The pants were slightly big, causing them to sag, as he shuffled his feet through the main hall. The hall had very few amenities, no tables, no furniture, just a great open expanse with dark wooden floors and white walls.

He guided them to a parlor just off the main hall. Not a lick of feminine touch anywhere. The air smelled stale in the room, from years of cigars being smoked in it. The walls were dingy yellow from the smoke. She was happy that the brown curtains were closed, keeping the sun out. Every surface had a few layers of dust. It seemed as if the couches had never seen a scrub brush. Sitting down on the edge of the chair to avoid getting as little dirt on herself as possible, thankful she had thrown on a pair of jeans. She sat there with Elwyn next to her, his hand on her thigh. She looked at that hand and wondered what the other fae thought. There was a time when such things as showing emotion towards someone before marriage was frowned upon. She wondered how many faes thinking had advanced with the modern times.

The door opened and a man she assumed was Reece came in. He was a dowdy, short fae. He probably stood about 5'5". Brown scraggly hair and a brown scraggly beard looked like it had been a while since a comb had been through it. His muddy brown eyes surveyed the room, obvious confusion why they were there. His blue suit had seen better days, and he looked sorely out of place in it. The seams were pulling tight as he must have gained weight since he first got the suit. He squirmed, obviously not used to dressing up. She wondered if he putting the suit on was why he had taken so long.

Elwyn jumped up and extended his hand out to him.

"Reece," Elwyn said, cheerfully. "Long time no see. I was in your neighborhood yesterday and was wondering what you had been up to."

"Alright," Reece said, skeptically.

"This is Feya Annwen of clan Talamh," Elwyn introduced. Feya stood up and extended her hand out. "She has been staying with me. I have been showing her around."

Reece took her hand and shook it briskly before letting it go. He eyed her up and down while frowning.

"Hmmm," Reece said.

Feya smiled at him, trying her best to be charming. "It's nice to meet you."

Reece nodded at her, then walked to a chair by the fireplace. He opened a box of cigars up on the table next to the chair. Pulling one out, he cut the tip and lit it up. He took a few puffs before looking back at them through a billow of smoke.

"Cut the bullshit. Why don't you tell me why you're really here?" he said, puffing out another cloud.

Elwyn laughed at Reece. Putting his arm around Feya's shoulders. He knew he could not get one past the old coot. He would need to just skirt the truth for this fae to believe what he said.

"Queen's business," he said, grinning. It was time to change tactics. Come up with something more believable than a social visit.

He heard Feya inhale in surprise. He pulled her close to him, squeezing her shoulder, hoping she would play along with whatever story he pulled out of his ass right now. He knew Feya was tired and not feeling well, and was not sure how well her powers would work under the circumstances. Mentally adding sunglasses to his list of things he needed to carry with him. So it was time to implement Plan B and Plan B was to ad lib.

"And what does the Queen want?" Reece grumbled, his temper showing as he sneered her title.

Elwyn stood there staring at him, debating whether angering him or joking with him would work better. Anger, he decided.

"She got word," Elwyn started. Taking a deep breath as he planned his response. "That you have intentions of attacking the border again. We are here to stop that before it starts. We would hate for more of your fae clan to die in such a childish endeavor to smite the Queen. You always seem to lose these little childish squabbles you start."

Reece took another puff of his cigar, releasing a puff cloud. The smoke wafted around his face a moment as he tried his best to stare Elwyn down. Elwyn smirked at Reece. He had spared with the old coot before and knew what buttons to push. Elwyn never blinked or backed down from that stare. He stood there grinning, like nothing was wrong. Reece, for some reason, hated Elwyn's cheery mood.

Reece took one more puff and blew smoke out before stating, "I don't know what you're talking about."

Laughing, Elwyn shook his head. "Come on, Reece. We both know you have something planned. No need to lie. You're always starting these annoying little skirmishes and they never end well for you. Lack of proper organization, I say."

"I do not skirmish," Reece growled, quietly. He leaned forward in his chair, punctuating each word with his cigar as ashes fell to the floor.

"Are you really going to lie to my face?" Elwyn laughed. He nudged Feya behind him. Feya stiffened behind him. He knew this was the point where she was going to stop being quiet. "Come on. We have word from a reliable source of what you have been up to and what you have planned. You can quit the bullshit and stop lying."

"How dare you say I am lying, you little pansy assed ballarag," Reece huffed, sitting forward in his chair. "You can take…"

"Gentleman," Feya interjected. She looked at Elwyn, those misty green eyes sparkling with annoyance. "We need not bicker."

She pushed past Elwyn, grabbing her wrist and shook his head at her. He did not know how Reece would act towards her, and he was not taking any chances. She turned and winked at Elwyn.

"Reece," she said, breathlessly. He knew that tone of voice. She was going to try to charm Reece. "You need not be mad at Elwyn anymore. Just tell us what your intentions are."

Reece blinked a few times. Elwyn could see that he was trying to fight the spell. Reece had always been strong of mind and character. They did not easily sway him. Anger, on the other hand, was different. Reece was very easy to trigger his anger response. Elwyn hoped Feya could hold the spell.

"I…" Reece stammered. The confusion in his eyes was clear as he starred at Feya.

"Come now," she breathed. "Tell us your intentions with these battles you keep doing."

Reece shook his head like he was trying to shake Feya out of it. His eyes clouded as he let the cigar burn in his hand unnoticed.

Feya walked closer to him. Resting her hand softly on his cheek. Reece's eyes locked with hers. "Why are you starting these battles?"

"The queen is weak and the people need to see it," Reece whispered back. He was still trying to fight the charm spell, but now he was failing. His eyes slowly became glassy. "Her husband was weak. Our people have grown weak under both of their rules. We are no longer mighty. We are pathetic. A simple invasion from another magical clan could weaken our defenses. We need a strong and decisive ruler. Not a pansy who caters to every whiney lil clan leader's demands."

Elwyn stood where he was, afraid if he moved, the delicate spell would be broken. Every fiber of his being wanted to protect Feya. He watched Reece like a hawk for any movement that he might attack Feya. Any motion that the spell was broken.

He could see the confusion in Reece's eyes as he tried to fight the spell and figure out why he felt compelled to answer her questions.

"What would you do to remedy the situation?" Feya whispered huskily.

"Show the faes how weak she is," Reece whispered in bewilderment. "Once they see that, they will elect someone new, hopefully not that fool of a son of hers. Her lineage has always been weak and needs to be put to pasture."

"Put to pasture?" Feya queried.

"Retire," Reece whispered.

"You will forget this conversation," Feya said, her eyes still locked with Reece's. Her hand was still touching his check.

Reece's eyes glazed over for a second, then snapped back as Feya dropped her hand to her side. Reece's eyes traveling from Feya to Elwyn. A look of confusion appeared on his face as he tried to pretend he knew what was going on. Elwyn always marveled at what she could do with that spell charm. He had not thought that Reece was the one, but part hoped he was. Then he could focus his time on Feya. He could not wait to spend time with her alone. He would need a break after this. Hopefully, without her father, he was making sure they got very little time alone.

Soon, he was going to have to get this rune tattooed. That way, it was on permanently. He knew she would honor her word, but her father… He debated having his mother get the tattoo as well. He knew she would come around to Feya and her family once she got to know them. Well, maybe not Redd so much.

"Ummm…" Reece muttered, looking down at the cigar in his hand.

"So," Elwyn started. "As we discussed, will you be attending the ball next month?"

"Why would I attend such a stupid, vapid event?" Reece growled, confusion giving way to anger.

Elwyn knew Reece knew something had happened. Reece would not admit that or ask questions. Too much pride. Reece's eyes looked around, trying to figure out what had happened and why he was missing part of the conversation. Feya must be tired, she had been so much more careful the other times she cast the spell.

"Well then, we will be off," Elwyn stated. He just could not help putting in one more jab. "It was such a pleasure talking with you. You are always such a gracious well of knowledge. I hope you change your mind and attend to the ball. The queen would love for you to come."

Elwyn's mischievous grin spread wide across his face. The confusion and anger on Reece's face were worth it. The old coot could sit there and stew in trying to remember what they had discussed. Elwyn secretly hoped Reece thought he was going crazy. The mean old bastard deserved to be knocked down a few pegs. When he went to bi-annual clan discussions, he always started a ruckus. These meetings were for the clans to each talk over grievances and work them out peacefully. Every time, this bastard would intentionally goad and rile up other clans. Encouraged fights and discord amongst them.

Elwyn's grin stayed in place even when Feya pinched him. She grabbed his hand and dragged him out the door.

"Why?" Feya grumbled as soon as they were outside. "Why would you egg him on? We could have just left, instead you make cryptic comments."

"I have always disliked him," Elwyn stated. "But you, on the other hand…"

He grabbed her, tugging her into his arms. His lips sought the warmth of hers. She sighed into his mouth as his tongue opened her lips. As his tongue explored her open mouth, he realized he would never get enough of the taste of her. Like sipping a smooth shot of Rougarou Whiskey, she was intoxicating.

A coughing noise brought him back to reality.

"Yes?" he growled at the old fae. He knew the old man was being polite by letting them know he was there. He just wished he had gone away instead.

"My Lord," he said, drolly. "Wishes you to never come back here."

Laughing, Elwyn stated. "No can do. If the queen wishes me to, then I shall do."

He grinned at the old fae. Reaching his hand up, he patted him on the head condescendingly. The old fae's eyes lit up with indignation.

Feya grabbed Elwyn's hand, dragging him down the walkway.

"You," she sputtered. "Could you not play nice for 5 seconds, even?"

"I played nice the whole time," Elwyn stated. She had not been a part of the royal court, so did not know what kind of verbal sparring needed to go on. "You have been here for just a moment. You don't know what these people are truly like or what they have done. I unfortunately do. We should go somewhere quiet, just the two of us."

"Shit," Elwyn muttered. As he noticed an alert and looked down at his phone. Lucian, his fae that he had watching Sen Jogah, the man who attacked him the other day, had messaged:

He got another letter. I was able to look over his shoulder. They are meeting tonight at 11pm at the tavern.

Elwyn sighed. So much for spending time with Feya alone. Maybe they would resolve this sooner than he thought. He handed the phone over to Feya to read the message. He watched as her eyes lit up. What surprised him most was they looked sad when she read it. *Why would she be sad that they had a new clue?* He wondered.

Chapter 23

Feya sat in the corner quietly at Ballybog's Tavern. Elwyn by her side in the booth. It had taken a lot of fighting, but her father and Aguya stayed in their quarters. Brady had managed, with a little charm, to work as a waitress in Sen's section for the night.

With the ease that Brady walked through the fae's, she wondered if this was the life she should have had. A quiet life with her own kind. Would Brady have been happier here? She mused. Knowing her father had done everything that he could to make all their lives as normal as possible. She had spent so much time stressing about always being the kid of the group and treated as such. It had played a hand in her own lack of confidence in herself and her abilities.

Shaking her head to brush the thoughts away, she looked at her phone to check the time. They still had a few minutes till 11:00 pm. She had hoped the perpetrator would be early, then she would have more time this evening to spend with Elwyn before she had to depart. She had not realized how much it would hurt leaving him. The idea was tearing her soul apart. She felt ill at the idea of leaving him, but knew it was what must be done. She could not stay here, and he must stay here. He had worked hard to build this life here.

To distract herself and escape the mire of her own thoughts, she glanced around the bar. The bar was smokey from some fae's smoking, Green Lust, in the far corner. The smell it

left in the air was rancid. She knew the narcotic was illegal in the vale, but apparently there were those who did it, anyway. The bar was packed with many fae patrons. No other magicals were here since they could not cross the vale. Her father still had not told them how he crossed through. He refused to let Elwyn know of this new trick.

They placed themselves about fifteen feet from Sen, and he faced away from them. When they entered the bar, he glanced up at them with no recognition in those muddy brown eyes. The charm spell she had cast was working its magic. They wanted to make sure they saw who came in to greet him and hear the conversation. She wished Leo had come. His hearing was the best of them all. Sighing, she continued to watch Sen. He just kept sipping his Alfheimr ale.

Brady came over, dropping some ale off for them. Time to blend in and stay in the shadows. Pretend to be just a normal fae at the bar with her mate.

Glancing over at Elwyn, his face covered in shadows, she could make out the line of his jaw. A hint of stubble covering it. The bruises on his face were almost gone, faded to a light yellow. He turned his face and smiled at her. She could not help but smile back at that warm expression. His hand caressing her shoulder gently. He turned back towards the doors when they heard them open. A bit of fresh air wafted in for a second, then vanished. Feya sighed in relief at the scent.

Elwyn stiffen up next to her. She turned to follow his gaze. Her breath caught when she saw who was confidently approaching Sen.

Elwyn stared down at Feya's face, partially covered in shadows. She was leaning into him as his arm draped it across her shoulders. Her hand gently sat on his thigh. After this mission, they would have to sit and figure out the future. He wondered how much time she would be willing to spend in court with him. He doubted much since it was an enormous risk if she was exposed.

Plus, he knew she had missed her family and there was no way they could stay in the vale.

How much of my life was I willing to give up? He thought. *So that I can be with her. Would I be willing to give up my status in court and follow her going from one mission to another? Working as a mercenary for the church?* Getting lost in the misty green eyes, he knew there was no decision to make.

Glancing away, he looked up as the doors opened and two fae women walked in. He felt his heart stop and then start again racing. The rush of betrayal robbing him of his breath. It must be a mistake, his brain screamed. He watched as she gracefully walked through the room heading towards Sen, her companion following meekly behind. She stood out like a sore thumb, her head raised high with dignity. Acting like what she was doing was nothing out of the ordinary. Strolling through the tavern like it was just a daily occurrence.

He tried to find a rational reason she would be here. A million thoughts raced with excuses through his head. Maybe it was just a weird coincidence. Perhaps she was looking for some Green Lust. Maybe she was meeting a man. Maybe she was lost and came in to get directions. None of the excuses sounded plausible, even to his racing brain.

His mother, Olette, and Deema sat at the table with Sen. He went to stand up, but Feya's hand on his thigh squeezed tight. He paused. Maybe it was not what he thought. He slouched back down in the chair. Every fiber of his being focused on the table fifteen feet away. Straining his heightened hearing, to listen to every word said. He put all his energy into blocking out all the din from the other patrons.

"Hello," Sen said, just barely audible over the din of the bar.

"I have a new mission for you," Olette said, her eyes looking around the tavern with disgust. "I will triple the pay if you get it done quickly and quietly."

"I am listening," Sen said, nodding his head, scraggly brown hair bouncing.

Olette turned her head towards the door to watch a fae enter. Her words got lost as she turned her head.

"Just spill it," Sen stated.

"Show respect," Deema stated. Olette turned back, her lips curled up in a sneer

"I need you to eliminate a fae for me," Olette said, passing what looked like a picture over to Sen. Elwyn craned his neck to try to see the picture, but could not.

Whistling, Sen said, "Well, isn't she a pretty one? Are ya sure you want to be rid of this one?"

"Yes," Olette sneered. Looking away, she waved her hand in the air, the smell obviously getting to her. "Her name is Feya Annwen."

Elwyn's body went on full alert. Why was his mother talking to a thug? Why would she want the thug to kill his Feya? She had to have known how Elwyn felt about her. He never introduced his mother to women in all his years alive, let alone brought them to stay with them. It hit him suddenly. He had put Feya in danger. His mother wanted to kill her, and he did not know what he would have to do. Plus, his mother had hired not one, but two faes to attack him. Her own son, she had hired these people to come after him. She had also hired someone to kill his stepfather and the queen's cousin. He did not know how to proceed from here. She was his mother, for fuck's sake. It just made little sense. What was her end game? Maybe he was misreading the situation. Maybe she was here just to get rid of Feya, but he knew that was not true. HIs gut felt like it was twisting in knots. He just knew that no matter what choice he made, he was going to lose.

Feya's hand squeezed his leg tight. Rubbing her arm, he wanted to tell her that there was no way in hell this man would survive the night if he took the mission. Elwyn would see to it. He might see to it even if he didn't.

"When can it be done?" Deema spoke up. He had disliked Deema from the day he met her. His mother had brought her in as a handmaiden when she first married his stepfather, Healfdene. She had been his mother's shadow ever since. Always gave him the creeps from day one.

"When do you want it done?" Sen said, sipping his ale.

"Tonight," Olette stated. "Do it tonight and I will quadruple the money."

Choking for a moment on his ale, Sen nodded. "Aight, I can get 'er done tonight. I expect half up front."

"You will get a quarter," Deema said, shrewdly. "The rest when the job is done."

Deema tossed an envelope, most likely filled with cash, onto the table. Olette and Deema both got up from the table. Before they exited the bar, Elwyn jumped up. He quickly caught up with his mother, grabbing her arm and spinning her around. He just stared into the eyes that were mirrors of his own, not uttering a single word.

She stood there looking up at him, shocked. Her mouth hung open before she turned and ran out of the bar. Deema hot on her heels.

Elwyn turned to see Feya and Brady standing behind him with looks of concern on their faces. He strolled past them to Sen's table.

Grabbing the fae by the front of his shirt, lifting him out of his chair. "I will say this once. If you come after Feya, the fae in the picture, I will make your life a living hell. There is a fate worse than death, and I will make sure you experience it every day for all eternity. Keep the money and leave this vale. Never come back, never come by one of mine, and mark my words, Feya is mine. Do you understand me?"

Sen nodded as much as his head could move with the tight grip Elwyn had on him.

"Say it out loud," Elwyn growled.

"Yes," Sen mumbled.

Staring into Sen's eyes, Elwyn deciphered that he truly understood. Elwyn dropped him unceremoniously on the tavern floor. He turned back to Feya and Brady. Grabbing Feya's hand.

"Let's go," Elwyn growled.

Brady followed as Elwyn dragged Feya out. He felt such a ball of icy rage rolling through him and a giant well of sadness all

at once. His own mother tried to have his life mate killed and had hired several people to attack him. Not knowing why she would do this was eating him up.

Feya followed through the streets to where she assumed was to return to the castle. Brady ran behind them, trying to keep up with Elwyn's long strides. His mother's betrayal of Elwyn left her speechless, and her heart ached for him. She looked at him, trying to say something comforting, but her mouth could not form the words. So she ran quietly behind him.

The guards opened the front doors with no questions, having recognized them. They ran up the stairs to their wing. She could hear Olette's heart in the dining room with her father and Aguya. It was pounding a song of fear.

"Dining room," she stated.

Elwyn continued on towards the dining room. Throwing the door open, Olette stood by the window, Deema being held in front of her as a shield.

"How did a vampire get in here?" Olette stammered, looking to Elwyn for help.

"Who the fuck cares?" Elwyn yelled, releasing Feya's hand. He walked over to them, shoving Redd out of his way. Olette's eyes grew wide, as her hands trembled on Deema's shoulders. Deema quivered as she leaned back into Olette.

"I am not..." Red started.

"I will handle this," Elwyn said, his voice lowered to a normal pitch, but dripping with icy rage. He turned back to his mother.

Redd came to stand next to Feya. He tapped a finger on her nose. Mouthing I love you. She mouthed it back, remembering back to the first time he had done that silly gesture.

She turned back to where Elwyn stood staring down at his

mother. Deema stood between them still. The room was quiet as no one moved or spoke.

Finally, Elwyn broke the silence with a whisper. "Why?" His voice filled with so much raw anger and pain.

Redd nudged Feya with his elbow, a questioning look in his eyes. Feya shook her head.

Olette stood there a moment, looking unsure of herself for the first time since Feya had known her. She looked around the room as if asking them to help her. No one was coming to her rescue, and no one was going to speak until she answered.

Chapter 24

$\mathcal{O}$lette opened and closed her mouth a few times, her blue eyes glossy from unshed tears. Before finally whispering. "I did it for you."

"Bullshit!" Elwyn screamed, before taking a deep breath. He looked towards the wall as he composed himself. Running his hand through his hair as he turned back towards his mother. Feya wanted to rush over to him and hug him, but her dad's firm grip on her arm told her not to. Her heart ached for him.

Finally through gritted teeth, he said. "I want the truth."

"Please," Olette pleaded. Her eyes beseeching Elwyn to buy into her lies.

"The. Truth." Elwyn carefully enunciated both words. He clenched his hands at his sides in fists. She felt the frustration in those words. Her heart ached to hold him. If she could have wished it to be anyone else, she would have.

"I am," Olette whispered. Looking so small and frail, as she continued to hide behind Deema. "Healfdene was going to retire. You knew this."

Olette paused, looking at Elwyn as if waiting for an answer, but he stayed quiet. Olette searched his face imploringly. Feya couldn't comprehend why she thought that was a sufficient answer.

Olette sighed before continuing. "He raised you like you

were his own son. You stood by his side through thick and thin. You were loyal and the best son that fool could ever have. I found out he was not choosing you as his heir. He was choosing his nephew Finbar, that ungrateful sniveling twat."

"So," Elwyn shrugged. Feya heard so much hurt and rage in that one word.

"I could not let this stand," Olette said, louder. "Don't you see?"

Olette, pausing for dramatic effect, she grew bolder as she stood taller. Deema was still standing as a shield in front of her.

"You were the closest thing to a son," Olette sneered. "That male would ever have. He wasn't man enough to make a son with his own seed, so he married me for mine. Then, after all these years of waiting for him to put you in the spot where you belong, he decides to give his place to that bumbling idiot his sister gave birth to. She could not even produce a worthy heir. Her son's magic is weak, his body is weak, and he has the mind of driveling hippalectryon. Their lineage was pathetic and weak. Just as Healfdene was. I hated every time I let that poor excuse for a male touch me. He was disgusting. But for you I did it. I knew he was the way to improve your future and get us out of that hovel your father left us in."

Olette stepped out from behind Deema, lifting her hands up to cradle Elwyn's face. She could see that with each word, Olette's confidence grew. Feya could not see Elwyn's face, but his body did not move an inch. He stood rigid. Hoping he would not fall for her words. She sounded so convincing, even her eyes looked convincing with that wide-eyed innocent look. Feya knew that had to be a ruse. Her heartbeat was so erratic as she talked to Elwyn. Olette's face glowed with certainty as she continued her story.

"My love," Olette continued, biting her lip. "Since the day you were born, I have done everything I could to make sure you had a better life. I could not let this injustice stand. So, I took matters into my own hands before the paperwork could be completed. I had to work fast to ensure your future, your rightful place. You must see this? After his death, so many in the court were suspicious. That bumbling fool I hired was to make it look like an accident and he failed. So, I had to do something to distract them and change the narrative. So the queen's favorite cousin just so happened to come into my sights while on the hunt. It was so easy to have an arrow that no one recognized. Many faes are dissatisfied with the queen, especially since the king's death, so I took matters into my own hands. She has made many enemies, powerful enemies. I just needed to talk to the right people. I made quite a few friends, useful friends. They wish to bring the queen and regime down. I only hired those men to attack you to throw people from the scent. I did not want them to think it was you, but if they attacked you… Then if you find the fae's responsible, you could gain favor with the queen. Maybe even be king, my love."

Olette stopped talking, searching Elwyn's imploringly. Tears finally falling down her cheeks. Feya knew they were fake, the consummate actress. She wondered how long Olette had been lying to all those around her. She tried to go back to her own memories of Olette to remember what she used to be, but no memories came to mind.

"You could be king," she whispered. "We just need to play our cards right. I did this all for you. If you want, I have many contacts. We can easily overthrow the queen and you can be king that way. I have an army at the ready. They are waiting for the word. Whatever you want, we can do this together, my love. Or we can find a scapegoat."

Olette's eyes veered towards Feya and Redd. Feya's eyes locked with Olette's. Feya hoped Olette sensed every ounce of hatred she felt for her in that gaze.

Continuing her story, Olette said. "Or if you want, we can gain favor with the queen and you can woo her. Feya can even stay in court as your mistress. Whichever plan you want, we can go with. We can do this together now."

The room grew quiet once again. There was no way Elwyn expected Feya to be just his mistress. Feya waited with bated breath to see what Elwyn would do. The moment seemed to last forever as he stood there with his back to her.

Finally, Elwyn reached up and yanked his mother's hands away from his face. He stood rigid with rage still.

"I never wanted Healfdene's seat," he whispered. "I never wanted to be king. None of this was for me. It was all for you and the status you so desperately crave. You wanted this power, never me."

Feya inhaled, her heart aching for Elwyn. Part of her was so proud that he did not fall for his mother's deception. Stepping forward, she wanted to go to his side, but her father jerked her back again. The room was dead silent once again as Elwyn and his mother stared at each other. Olette silently pleading with her son.

"My love," Olette implored. "I am doing this for you. You can be the hero in this. I have everything planned out. We can play the plan any way you want. Just let me know how you want to go from here."

"You really think I would believe this…" Elwyn said, waving his hand in the air. "I know that this isn't for me. So tell me the truth now."

"I am," Olette pleaded.

"Stop lying!" Elwyn screamed. Taking a step towards his mother.

Feya had never seen him lose his temper before. Even with her dad the other night, he had stayed cool and collected.

Olette bit her lip, looking up at Elwyn with her most innocent look she could muster. Her blue eyes shining with the dew of tears. Her nose had the slightest blush to it. Tilting her head to the side, the light caught the trail her crocodile tears had left.

"My love," she whispered. "Everything I do is for you, from the day you were born till the day I die."

"Go to your room," Elwyn growled. "Do not leave it. I will talk to you in the morning. I need time to think."

Feya watched as Elwyn's trembling hands ran through his hair. Olette stood there a moment longer before leaving the room with Deema close on her heels.

They all stood still as Elwyn went to stand in front of the window. His reflection in the window shows a tense jaw and clenched lips. Blue eyes that changed like the ocean waves, one second sad, the next angry.

"I need to know what happened," Redd muttered.

"I am also curious," Aguya grumbled.

"I'll catch you guys up," Brady mumbled.

Redd nodded. Her father released her arm. She ran to Elwyn. Flinging her arms around him. She heard the door quietly open and shut as everyone left the room

"Elly," she whispered, using her childhood nickname for him.

He turned in her arms burying his head in her hair.

"Fe," he whispered back.

Chapter 25

*T*hey spoke no more words as he lifted his head and stared into her eyes. The anger and sadness in those dark blue eyes tore her to pieces. Standing on tiptoes, she planted her mouth on his. Trying to convey how much she felt for him in this one kiss. What was an innocent gesture turned carnal in a flash.

"Mmm," Elwyn whispered. "You sure like to bite."

Laughing, Feya licked his lip, tasting another drop of blood. The heady taste of the blood went to her head.

He aggressively brought his mouth back to hers. Their tongues wrestled as the taste of blood lingered on his lips and mouth. His hands grabbed her ass and lifted her up. She wrapped her legs around his waist. He was already rock hard, nestled between her thighs. Turning around, he slammed her up against the wall as his mouth left hers. He nibbled her chin, working his way to her neck. Sucking the delicate flesh of her neck in between his teeth, his hand came gripping her chin, shoving it up for better access.

Scratching at his shirt, she tried to pull it off. He pulled his mouth away and let her tug the shirt off. She went to lower her hands, but he grabbed them and held them above her head. He held her wrists bound in one of his firm hands. His free hand went, grabbing her hair and tugging her head back, gaining access to the delicate skin of her throat again. His teeth scraped across the pale skin before sucking in a bit of flesh. Goosebumps shivered down her spine as he suckled on her flesh. Releasing her hair, his hand went to her shirt. Ripping it open, exposing her breasts. Her breasts heaved with every breath she took, his eyes devouring them as they moved. His mouth came down, biting her nipple. She arched her back, pressing against the wall as his teeth scraped her nipple, releasing it. He moved his mouth to the other breast, sucking it in his mouth roughly.

As his mouth ravaged her breast, his free hand moved down and tugged at the button and zipper of her slacks. After a few tugs, the button snapped off and her slacks fell open. He slipped his hands in and under her panties as he thrust his fingers in her. Her wetness growing as his fingers glided in and out of her, the fire growing in her core was raging out of control. She tried to jerk her hands free, but he just gripped them tighter. Her breath was catching in her throat as her hips thrust up against his hand.

She wanted more of him, but the words caught in the back of her throat. The only sounds that came out were groans.

Just when she thought she could not take any more, he stopped his fingers from thrusting inside her. His eyes locked with hers, before he sucked his finger into his mouth, tasting her. That hand then went down and unzipped his pants. She felt his stiff erection throbbing between them before he shifted his hips and thrust into her. She gasped as the fireworks exploded, rocking her to her core. He released her hands, and they limply went around his shoulders. His hand came to her throat just under her chin as his tongue shoved into her mouth. Hips continued to thrust in and out of her. His tongue plunging into the depths of her mouth to the same beat as his hips. He bit her lip gently before he finished. She felt his shaft throbbing from his release.

His head came to rest on her shoulder. She gently started rubbing his back. Her eyes drifted to the vein in his throat as she watched it slowly beat back to a normal pace. Slowly, everything came back to her. She knew that she may have distracted him for a while, but his mind would drift back to what was happening.

She heard him mutter something, but could not make out the words. "What?" she muttered.

He lifted his head up, but did not make eye contact. "I am sorry if I hurt you."

Laughing, she said. "You did not hurt me at all. I quite enjoyed it."

His eyes locked with hers, he brushed a stray hair out of her face and said. "My beautiful Fe. I have put you in danger. Truly, I am sorry for that. I would never let or want anything to happen to you, ever."

He gently kissed her lips, sighing into her mouth he continued, "I meant sorry for everything tonight, my mother, just everything. If I had known she would try to hire someone to hurt you, I would never have involved you."

"I am glad you involved me," she whispered, her lips hovering next to his. "No regrets in coming here to help you. I am glad you asked for my help. Though I think we need to renegotiate the terms of our contract. I have decided I don't like the terms we previously agreed to."

She watched as he moved his head back to search her eyes better. The dark eyes filled with worry before he smirked. He whispered. "Do we now?"

"Yes" she smirked. "Elly, I have decided the first contract is null and void. So we should discuss a new one."

Throwing his head back, he laughed. "What does my Fe want?"

"Well," she said, running a hand through his hair. "I want to put my clothes back on somehow and go to our room."

"That can be arranged," he said, kissing the tip of her nose.

He gently set her down. Taking a step back, he grabbed his shirt off the floor where it had been tossed, then tugged it down over her head.

"See," he smirked.

Her eyes roamed his body, his slacks still open, his manhood hanging out, his bare muscular torso and then his eyes. His eyes were filled with such sadness again. She wished she could push that sadness away. A word, a gesture, anything. She knew that nothing, but time could heal this wound.

He whispered. "First item of the newly negotiated contract is done."

Laughing, she shook her head. She kicked her slacks off since the zipper and button were goners and they would not stay up, anyway. Luckily, his shirt was long enough to cover up her goodies. Picking up her slacks and heels. Elwyn held his hand out to her. She grabbed it and followed him out of the room.

Feya woke up, with Elwyn's arm strewn across her chest. She felt so cozy and snug. She did not want to leave the bed. Elwyn had tossed and turned and took forever to fall asleep. She sat there as he wrestled the demons in his head, offering what comfort she could. Knowing she should get up, instead she burrowed deeper in the blankets. Elwyn's arm pulled her closer to nuzzle her neck.

"Fe," he whispered.

"Yes?" she replied.

She looked into his sleepy blue eyes. He smiled at her, like the old Elwyn would, the one before his mother's betrayal. She smiled back up at him. He turned, his face hovering over hers. Brushing a gentle kiss across her lips.

"Good morning," he said, brushing another kiss across her lips. "My beautiful Fe, did you sleep well?"

"Yes," she breathed as his lips came to hover over her again. She inhaled his breath as he exhaled. The tension building between them was palpable. "What about you?"

"Cuddling," he said, his nose nuzzling hers. "With you made it easy to sleep. Waking up to you also…"

Laughing, she wrapped her arms around his neck, tugging him down to her mouth. Before their lips could meet, there was a bang on the door.

Groaning, she listened. Hearing her father's heartbeat was erratic, telling her he was angry over something.

"Go away," Elwyn grumbled, flinging himself back onto the bed. He rubbed his furrowed brow.

"Get up," Redd growled. "We have a situation."

"Too good to be true," Elwyn muttered, before jumping out of bed.

She looked over at him, seeing his face screwed up in an indiscernible expression. For a moment, he had forgotten and now the problems came back to him. Jumping out of bed, she walked up and wrapped her arms around him from behind. Burying her face between his shoulder blades.

"Just a moment longer," she whispered.

He paused before turning in her arms. He buried his head in her hair, his arms wrapped around holding her tight.

"I need you, Fe," he whispered.

"I need you too," she whispered back.

They stayed wrapped in each other's arms for a moment before breaking apart and getting dressed. They dressed in silence, neither sure how the day would come. Feya knew soon she would be leaving. It tore her heart to know she would not be seeing Elwyn daily. She would miss him till the day she died. She had always assumed she would never have these feelings for anyone.

She glanced at Elwyn as he buttoned up his gray shirt. The filtered sunrays coming through the curtains showed off blonde highlights in his brown hair. She walked over, brushing a strand of hair off his forehead. He stopped and looked down at her. Gently, he bent down and kissed her lips.

They left the room, hearing Redd in the dining hall pacing. They walked into the dining room. Only the three of them were in there: Redd, Aguya and Brady.

"I knew you were too fucking soft, boy," Redd growled when they walked in. He stalking across the room like a caged tiger. His angry strides made the room look small.

Brady stood at the window, staring at the dark curtains that were drawn across them. Aguya stood in front of the barren fireplace, seeming to zone out, staring at the ashen floor bed.

"I am really not in the mood," Elwyn sneered, his blue eyes shooting icy daggers. "For your half assed cryptic insults this morning."

Feya stopped looking around the room as it registered what would make her father so mad. She focused on heartbeats. One, two, three, and four. The only heartbeats in the wing were the people in this room. No wonder her father was upset. The mission was no longer over. Olette and Deema had run while they all slept.

"Elwyn," Feya stated.

He turned to look at her. His eyes were dead as they locked with hers. A twinge of pain shot through her as she stared into those cold eyes.

"Boy," Redd said.

"Father, no," Feya stated. Turning to Elwyn, she screwed up the courage to tell him. Taking a deep breath, she put both her hands on his cheek. "Your mother has run. She is no longer here."

He stared at Feya, his expression never changing. She waited for some flicker of emotion, but none came. He nodded and turned back to Redd. He had known his mother would run, and he had let it happen. Feya sat there as the information sunk in. She had a feeling if the roles were reversed, she would have done the same thing.

"Okay," Elwyn growled. "There's no subtle way to say this. I am fucking tired of your constant insults. So you take those insults and…"

"Hey," Feya said, calmly. "There is no time to fight among ourselves. We need to come up with a plan."

"There is no need," Elwyn said. "My job was to find the culprit. I now know and can report it to the queen."

"That's it, boy?" Redd said, storming over to Elwyn.

Feya went to jump between them, but Brady grabbed her. She had been so distracted she had not realized Brady had moved towards her. She brushed off Brady as she stared at Elwyn and her father. Elwyn just stared at Redd, not saying a thing.

"She hired someone to kill Feya!" Redd screamed. "Are you going to just let that stand? I knew you were a pansy ass fae. I just didn't realize how much till now."

"I took care of it already," Elwyn growled back.

Feya could tell Elwyn was close to snapping. His heart was racing, his breath hurried. The coldness in his eyes went no further. He was masking the rage and turmoil inside him. She just needed to redirect at someone other than her father.

"Elwyn," Feya said, quietly. "Let us go talk to the queen."

"Fine," Elwyn snarled. Turning, he exited the room. Feya followed behind him. Glancing back at her father, she gave him a worried glance.

""Feya," Redd stated. "You are to stay here. We are leaving to…"

Feya did not wait for the rest of the sentence before slamming the door shut and following Elwyn through the hallways. She knew her father worried about her, so he wanted her away from here and safe. She wanted to finish the job she started. So far, she had blended in with no issues. Her whole life, she had to hide from half of what she was. Now she knew she would not have to always hide.

Taking a deep breath as she followed Elwyn, she knew there was more to it. She would not leave while Elwyn was in this much pain. He needed her, at least for now. She would leave soon enough to go back to her old life.

Chapter 26

Elwyn stood outside the queen's office. He should feel nervous with what he was going to tell her, but all he felt was numbness. Once he let the queen know who had done this, he was not sure what the consequences of his mother's action would be. Probably going to lose his place in the court, but he did not care. A month ago, it would have devastated him. He had spent years trying to get to where he was. Schooling, training, fighting tooth and nail for this position, it no longer meant anything. Knowing Feya could not stay at court made the idea of leaving easier. He would have to learn how to get along with Redd somehow, though. That was a task he was not sure he was up to right now.

He paced the hallway restlessly. Just wanting to get this over with so he could move on with his life. The betrayal he felt from his mother still stung so much. In his heart, he knew she had not done this for him. She had wanted the status in the court. She had always been trying to climb that ladder since the day she met Healfdene. He had just never realized she would use him as a tool to get there. He felt such a rage he had wanted to shake his mother last night and at the same time give her the chance to run. When he looked in Feya's eyes, he knew she knew the truth. He had let his mother run. He felt guilty for not telling her the truth beforehand, he had feared she would try to stop his mother.

He stopped pacing when he felt a hand touch his arm. Glancing down at Feya, he saw the worry in her eyes. Knowing it was aimed at him, he tried to smile at her, but it did not reach his eyes. Seeing that it did not placate her, he bent down and kissed her forehead. He had been worried she would be mad at him. She was not.

"It's going to be alright," he whispered.

"Will it?" she whispered.

"It will," he whispered back. "Just be patient."

"How do you think she will react?" she asked, hesitantly.

"Most likely," he said, pausing for a moment. He pulled her close, needing her warmth. A coldness had settled him, like he had never felt before. "I will lose my status in court. They will hunt her down and she will be put on trial for her crimes."

Nodding her head against his chest. She sat there quietly, nestled in his arms. Not ready to talk, he just wished she would wait till after this to ask the questions. He was going to need to be in the right headspace to explain this betrayal to the crown, to his family, to him. He did not need to be thinking about anything else.

"What will you do?" she whispered, her hand sliding up and down his back comfortingly.

"You guys need another fae to help you out?" he said, laughing.

He knew Redd would not stand for that. It would be a daily fight with Redd to be with Feya. He patiently waited for an answer, but Feya stayed quiet. The numbness faded at her lake of response. He felt the pain stabbing at him again.

Pushing away, he turned from her to stare at the door. He willed the door open so he could get this done. Maybe he would just retire to one of his estates after all. He was tired of chasing someone who constantly ran hot and cold. He was just tired in general. Closing his eyes, he rolled his head back and forth, trying to release the tension in his shoulders and neck. Now if he could just release the tension in his heart.

Laughing coldly, he opened his eyes. A guard stood in front of him, ready to let him in to see the queen.

"I hear you have news," Queen Cassada muttered, never

looking up from her books. Her curly brown hair bounced while she talked. She wore a casual cream-colored blouse, as she made notes in the ledger.

He walked closer to her desk, stopping a few feet away. Feya hot on his heels. He could practically feel her breathing down his neck. Wished she had just stayed in the hall. He did not need her here, distracting him from what needed to be done.

"I found the culprit," he said, gearing up for what he had to say next. Taking a deep breath, he steeled himself. "My mother."

The queen looked, her eyes growing bigger. He stared into the queen's eyes as a range of emotion crossed her face. Surprise, confusion, and finally anger.

He waited for her to yell, to call her guards, to throw him in a dark cell. Would they put him on trial for this? None of that came.

Queen Cassada sat back in her chair, looking contemplative. Her fingers tapping on the ledger.

"Why did she kill her husband?" She whispered. That earnest brown eyed stare making him feel foolish.

Nodding, Elwyn stated. "He had chosen a new heir, his nephew. She wanted to kill him before he changed his will. Wanting to make sure everything stayed with her, and I guess myself. The money, the status, and such."

Looking down at her desk, her fingers continued to tap mindlessly as she contemplated what he said.

Feya put a hand gently on Elwyn's back. Closing his eyes, he held his tongue. He wanted to yell at her. If this was nothing but a fling, she could leave now. He did not need her pity or her father's constant belittlement.

Opening his eyes, he saw the queen was staring at him.

"Why my cousin?" she whispered, anguished. Tears welled up in her brown eyes. His breath caught as he stared into them.

"To throw us off the scent," he whispered back. Taking a deep breath, it was now or never to tell her the rest. "I fear she has an alliance with some of your enemies and will not run and hide quietly. My fear is she will escalate this. I am not sure whom she built an alliance with. I just found out last night when she tried to hire someone to kill Feya."

The queen nodded. "Anything else I should be apprised of at this moment?"

"I don't know," Elwyn muttered. "I was unable to get the entire story from her."

The queen nodded again before staring out the window to her right. The kingdom stood quiet as the sun rose in the sky. Colors of oranges and blues shooting through the sky. A few faes ran about starting their day.

Everything he thought was going to happen had not. He felt on edge as he kept expecting the next shoe to drop. Feya's hand on his back, the queen not raging at him, and knowing the truth about his own mother was all giving him anxiety. They all needed to stop being so nice. Yell, scream, do anything but offer sympathy.

"Alright," the queen said, after contemplating. "You will speak with the captain of the guard tonight. Provide him with all the details on Olette that will be needed for us to pursue this. I will put the castle on lockdown. No one in and no one out. Do you feel this will cause a conflict with you?"

"No," Elwyn stated. "My commitment is to you and the crown, your highness."

Nodding, the queen said. "You are dismissed. Captain Wallace will call for you."

The queen looked back at books. Without seeming to be bothered by the situation, she started back working.

Elwyn stared at her a moment, unsure if he should say something else. Elwyn turned and left the room, not sure how to respond to this. He stalked the halls, heading to his wing, Feya following close on his heels. He assumed he would remain there until they invited him to talk to the captain.

He had been so sure they would blame him, and he would have to fight to prove his innocence. Having geared up for the battle to come, even though he knew he was ill prepared for that battle, he still had been ready for it. No one blamed him, no one fought him. They should. He should have seen what she was up to. She was his mother, for fuck's sake. He should have known she was up to something. How could he have been so blind? Should have known she had murdered his stepfather, but he had not. Blinded to the fact that she hated his stepfather so much that she would have him murdered. He knew even at a young age that it was an arranged marriage, but he assumed since they never fought, they eventually grew to love each other. Never looked too deeply under the depths of who she was, just saw the frivolous socialite she had been pretending to be.

Opening the bedroom door, he slammed it shut before Feya could walk in. He heard her stop outside the door. He just needed to be alone, and he hoped she would just go be with her family. They would probably want to leave, anyway. Plus, they would need to hurry before they locked the vale down. She would need to go update her father. He would want to know what had happened either way. Most importantly, he needed to be alone.

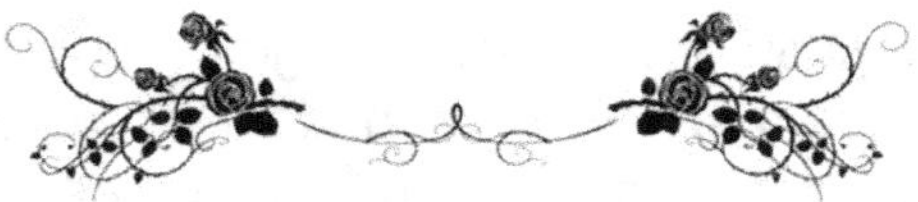

Feya stood outside the door that was just slammed in her face. She knew he was angry with her. She just could not figure out why. Outside the queen's office, he had pushed her away and would not look at her again. When she touched him in the queen's office, he had stiffened up. Standing there, she debated if she should walk in or walk away.

"Come with me," Brady whispered. She gently grabbed Feya's hand and tugged her away.

Feya let Brady drag her along as they walked down the halls. They went through the kitchen and walked out to the garden. Brady guided her through them, not speaking a word, just holding her hand.

A lump built in her throat as she halted, tears welling up in her eyes. Biting her lip to stop the sounds that wanted to escape.

Brady turned to her. "Let it out, muffin," she whispered,

pulling Feya into her warm embrace.

"I don't know why he is mad at me," Feya whined.

She hated crying, especially if she knew someone would see her. The odds were high that someone would spot them since they were in the herb garden. She was just so confused and tired and just emotionally drained. Plus, she once again forgot her sunglasses, and she felt the beginning of a migraine coming. She missed living in the night and not having to worry about such things. She felt so whiney right now.

"Tell me what happened when you were gone," Brady said, hugging Feya tighter.

Feya told her everything that had happened outside the queen's office. The conversation they had, the moment he pushed her away, how he stiffened when she tried to comfort him in the queen's office, finally ending with him slamming the door in her face.

Feya told her everything that had happened at the queen's office.

Brady pulled back, looking into Feya's eyes as she said, "Muffin, you are a fool."

Feya stood aghast staring at Brady.

"What?" she muttered in confusion.

Startled at Brady's response. She thought Brady would be on her side; she felt slighted that Brady called her an insult instead. Sniffling, she glared at Brady, her betrayer.

"That boy," Brady started. "Stood there in his darkest hour asking you if he could join you and you said nothing. No wonder he is mad at you. He was expressing his feelings, and you just sat there saying nothing. Do you not realize how hard it is for some people to tell others their feelings?"

Feya stood staring at Brady as the implication of her words sunk in. She remembered all the times Elwyn had been nice and gentle with her, and she had pushed him away. She had been so wrapped up in her own feelings of trying to prove herself, of trying to get him out of her head and heart, she had not stopped to think he might be going through the same thing. No matter what she said or did, he never snapped; he just stood there patiently. She had not meant to hurt him with her silence. She had just stayed quiet because she assumed he had not meant it. Closing her eyes, she remembered that was the point when he pushed her away, when he gave her the cold shoulder. No matter how much she hated it, she deserved his anger.

She opened her eyes and met Brady's gray eyes. She saw the sympathy in there.

Giving a self-deprecating smile, Feya muttered, "I am not very good at this relationship thing."

Laughing, Brady said. "You get that from your father. He is not emotionally intelligent with others either. The point is, you know now what is wrong and you can go fix it."

Feya stared at Brady before nodding. She was not sure she could or should fix it. He would never be happy living the nomad life. Plus, he said that, thinking the queen would exile him. Obviously, that would not happen.

"You march up there and tell him how you feel," Brady smiled sweetly.

Feya stared at Brady, muttering. "Easier said than done."

"Hush," Brady said, a fake frown flashing across her face. "Your mouth. You can fix this by being honest with him."

Brady grabbed her hand and led her through the gardens to the wing. Feya tried to figure out what was the best thing to do, but nothing came to mind. Her heart sank at the idea of leaving Elwyn, but she knew she could not stay. Her thoughts kept going back and forth. If he was mad, it would be easier when she had to leave. The idea of leaving and him hating her tore her apart. Why had she let him into her heart? This was to be a mission and nothing else. She was to prove she could handle herself. All she proved was that she would fall at the first opportunity.

She stopped walking as her own thoughts sunk in. Closing her eyes, pushing the thoughts away, racing through her mind. She was not ready to face them. She now knew she needed to make it up to Elwyn, though.

"You ok?" Brady whispered.

Nodding Feya, started walking again. She felt like a child holding her mother's hand, though. She gently shook Brady's hand off. Brady laughed as they continued the walk up the stairs.

At the top of the stairs, Feya made the trek to the bedroom. She could hear Elwyn's heartbeat there. She tentatively opened the door.

Elwyn sat in the chair in front of the fireplace, staring at the small fire in it. HIs flickering a flame on and off absentmindedly. He did not look up or acknowledge her. She walked over, standing in front of him. Waiting for him to look up at her, but he did not.

Sighing, she started. "I am no good at these things. Didn't know how to respond to your question earlier so I sat quietly. I knew the queen would not find you at fault, just as I know you had nothing to do with your…"

She faltered for a moment, pausing as she tried to think of what to say as he continued to look through her.

She bent down to be in line with his eyes. He finally looked at her, his eyes icy cold. She shivered, knowing she had made things worse. Her tumbling words were not helping either. Sighing, she reached her hand up to touch his face, then dropped it. His face was not welcoming.

"Elly," she whispered. "Do you really think you'd want to leave here and travel with my family?"

His eyes locked with hers. "What I want doesn't really matter, does it?"

She stood up and stared down at him. He had finally looked up at her; the coldness gone and in place was anger instead. Anger she could handle.

She plopped herself down on his lap as he stared at her in surprise.

"Elly," she whispered as she brought her mouth close to his. Her lips hovered a breath away as she locked her eyes with his. "Don't be mad at me."

She watched as his eyes traveled to her lips. Sighing, he brought his mouth to hers. Kissing her roughly before pulling away.

"Damn you, Fe," he muttered.

Chapter 27

Elwyn sat there holding Feya in his lap. He tried to stay mad at her, knew he should, but she flashed those damn misty green eyes and all his resolve was lost. He must have lost his ever loving mind. Burying his head in her neck, he tried to let the anger and frustration with everyone go. He stayed buried inside him. He could not remember the last time he had felt this way.

Sighing, he tried to figure out where he would go from here. If the queen allowed it, should he just stay at the court? Obviously, Feya did not want him to join her. He did not know how he would enjoy what little time they had left with everything going on. She and her family would probably leave as soon as they lifted the restrictions. Maybe it had always been this way, him chasing her and her running away. Even when they were kids, he had known she was it for him. That's why he had told her to run. He could not stand the thought of losing her. Even knowing the horror stories, he told her to leave. Thankfully they had all turned out to be a fae urban legend. He had spent years secretly searching for her, never telling a soul. Paying one investigator after another. Fearing she had died that night, but still never giving up hope he would find her one day. Then a few years ago he found her, just by chance. He spotted her across the street in a small town in Italy. She seemed so happy with her family exploring the town. He had stood back, studying her and trying to find the best time to approach her. He had felt so insecure about disrupting her life. Every time, it felt like it was not the right time. He was attacked and came up with the stupid idea of requesting her help in solving the crime. Not even really thinking he needed the help, though she came quite in handy after all. He had not gone to see a healer once he had the idea, just went straight to where he knew she was at. He wondered if, under different circumstances, she would ever feel the same for him.

A knock on the door dragged him from his reverie. He thought back to Redd there was no way he could pass off. The witch may be on a bad day could pass off. With how much traffic he was going to get, he was not sure how much longer they could hide here in his wing. Luckily, they had given him privacy so far, but who knew how long that would last. They would probably want to investigate his mother's room soon.

He gently nudged Feya off his lap as he went to the door. Opening it, he saw Wallace, the general of the fae army. He stood about 5'8" with chocolate brown eyes. Jet black hair slicked back underneath his gray beret. HIs mahogany skin stood in contrast to the gray uniform. His gray uniform was perfectly impeccable, making Elwyn feel like a slug in his jeans and shirt. He should have dressed in uniform, but his head and heart had been elsewhere.

"Hey," Wallace muttered. His eyes darted past Elwyn to where Feya stood. "Let's go somewhere private."

He shut the door, leaving Feya in the room. Wallace, without speaking, followed him down the hall as he left his wing and went down the stairs. He had left his wing to help keep the others hidden, no destination in mind.

"Where should we go?" Elwyn grumbled. He should probably start focusing on how to get Feya and her family out of the vale safely. Shove his emotions down and do what needed to be done. He could face what was to come once he was alone, probably for the best that way.

"Let's go to the barracks," Wallace said in his gravelly voice. Elwyn always thought his gravelly voice sounded like he had been punched too many times in the throat.

Briskly walking, they left the castle. Crossing a grassy

knoll, they made the trek to the barracks just to the left of the castle. Elwyn glanced around, noting the fae soldiers were running around, preparing for whatever was to come. Knowing his mother had started this, ate at his soul.

He kept waiting for everyone to hate him. His own mother had betrayed them all. They should hate him. At this moment, he hated himself, if he was honest. He wished he had seen it, could have prepared for it, stopped it before it happened, he wished he could have done anything, but the nothing he had done. He felt like a fool right now.

They entered a meeting room on the first floor of the barracks. Elwyn steeled himself for the hours to come of interrogation.

Feya paced the room after Elwyn left, restlessly. She knew in her heart that he had not really forgiven her. She was attempting to think of the words to say when someone knocked on the door. He looked like just another fae guard, but Elwyn never introduced her. He just left without saying a word. There had been hope they would have more time to talk before they hailed him to be interrogated.

Elwyn had been gone for hours. Elwyn had left before lunch and was still not back. Glancing out the window, she saw that the sun was setting. Guards were running around the gardens. The castle had been on high alert. So far, no one had come to their wing. She had not been sure what she would do when they came to search the wing with her family.

It worried her how long He had been gone. What if the queen had arrested him? What if they had beaten him up during the interrogation? So many worst-case scenarios played through her mind. She wanted to be sure of his whereabouts and if he was safe. Closing her eyes, trying to sense his blood, but the pull was fading. She sensed he was still alive, but nothing else. Not enough of his blood had been drunk to be able to follow him. She turned from the window, deciding it was time to search for him. She would enlist Aguya's help. Aguya was better at tracking spells and could find him faster than Feya could.

Leaving the room, she walked to where Aguya and Brady were staying. It surprised her they were peacefully staying in the room together. She paused outside the door, thinking about the day's events. Her father had wanted to drag her out of here today. Explaining the lockdown and why they could not leave took a while since he was hardheaded and would not listen. Brady had left to confirm that the vale was closed and they could not leave. Fighting with her dad had been a distraction for a while, but now that she was alone in her head again, she could not stop thinking of Elwyn.

The one and only portal gone. Powerful faes had shut it down so no new soldiers could enter and none could leave. With the portal closed, the air had changed in the vale. Atmosphere around them felt electrified. The air had lost its freshness. The faes were even acting on edge, nervous and anxious as they tried to figure out what was happening. They made no announcement about why they had done the lockdown. All was just shutdown. Most faes locked themselves in their homes or businesses, unsure what to do.

Lifting her hand to knock, she heard a heartbeat approaching the wing. Pausing, she listened. It was Elwyn's.

Running to the top of the stairs, she anxiously waited for him to climb the stairs. He looked emotionally beat and exhausted, but he had no new bruises. He nodded at her as he walked past her, heading to their shared room. This time, he did not shut the door in her face. It was a minor victory.

After she shut the door behind her, she asked. "Do you want to talk about it?"

"No," he grumbled. He took his shirt and pants off the climb into bed.

She stared at him, feeling unsure of herself. She did not know how to react to this, Elwyn. He was usually so talkative and cheery. This was out of character. Deciding to not talk, she stripped and then climbed into bed next to him. She gently touched his back. Rolling over, he pulled her into his arms. A moment later, she heard him snoring softly. Snuggling deeper into his arms, she closed her eyes to sleep.

Chapter 28

*I*n the middle of the night, a banging on the door woke them. Feya sat up startled, listening she did not recognize the heartbeat.

"I don't know who it is," Feya whispered, grabbing Elwyn's hand.

Elwyn nodded, squeezing her hand before releasing it. Jumping up, he yelled, "One second!"

He grabbed the jeans he had dropped the night before on the ground and pulled them on. Feya used the blanket to cover herself up as she walked behind Elwyn. He opened the door. A different guard from earlier stood there, looking somber in his gray uniform.

"Olette has attacked with Reece Pellings and Clan Ailil. The queen wishes to see you in the war room." the guard said, before leaving.

"I have to get ready," Elwyn stated. Going to the closet for clothes. She watched as he pulled his guard uniform out

"I'll go with you," Feya stated.

"I would prefer you didn't," Elwyn said, stopping getting ready.

"I will not stay behind," Feya stated. Staring directly into his eyes, she would fight by his side, no matter what happened.

"Stay," he whispered. "If something happens to you, if you

get—"

Feya stared at him, knowing he was worried about her. She smiled up at him. Reaching up, she brushed a stray hair out of his face. "I am going."

Sighing, he nodded, then went back to dressing in his uniform. Feya grabbed some jeans and a gray blouse. She had never had a uniform. Her family just wore whatever they wanted when they were on missions.

She looked at Elwyn. He was buttoning up his impeccable coat. The dark gray coat was form fitting, with gold cording embellishments dangling from the epaulets. The tree of life was hand woven into the front right breast of the jacket, the queen's logo. He had many badges on his left breast pocket. She wondered what he had done to earn those badges. His matching gray slacks fit snuggly. There was a peak of the crisp white button-up shirt just above the collar of his jacket.

"You look handsome," Feya said, at a loss for words. What do you say to someone who found out his mother betrayed him and his beliefs? What do you say to him when 24 hours after that betrayal she attacks the castle he is in? She reached up and stroked his cheek.

Half ass grinning at her made her heart skip a beat. Pausing when she saw the grin did not reach his eyes. She grabbed his cheeks, bringing his mouth to hers. The kiss felt haunting. No other words could describe it. She pulled away, feeling bereft. He was pulling away, and she did not know what to do to fix it.

They left the room and entered the hall.

"We're ready," Redd said from the shadows.

"Stay here," Elwyn growled. "It will cause more drama if you come, then if you just stay out of the way."

Redd stepped into the moonlight shining through the windows. Arched one red eyebrow and stood there sternly.

"I mean it," Elwyn stated, walking away before Redd could respond.

Feya looked at her father, pleading with her eyes to just

be patient. She followed Elwyn down the stairs and through the winding halls. As they got closer to the first floor, she heard the sounds of battle going on outside the castle walls. What felt weird to her was there were no sounds of gunfire, just metal on metal, earth shifting, fire crackling, swooshing of air. A magical fight raging just outside the walls.

Feya sighed as they turned into a room. Inside, the queen stood front and center behind a long wooden table. On her right stood the man who came to grab Elwyn earlier. Other faes she had not met before stood around the table. She hoped Elwyn would introduce her, but he just started talking.

"Can I get an update?" Elwyn asked. He stood erect. The happy-go-lucky Elwyn gone, the stern, cold new Elwyn in his place. His blue eyes looked dark and cold.

"Pellings and his clan," the fae guard who picked him up earlier said. His uniform had more badges than Elwyn's. "Are working with her outside. There are also a couple stragglers in with the group, it seems. They must have been slowly trickling people into the vale for a while now. We are trying to calculate how many they have and the powers they possess."

Nodding, Elwyn looked at the queen. "What is our strategy?"

"I will not lie," Queen Cassada stated. "I have never been a warrior. So I cannot tell you what to do, but I can put this in the best hands. Wallace will be in charge henceforth."

"Of course, my queen," Wallace humbled. "So far, we know they have snuck in some extremely powerful earth faes. We know Pellings are known for their earth magic. We need to contradict that magic. I have sent the top water magics to fight by using their powers to shift the earth. Goal is to undermine their powers and then take them out…"

Feya zoned out as they droned on. As what they considered a novice and an outsider, they would not listen to her or appreciate her help. Closing her eyes, she let the surrounding room and drifted away. Focusing on the walls of the castle and what was out there. Too many heartbeats to count and she could not differentiate between friend and foe, but she listened to them.

Hearing their thunder as she mentally prepared herself for the battle to come. Searching through the beat, she tried to hear Olette's, but there were too many to find just hers alone.

Kicking her sandals off, she rested her bare feet on the wooden floors, feeling the rumble of the feet storming through the halls. Inhaling, she could smell the upturned earth from the earth's faes' magic, the mist in the air from the water faes' magic, the smoke from the fire faes' magic, the wind from the air fea's magic blowing it around. Quieting her senses, she took a deep breath. She then focused on her own heartbeat Counting one, two, three beats. She counted each beat to center herself for the battle to come. Here and now she would prove herself to everyone. She just had to remember to not bite anyone. She laughed to herself.

Opening her eyes, she came back to the present. Listening as Wallace continued to go over a plan, she would not be a part of. It reminded her of all the times her father made plans and she was not involved in them. Today she would walk her own path, fight her fight. She was ready, and she was confident in her own abilities.

"Get to your stations!" Wallace roared as the fae soldiers saluted and ran off.

Feya followed Elwyn as he left the room, her shoes forgotten in the war room.

Turning, Elwyn said. "Go back to the room and stay with your family."

Feya stared at him for a moment, debating if she should talk back or leave. Deciding it was best to just walk away, she turned away. She hoped he would stay safe, but there was no way in hell she was going to hide.

Walking down the hall, she searched for a room that was empty. She found a window where she could jump out. The sounds of battle growing closer and closer to the castle. Soon they would be upon them here. Curling her toes in the earth, hearing the hum beneath her. She was crying in pain at the damage they were doing to her with this battle.

Feya grabbed her ponytail off her wrist, throwing her up in

a messy bun. She wished she had grabbed some extra ones so she could keep it out of her face better. Turning the corner, she saw the full bloom of the battle in front of her.

Searching the crowds of fae, she tried to find Elwyn. She recognized Elwyn standing next to the Wallace guy and some others. The fool had seriously believed she would run and hide. She shook her head in disappointment. Maybe he did not know her so well after all. At least she knew he was safe.

Scanning the battlefield behind the castle. Earth faes bent and shifted the earth, tearing up the land. The green grass was a mess of char from the fire faes. The atmosphere was parched, as the water faes greedily grabbed up all the surrounding water for the battle magic.

Hearing the boom, a massive flame ball was met with water. Steam drifted up from the explosion, creating a crater in the earth, as Gaia cried in pain. Feya felt that pain wrenching at her soul, as he traveled from the soles of her feet to her the core of her soul.

Taking a deep breath, she pushed the pain aside. She searched the field, trying to find Olette. She had a sinking feeling Olette was more of a behind-the-scenes kind of fae, probably tucked away somewhere safe. Letting others get hurt for her greed. She saw no sign of Olette in the moonlit field.

Glancing up through a haze of dust and smoke, she could see the full moon shining.

"Arianrhod," she whispered, staring up. "Protect Elwyn and watch over him this night."

"Ahem," Redd said, standing behind Feya.

Turning, she saw Redd, Aguya, and Brady ready for a fight. Redd leaning on the wall of the castle casually, smiling. He was always ready for a fight. The surrounding air sparked from the heat Aguya put out. Brady stayed calm, smiling as she walked up and smoothed Feya's hair down and adjusted the bun.

"You really think you would go into this alone?" Redd said, raising an eyebrow.

"I never thought I would go alone," Feya said. "But I can

blend in. Both sides would try to kill you. Maybe you should stay back."

"I don't need to be out there in the center," Aguya said, looking at her nails. "To bring a little warmth into these faes lives."

"I will stay back," Redd said. "Until…"

Feya waited as he paused for dramatic effect. He seemed to think they had all the time on earth here.

"Until I feel you need my help, Aguya will be with you, though. They will be so busy they will not notice what Aguya is. You will not go into this battle alone. Do you hear me?" Redd said.

Nodding her head, Feya knew it was for the best to give in. Turning, Feya walked towards the battle, her feet sinking into the soft soil, feeling the earth beneath her. Aguya walked behind her as she worked her way through the throng of soldiers to the front line. The two of them stood to the right flank of the battle. No one paying them mind, too busy focusing on their own tasks. She stopped when they were well entrenched in the battlefield.

Turning, Feya walked towards the battle, her feet sinking and feeling the earth beneath her. Aguya walked behind her as she worked her way through the throng of soldiers to the front line. The two of them stood to the right flank of the battle. No one paying them mind.

She looked at her feet, her toes curled in the earth. She heard the hum of the dirt, the whisper of the grass, the whispering of the trees. She felt the rumble start in her core as it spread throughout her to the earth. She heard faes yelling as the earth shook. Aguya grabbed onto Feya as the earthquake made the land tremble.

Looking down at her feet, her toes curled into the earth. Listening to the hum of the dirt, the whisper of the grass, the shuffling of the trees. She felt the rumble start in her core as it spread throughout her to the earth. The earth trembled beneath her feet. As she released the magic within and felt it spread. She heard faes yelling as the earth shook. Aguya clasped Feya as the land shook due to the earthquake of Feya's magic

It had been so long since she had unleashed her earth magic. She felt triumph as she looked around and saw soldiers on both sides falling to the ground.

Turning her eyes, she found the most likely spot for the leaders of the resistance. Calling to the earth, she felt the sink hole open as the earth tried to swallow them up.

Walking forward, Aguya's hand dropped off. Aguya shouted, "Feya, stay by me!"

The words faded as Feya walked on, her eyes and magic focused on Reece as she singled him out in the crowd. She knew she should have questioned him further that day, but she had let a headache and let weariness get to her. She would not make that mistake again. Today was when she made him regret starting this battle.

Reece's eyes grew wide as he stared at her and the earth twitched and shook with every step of her feet as she walked towards him. Soldiers on both sides ran away from her, stumbling to get out of her path of destruction. Reece stumbled backwards, falling as he tried to run, but a tree root shot up and curled around his foot. Dragging him back towards her. His hands clawed at the loose dirt as he tried to fight to escape. Guttural noises escaping his mouth. His soldiers ran and crawled away to escape the fate that was coming to their leader.

She stood above him as the root stopped dragging him. With a flick of Feya's wrist, the root flipped Reece back onto his back. The earth stopped trembling when she stopped walking.

"What the fuck are you?" Reece asked, stunned.

Feya coldly laughed. No words to describe what she was. Plus, how could she when she knew they would hunt her down and kill her? She smelled the blood in the air from wounded soldiers. It filled her nostrils as she bit her lip to control the blood rage rising in her. He had scrapped his hands when he fell and clawed at the ground. She feared if she opened her mouth, she would jump for his throat. Her eyes shooting to the vein throbbing in his throat, as anger had given way to fear. She could see the beats as the jugular vein pumped. Her teeth itched and ached to sink into it.

She called forth another root to wrap around his throat, not enough to choke him, just enough to make it so he could not talk. More roots to bind his wrists and ankles.

She heard Reece gasp and as he struggled to free himself.

"Feya," Elwyn said.

She had been so focused she had not heard him approach. Next to him stood Aguya, Wallace and others. Many of their eyes were wide with fear as they stared at her.

Sighing, she was happy it was over her earthbound magic and not that she had eaten a snack she was craving with every fiber of her being. Her hands trembled from the blood lust as she released the vine spell. Reece stood up as soldiers descended on him and arrested him.

Looking around, she tried to focus. Her breath heaving as hunger raced through her. Her knees felt weak, as she felt the punch in the gut from the blood lust. She knew she could not stay here with them any longer. She had used too much magic and now she was hungry.

Turning she ran off to the shadows where her father was. Aguya hot on her heels.

"Little one," Redd whispered as he pulled her into his arms. "We cannot stay here any longer. You are no longer built for this world. It is time we return to ours."

Chapter 29

"*I* can't control it, daddy," Feya gasped.

Feya trembled in her father's arms as the blood lust coursed through her veins. Her mouth was dry as she craved the warmth of blood to quench her thirst. Every heartbeat sounded like a drum pounding into her temples. Using her hands, she covered her ears, trying to quiet the noise.

Gently Redd pushed her away as he turned. He grabbed an unconscious soldier by the scruff of his neck. His navy blue uniform showed he was one of Reece's soldiers. His brown hair hung limply across his face, obscuring most of it. He was built like a string bean, tall and skinny.

"Good thing I grabbed take out," Redd said, sinking his fangs into his neck.

The soldier's eyes grew to saucers as he came to from the pain. Feya ran over as the scent of blood filled her senses. She sank her teeth into the other side of his neck.

She tried to pull away, but could not, no longer in control. The warmth of the blood gave as it slid down her throat, making her feel like she was floating. As his lifeblood drained from him, a fleeting memory of him beating his wife flashed before her eyes. Another of him holding a baby cradled in his arms. One more of him on the field of battle, sinking his knife into the gullet of an enemy. The memories stopped flashing as he went limp in their arms.

"Better?" Redd whispered.

Feya nodded as she wiped the blood that had dripped from her mouth onto her chin. Looking at her hand covered in blood, she knew she had made it worse. It was all over her sleeve now. She could feel it dripping from her chin, knowing the front of her blouse drenched in his life's essence.

Laughing, Redd used his shirt to wipe some of the blood off her face. Just a couple of drips of blood ran down Redd's chin. Barely a mess made.

"I swear," Redd stated. "You have always been the messiest of eaters. How you can't keep your dinner in your mouth is beyond me."

Rolling her eyes, Feya glared at her father as he wiped the blood off her chin.

Feya smelled the burning flesh as she turned to see Aguya burning the dead fae from the inside out. Sighing, it was time to eliminate the evidence. Feya opened a hole in the earth, perfect to put the ashes and pieces of him that had not disintegrated in. Brady using her air magic to push the pieces into the hole. Feya settled the earth on top and made the grass grow back. This way, there was nothing to tie them to him.

"Look at us," Brady cheered. "Working so well together. Leo would be proud of us."

"I miss Uncle Leo," Feya sighed. "We should sneak up to the wing somehow. I need a shower. Plus, soor we will have to search for Olette. If Leo was here, we could have had him sniff her out."

"We will find her," Redd grunted. "Plus, sneak is the right word. You look an absolute fright."

"Screw you, father," Feya said, shaking her head.

Laughing, Redd tapped his finger on her nose. "Let's head up."

They walked to stand under the window of where their wing was. Feya knew she would need to fly her father up. The self-consciousness washed over her as she looked around before crossing the charm that bound her wings. Fearing more the

reactions of people seeing her wings, she had rarely flown with them unless she knew she was alone. She grabbed her dad's armpits as she pushed off of the earth, lifting.

The rush of the wind on her wings was a type of freedom she rarely allowed herself. It made her feel lighter as she lifted off the ground. Her wings drifted up and down, propelling her upwards. For a moment, she closed her eyes to feel the wind caressing her wings. The coolness of the breeze hit her wet blouse, causing a shiver to run through her spine.

They got to the window, Redd kicked it, breaking the window. Sticking his arm through the broken glass, he unlocked and opened it. Feya rolled her eyes as she tossed her father through the window. He could have at least tried to open the window first. Climbing into the dining room, she jumped over the broken glass, avoiding cutting her bare feet.

Brady and Aguya soaring in next.

"Have you gained weight?" Brady asked, panting. Brady dumped Aguya on the floor unceremoniously.

"Ha," Aguya said, before releasing a tirade in a long dead language. A language only she understood.

"Did you lose another pair of shoes?" Redd asked, his brow furrowing up. As he attempted to change the subject, Feya just wished he had not directed it at herself.

Feya glanced down at her feet, covered in dirt and grass.

Shrugging, she said. "I guess I did."

Laughing, Red grabbed her by the shoulders. "What am I going to do with you? A messy eater, always losing her damn shoes, and the strongest damn earth fae any of those bastards have ever seen."

Startled Feya looked up at her father. This was the first time he had complimented on her magic. A swelling of pride went through her as she reached up to retract her wings.

Brady came over, placing both hands on her cheeks. "We are all so proud of how you handled yourself tonight. You are a force to be reckoned with."

"Eh," Aguya said, before leaving the room.

Feya laughed as she headed to her and Elwyn's room. She climbed into the shower to take her clothes off in there. That way, it was easier to clean the mess up.

As she unbuttoned her shirt, she heard the door. Hearing Elwyn's heart, she continued to undress. He entered the bathroom, halting as he stared in surprise.

"Do I want to know whose blood that is?" He grumbled.

Stopping removing her clothes, she looked at him, trying to gauge his reaction. All she saw was shook, his heart rate was normal. His eyes, his demeanor normal. So she went back to removing her blood-soaked clothes.

"I am almost for certain," Feya stated. "You have never met this soldier of Reece's. I had to eat."

Searching his dark blue eyes, she waited for some emotion to flicker there, but none came.

"Get dressed," Elwyn stated, waving his hand at her. "And washed up, the queen wishes to meet with you. They are rounding up the dissidents as we speak. They still haven't found my mother or Deema."

"Want to join me?" Feya whispered huskily, as the last of her clothes slipped down her body.

His eyes traveled up and down her. She heard his heartbeat sped up as his eyes dilated.

"No," he said as he turned and left the room.

A rush of hurt shot through her. Trying to tamp it down with the knowledge he still lusted after her. Maybe it was for the best. She will leave soon. She knew she could not stay. It had taken every ounce of her willpower not to grab the nearest fae and drink her fill earlier. If they had not stopped her, she might have drank Reece's blood in front of everyone. Looking down at herself, seeing the blood that stained her skin that had seeped through her clothes, maybe he was not a fan of blood. Shaking her head to shake off the thoughts, she turned the water on.

She rinsed the blood off. The cold water blending in with

the icy pain raging in her heart. Trying to wash her clothes the best she could, trying to get as much blood out as she could. The shirt would forever have the stain, unless Brady could work her magic.

Grabbing a towel, she dried herself off. Entering the room, Elwyn had already left the suite. Grabbing a fresh pair of jeans and a black tank top, she decided it was time to be her casual self. She was not in the mood to impress the queen. Brushing her damp hair, she threw it up into a ponytail.

Exiting the room, she figured time to head to the queen to answer questions. Elwyn stood in the hallway waiting for her.

"I figured," Feya whispered. "You had left."

"Nope," Elwyn stated. "I waited for you. Ready to head down?"

His voice sounded horse and distant, his heartbeat calm.

Nodded, she followed as he led the way. They took the same path as earlier that day to the queen's office. Guards running up and down the halls as they prepared for the dawn approaching. The search would start anew for Olette. At least, half of what they needed to find out was done.

Earlier, she had not looked around or noticed anything. The waiting area outside the queen's office was quite masculine, leather chairs, dark wooden tables, the paintings were of hunting scenes. Taxidermy heads of rare and exotic magical creatures, a pure white unicorn, a basilisk, a barghest, etc. She wondered if this had been the king's office and the queen had taken it upon his death

It took only a moment before the office door was opened by two fae guards standing outside the queen's office. Two faes were in there: the queen and the captain.

She watched as the queen's shrewd eyes appraised her. It seemed like the first time the queen actually saw her. Fear settled into her soul as she watched Queen Cassada's eyes travel up and down Feya.

"Aren't you interesting?" the queen said, tilting her to the side. She walked closer, her hand reaching up and brushing a stray hair out of her face. A shiver went down Feya's spine as she looked into those big brown eyes.

"That is all," the queen said, turning away. "You are dismissed. Take your shoes with you when you leave."

Feya grabbed her shoes and did not hesitate to run out the door. The entire exchange with the queen had been calm, her heartbeat at rest, but Feya knew with certainty that the queen knew what she was. She did not wait for Elwyn as she ran up the stairs to the wing. Her heartbeat raced as she climbed the stairs two at a time. Her dad was at the top of the stairs waiting for her, having heard her thundering heartbeat.

"What's wrong?" Redd growled.

"I think," Feya whispered. As she heard Elwyn storming up behind her. "The queen knows."

She stared into her father's eyes waiting for the 'I told you so' lecture to come.

"Why did you run off like that?" Elwyn asked when he got to the top of the stairs.

"Not now, boy," Redd growled. "Pack your shit, Feya. No sassing back, you've proven your point. It is time we find a way out of this vale before sunrise."

Feya stood there staring at her dad, weighing her options. If the queen wanted her dead, it would already have happened. Now that the initial panic was over, rationality was kicking in. The queen did not want her dead because she had a new weapon to play with. One that she could weld against her enemies with no care if the weapon came out alive or not.

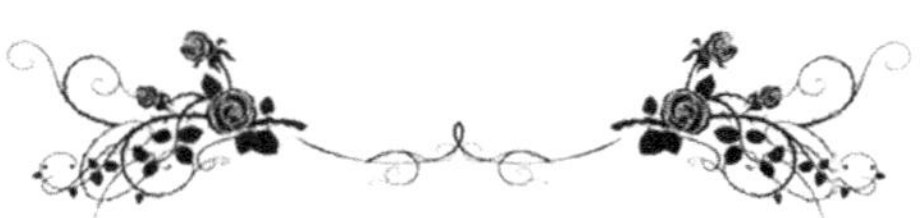

"For fuck's sake," Elwyn stated. "I am sick of you constantly belittling me. Plus, they still have the vale locked down. Redd, you can't get out. You need to hide and…"

"Boy," Redd growled, cutting Elwyn off. "My daughter is no longer safe. We will find a way out. I don't care if I have to burn

this whole place to the ground."

Elwyn stared at Redd as the words sunk in. He remembered the moment he noticed her on the battlefield. Barefoot walking across the field, his heart had stopped as he sprinted into the battlefield trying to get to her. Then the ground quacked with each step she took. He had never seen another fae make the earth tremble like she had. The damage from the earthquake she created was extensive. The reports of damage were still coming in and would take months to repair. Even more, it was over an entire square mile that was affected. It had not been centralized to the vicinity they were in. Other faes had created quakes, but always centralized to a smaller locale.

There was no way the queen would know unless…

"What…" Elwyn cleared his throat, trying to figure a delicate way to phrase the next part. "What did you do with your late night drink? Could they have found said drink?"

"Boy," Redd said, shaking his head. "You seem to think this is our first dance. There is no way in hell they find what little was left of our supper. We throw the scraps out when we are done with our meal."

Elwyn squinted at Redd, debating if he should insult him or set him on fire. The latter sounded more appealing as he felt the fire itching to escape. He had geared up for this battle, ready and willing to fight, but Feya ended it before he could release his pent up rage burning inside him. He rubbed his fingers together, feeling the spark lying beneath the surface. His whole being was on fire, ready to ignite at any moment.

Thinking back to the odd conversation they had with the queen, he could see why Feya thought she knew something. Maybe she was wrong, but thinking about it, he had a feeling she was right.

"Stop bickering like children," Feya interjected. "She doesn't want me dead, father. If she wanted me dead, she would have done it already. There is no need to run and hide from this. Plus, we both know there is no exit from the vale at this time."

Elwyn looked at Feya's face. She was calm now, no longer wide eyed and panicked. An icy chill went down his spine as he turned and looked away. It was taking everything he had to stay calm and not rage at her. One minute he wanted to hold her close, the next he wanted to run as fast and as far as he could. He had always assumed she would always feel the same as he did. That she had been looking for him. When she saw him, recognized, and whispered his name, he thought it was fate. Now he knew differently. She had not looked for him; she did not feel the same, and she would leave as soon as she could. It did not change his feelings for her, but his heart felt like there was a gaping hole in its place.

"Feya," Elwyn stated. "Is correct. Everyone should get some rest. Once they find my… Olette, the vale will open and you can be on your merry way."

Turning, he walked to his room, Feya a step behind. He just wanted to sleep. It seemed an eternity since he last slept. Glancing out the window, he saw the start of the sun coming up. He did not know how the fuck Redd thought they would get out of the vale. Maybe he was going to leave the same way he came in. Elwyn wished he could figure that out. Laughing, he shook his head and started taking his uniform off. Carefully, he hung it up. Usually, he just tossed his clothes on the floor, but this was something that was drilled into his head. Respect and care for the uniform.

Climbing into bed, he folded his hands behind his head as Feya climbed in next to him. The urge to pull her close and push her away warred inside him. So he just lay still, resting his head on his hands. He stared at the ceiling as Feya laid her head on his chest.

"Elwyn," she whispered huskily.

He debated ignoring her or not.

"What?" he muttered.

"Will you talk to me?" she whispered. He could hear the hesitancy and uncertainty in her voice.

"About what?" he grumbled. Trying his best to stay cold. He needed that armor right now. Just put distance between them now, so it was easier when she left.

"About what's going on in that head of yours?" Feya sighed.

Elwyn rubbed his brow as he said. "Nothing much, just tired."

Elwyn yawned dramatically and closed his eyes, hoping that would end the conversation.

"You're acting very distant," Feya mumbled. "We have little time left to spend together and I don't want to spend it fighting."

"We aren't fighting," Elwyn grumbled, knowing he could not escape this conversation no matter how much he wanted to.

"You Then why are you acting so…" Feya said, waving a hand in front of his face. He could feel tears hit his chest.

"Dammit, Fe," Elwyn growled, as he wrapped his arms around her. "Why the fuck do you have to do this now?"

"I am sorry," Feya said, hiccupping. "I don't understand why you're acting this way."

"Fe," he groaned, frustrated. "Why does how I'm acting matter? You have no intention of staying. You are going to leave the second you can. So my fucking attitude is irrelevant."

He felt rage bubbling up under the surface. He tried to tamp it down, but it boiled over.

"You really want to know how I am fucking feeling?" he growled.

Sitting up, Feya looked down at him. Tears streamed down her face. "Yes!"

"I am fucking pissed," Elwyn growled. "I am gutted. Everything in my life has been shattered to shit. Are you fucking happy? You and my mother have torn my fucking heart out, dropped kicked it, and stomped all over it. Is that what you wanted to hear? You plan to be here until you've completed your mission, then nothing. You will run off and not care about the fucking mess you made of my life. So why the fuck you give two shits about what I am feeling right now is beyond me."

"Do you think I don't care?" Feya whispered.

His heart tore as he stared into those dewy green eyes.

The moonlight streaming through the windows shined on her tears, making them sparkle like diamonds. He sat there, unsure how to respond.

Chapter 30

Feya stared down at Elwyn in the bed. It shocked her he thought she did not care. She had risked her life, exposed herself to someone who might kill her the instant she was no longer useful. Thinking back to the times she had been cold, or the time she cut him off when he was expressing his feelings. No wonder he thought she did not care. Turning away, she climbed out of the bed to pace the room.

Sighing, Elwyn said. "Come back to bed, Fe. I am tired and just want to sleep."

"Fine," Feya said. "Go to sleep, but think about this. If I did not care, I would not have entered a vale where everyone here, if they found out what I am, would not hesitate to kill me. If I did not care, I would have run off the instant we found out who was responsible."

"Then why is it so easy for you?" Elwyn growled, jumping out of bed.

"Why is what so easy?" Feya said with confusion. She tried to stop the flow of tears running down her cheeks, but could not.

"Leaving!" He yelled.

She inhaled as she saw the anguish cross his face again. Never having meant to hurt him. Walking to him, she wrapped her arms around his chest and buried her face in the crook of his shoulder.

"That's the thing," she whispered. "It isn't easy, but I can't stay here. As soon as I am no longer useful, the queen will have me executed."

"I would never allow that," Elwyn growled.

"You would not have a choice," Feya continued. "I would not make you choose between the life you built and the nomad life we have. I care enough to not force that choice on you."

"What if I told you there is no choice," he whispered.

He lifted her chin up, bringing his mouth to hers. Gently nibbling on her lip before his tongue explored the depths of her mouth. Sighing, she melted into him. Elwyn walked backwards towards the bed. When the backs of his legs hit the bed, he fell, pulling her with him.

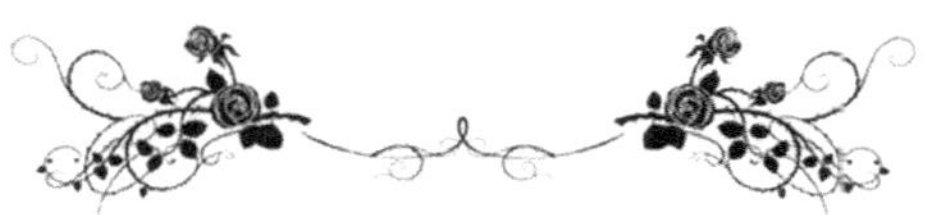

Feya slept most of the day, only awakening when Elwyn climbed out of bed. He kissed her on the forehead and suggested she go back to sleep. She was happy her Elwyn was back. Climbing out of bed, she opened the curtain to look out. The sun was setting on the horizon. No more declarations of war came throughout the day. From her vantage point, she could not see where the battlefield was, so did not know the extent of damage from the night before. Having been on the field and felt Gaia's pain, Feya knew the damage was probably bad.

She felt safer being back to her normal schedule. She had missed living in the night. Sunrises and sunsets were wonderful to watch, but the moon held a bit of her soul in her grasp.

Elwyn came up, wrapping his arm around her waist and kissing the top of her head.

"Good morning, Fe," he whispered.

"Good morning, Ellie," she whispered back. Turning in his arms, she looked into his deep blue eyes, smiling down at her. "You should have Brady heal that."

Feya gently tapped the two fang marks on his shoulder.

Laughing, he said. "I am pretty sure I am not any of your family's favorite fae. They will not want to help me out."

"Trust me," Feya said. "She will."

Reaching up, she brushed a kiss across his mouth. A moment later, she heard her father's heartbeat approaching the room. Sighing, she pulled away to throw some clothes on.

"Ugh," Elwyn growled when he heard the knock. "Go away."

Feya giggled at the teasing in Elwyn's voice. Her heart soared, knowing he was back to his old self.

"Boy," Redd growled. "We need to get to work so they can open that damn vale."

"You think if I just ignore him until he gets my name right, it would work?" Elwyn stated loudly.

"Doubtful," Feya said just as loudly. Giggling, she ran over and flung herself in Elwyn's arms. "But he is right. We should get to work."

Sighing dramatically, Elwyn threw a shirt and jeans on. They both made their way to the dining room where her family sat. Aguya and Brady chowing down on roast beef and potatoes, while Redd glowered at Elwyn.

"Took you long enough," Redd growled.

"You know what?" Elwyn said, laughing. "That face of yours is fine, but that personality… You sure need to put a bag over it."

Redd stared at Elwyn a moment before his eyes locked with Feya's. Trying to plead with her eyes to give Elwyn a break. She was tired of fighting her loved ones and just wanted there to be peace here.

"I guess I am an acquired taste," Redd growled. "If you don't like me, maybe you should get some taste."

Sighing, Feya knew her father was behaving as well as he could.

"Alrighty," Feya said, interjecting before the insult war progressed further. "Brady, Elwyn has two small wounds that

need attending to."

Elwyn turned to glare at Feya as she filled her plate with food.

"What, the boy can't handle a little bite?" Redd growled.

"Father," Feya huffed. Her face and neck burned as if they were on fire. She did not know why her father had to make the commentary.

"Oh my," Brady said, jumping up to come inspect Elwyn's neck.

Elwyn waved her away as his skin flushed, grumbling, "Dammit, Fe."

"His right shoulder," Feya smirked, taking a bite of food.

Brady tried to pull Elwyn's shirt off to get to the wounds. Elwyn fought to keep his shirt on and his chest covered. Redd and Aguya were laughing so hard they almost fell out of their chairs.

The sun had fully set. Her father refused to stay back this time. He was hunting for Olette, no matter the objections. Insisting they break up, Aguya with Elwyn and Feya with her father.

"Where are we going?" Feya asked. It did not feel like he was randomly roaming the streets. She knew he had a destination in mind. He had been acting weird since they all separated.

"Nowhere in particular," he muttered.

Feya stopped walking and stared at her father's back as he took a few more steps before stopping.

The vale was quiet. Since the battle, most faes were staying inside their homes. The tavern they passed by had even shut down early. All the faes were on edge, unable to run from a danger they were not fully aware of. Announcements from the

crown were few and far between, as they had kept tight-lipped on what truly was going on.

They were still hunting down turncoats, refusing to open the vale up until they had tracked every single one of them down. She had gotten to glimpse the missive the queen had sent out. It had been very vague.

There has been an uprising. All clan members of Ailil will be brought to the attention of the guard. Anyone who assists a member of clan Ailil will be held and put to the trial. NO quarter will be drawn. Reconstruction will start shortly to repair the damage Clan Ailil has done to our homes. Please see the bailiff, George Conry, to inform him of any repairs needed.

Nothing else. Just that vague response and the guard randomly bringing in members of Reece's clan. They were not even sure the amount of faes they were looking for, so who knew how long the lockdown would be in effect.

Part of her wanted the lockdown to last a while longer and part knew it was best that it ended sooner than later. Her family was in danger the longer they stayed here. She was in danger the longer she stayed here. There was no telling how long the queen would allow her to stay alive.

Her father finally turned and tried to stare her down. She remembered all the times she had broken under that gaze, but no longer would she do that. She stood her ground, not blinking or moving an inch.

Laughing, he took a few steps back to stand in front of her.

Taping her nose, he whispered. "Little one, you're all grown up now, I see."

Rolling her eyes, she said. "That happened over a hundred years ago, father."

Laughing, he shook his head. "Two weeks ago, you would not have stood up to me."

Shaking her head, Feya said. "That is beside the point. I

know you and I know when you know something. Spill the dirt."

"You think I have not had a…" he winked and smirked at her. "Snack this whole time I have been here?"

Feya paused as the realization hit her. She had not thought about her father needing to eat or whom he would 'snack' on. She opened and closed her mouth a few times as she processed this information.

"Who?" she finally whispered.

"Well," he chuckled. "I knew your mate would not be happy if I snacked on his mommy dearest. So I had a sip of dear bland tastes like dirt Deema."

Feya covered her mouth to stifle the giggle. "Her blood does smell like her personality."

Laughing, Redd shook his head. "I am not sure if they are still together, but I know where we can find the little dormouse."

"Lead the way," Feya said, her hand making a wide sweeping gesture to the path ahead. "So let me get this straight. Have you known where Deema was for the last few days?"

"Yes," Redd said. Turning, he winked at her again. "I am not a complete ass. I knew you wanted to spend more time with the boy. You realize we need to leave ASAP now? We can't stay hidden here forever."

"I know," Feya sighed.

"How will you handle that?" Redd asked, all traces of laughter gone.

"I don't know," Feya whispered. She tucked her arm in her father's as she followed him through alleys as they zig-zagged.

They stopped occasionally hiding when they ran into someone. Having to hide from guards and fae alike made the journey much longer. Finally, they stopped in front of a small ramshackle hut on the outskirts of the town. It stood a few miles away from Ballybog's tavern. Further they got into this area of the vale, the less clean it was. The stench of piss and stale Green Lust hung in the air. The hovels looked to be built from scraps of wood that did not seem to fit together properly. As they passed one place, the overwhelming stench of recently smoked Green Lust filled her nostrils, making her gag a bit. The scent of the unwashed mass of faes inside the hovels leached outside. Luckily, her father stopped at the one next to it.

She listened and could only hear two heartbeats. Deema was one and a stranger the other. They had not found Olette.

Feya sighed in frustration.

"Rein it in, little one," Redd whispered. "I have a feeling she knows where to find her."

Feya nodded, hoping her father was right.

Redd walked up and tapped on the door.

The door slowly opened and Deema's brown eyes widened.

"Attempt to scream and it will be the last breath you take," Redd whispered menacingly.

Deema nodded as tears streamed down her face. Feya almost had pity for her, then she remembered how rough she had brushed her hair and how demeaning she had been to Feya. It was petty, but she did not like her for that alone. Plus, through everything else, this fae had done helping Olette, and there was not an ounce of pity in her soul for this worthless fae.

Pushing into the hovel, Feya shoved past Deema to see who else was in the room. A fae who looked strikingly like Deema sat on the bed in a haze of Green Lust.

"Who is this?" Feya asked, flicking her wrist toward the woman on the bed. If you could call it a bed. More like a thin mattress roll that was on the ground.

"My sister Donella," Deema whispered as she shrunk into the corner.

"Another fucking addict," Redd said, as he eyed Deema. "Where's your mistress?"

"She abandoned you as soon as you were no longer useful?" Redd smirked.

"No... No," Deema said, trembling.

"I wanted to go to see my sister."

"Then you know where your mistress is," Redd stated.

"She did not tell me," Deema insisted.

"I... I," Deema stuttered as she shrank down into the corner. "Don't know."

"You would lie to me?" Redd said, pointing to his chest. "Do you really believe you can keep the truth from me? The same way I knew where you were is the same way I know that you're lying."

"I am not lying," Deema cried. Her trembling hands trying to pull the collar of her dress higher on her neck.

"You think I want to drink your blood?" Redd laughed. "Already tasted it. I've had piss-swallow that was better."

"Wh... What?" Deema stuttered.

"Tell me where Olette is," Redd growled. "Or I will slit your sister's throat in front of you. Let you watch as she limply lays there and her blood seeps from the slit in her throat. Then when I am done with her and her blood is pooled all over the floor of this hovel, I will turn to you. I will slowly torture you. I will start by..."

"Croi na Tine's temple," Deema cried. "She is at the temple of fire. Please don't hurt us."

"We should head there," Feya said.

"There's one thing that needs to be done," Redd stated.

Feya locked eyes with her father. She had no love for Deema. Knowing how many lives Deema was willing to help Olette end, she nodded at her father.

Turning he walked over, grabbing Deema by the front of her dress.

"No, please," she begged, her hands going to cover her neck.

"I already said I did not want your blood, damn bloody fool," Redd said as he made quick work of reaching up and twisting Deema's neck till it snapped.

She fell to the ground in a pile.

"I thought you would have had a sip," Feya said, tilting her head to the side to look at Donella. Her haze was so strong she had not moved from staring at the wall. She did not even know they were there. Feya made the mistake of drinking the blood of someone on drugs once before. She had tripped for hours.

"Less clean up and less questions this way," Redd said. "Plus, again, she tasted like dirt."

Feya could not help, giggle and shake her head. "How many times did you taste her blood?"

"Ummm," Redd stated. "Enough times to not want to try again.

She knew he would not answer and figured no point in pushing. They left the hovel to make the trek to the fire temple.

The temple stood in front of them. Red and Onyx marble walls surrounded the Croi na Tine Temple, shining in the dim moonlight. Six pillars of fire that were never to be extinguished stood along the path to the front doors. Three on each side of the path, each had a fire spell carved into the marble. The flames burning bright blue and orange lit by magic flickered in the light breeze. Red crushed glass at their bases. A lava stone path stood between the pillars leading to the front door. As they got closer to the doors, she could smell the sweet scent of the flame lilies. Blooming in pots next to the front doors. Their yellow and red petals looked like flickering flames. Carved in the massive oak doors was the fire emblem, an upside down half circle with the flame carved in its center. Inside the flame was a triangle with swirls extending from the tips of the triangle.

Looking to the horizon, she knew there was only about two hours left till sunrise. They had little time before her father would need a place to hide.

Placing her hand on the door handle, she closed her eyes. Listening, she heard five heartbeats and one of those was Olette's. She did not recognize the others.

"She's inside," Feya whispered.

"I know," Redd whispered back. "It looks like they are in some kind of basement."

She silently prayed that the hinges were lubed as she slowly pushed the door open to avoid any squeaking. Relief washed over her when the door opened silently. They silently creeped into the main hallway of the temple.

Feya kicked her sandals off to keep the heels from clicking on the red marble floors. A few candles flickered in sconces on the walls, otherwise no other light lead the way. The candles making the shadows dance. If she had not known that there was no one but them on this floor, she would have thought they were not alone. The flickering flames casting shadows that looked like faes moving. She wondered if this came from a spell cast. They quietly stalked the heartbeats to a stairway in the main chapel of the temple. It was hidden behind a curtain at the back of the altar. Blood on the altar showed there must have been a recent sacrifice. Sniffing the air, the sour gamey smell told her it was a female deer. Feya wondered what ritual Olette had performed. Had she made a sacrifice to Balor hoping to escape?

Feya leaned against the cold gray stone wall, slowly taking the spiral stairs down. Her father insisted on going first. She followed about two feet behind. Her feet tiptoeing down the stairs.

Reaching his hand back, he touched Feya's arm as he stopped. She could hear two male faes joking and drinking Alfheimr Ale. Their hearts were at rest as they sat guard. It was obvious they had drunk much from the scent of cloves, apples, and hops in the air.

The other two guards were in the room with Olette, who was being half-ass guarded. The oak wooden door closed.

"Alright I got a good joke for you. What do kids' movies, fairy tales, and porn have in common?" The first guard said.

"I don't know, Georgie," the second guard said. "What do they have in common?"

Feya pushed her father to hurry, but he shook his head. Swatted her arm gently.

"They all give unrealistic expectations of step moms," the first guard laughed.

Redd shook his head before stepping forward. He grabbed

the first guard and sunk his teeth into him while Feya grabbed the second. Drinking her fill, the warm honey filled her senses. A heady sense of being buzzed swirled through her head from the alcohol coursing through the guard's blood. Flashes of memories filled her mind as his life's blood filled her. Removing her fangs once his heart slowed down to a snail's pace, she slowly lowered him to the ground. Her father had already finished his meal, stared at her impatiently.

"Don't you dare look at me like that," she whispered. "You waited to hear the end of that stupid joke."

Redd shrugged while testing the doorknob and found it locked. The people in the room stopped their muffled chatting when Redd tested the doorknob.

"Yes," Olette scowled. "What do you imbeciles want?"

"Hello, mommy dearest," Redd growled. He threw his shoulder into the door as the lock gave and the door crashed open.

A guard came running towards Redd, his sword burning from the flame of his magic. He lifted his arm up to swoop the sword down. Redd grabbed his forearm, blocking the downswing of the sword. Once he had an opening, he grabbed him by the throat and picked him up. He slammed the fairy to the ground as he dropped the sword and the flame extinguished. Lifting the fairy up, Redd sunk his teeth in and ripped his throat out. Blood splattering across the room. Tossing the body down at the second guard's feet.

The second guard stumbled back, trying to run from the fight, but there was nowhere to go. Olette sunk into the corner, her tears streaming down her face, whimpers escaping her throat.

Feya walked to the guard, welding a dagger. She swatted his hand aside as he lifted it up to strike her. The dagger slid across the room. Grabbing him by the collar of his shirt, she dragged him to her as she sank her teeth into the flesh of his neck. Feya drank the blood of the guard's essence. Just enough to reach his mind. Sensing the click as he became under her control. She injected her venom into him, pushing him away. She stared into his hazel eyes, seeing the daze from her venom.

"Grab Olette and pin her down," she breathed.

Turning, he did as she commanded of him. Throwing Olette to the ground. She laid on her back screaming, kicking and begging for her life as he pinned her down.

"Please, Frank," Olette cried.

Feya frowned, saying. "His name isn't even Frank, you twat. It's Brad. Are you so narcissistic you could not bother to learn the name of the males you expected to keep you safe? Males that were supposed to give their life for your safety. Hold her arms above her head."

Olette kicked and screamed as Feya sat on her chest. Brad the guard grabbing her arms and pinning them above her head.

"Please don't," Olette pleaded. As blood dripped from Feya's chin onto Olette's chest. "What is wrong with you? Why would you do this? What the hell are you? Elwyn will not be happy that you hurt me."

"Do you remember that night so long ago?" Feya whispered as she brought her face close to Olette's. "The night your husband died? The night our little village was attacked by the vampire horde. Do you remember?"

Olette swallowed, then nodded. Tears coursing down her face.

"That was the night I got turned," she whispered, staring into those eyes that were so like Elwyn's, but different. A coldness that Elwyn's lacked had hidden just beneath the surface this whole time. Olette had just been so good at hiding it.

She watched as the knowledge sunk in. Olette's eyes dilated as a deeper fear sunk in. Feya figured since Olette saw her bite the guard, there was no use hiding her secret anymore. Might as well do the whole anti-hero reveal thing.

Feya grabbed her chin, turning her head to the side. She bent down, sniffing Olette's neck. The warm blood pumping so fast in her veins. Feya wanted to bite, draining her of her blood, all of it, but she waited. Enjoying the torture she was causing. Olette whimpered beneath her.

"Feya," Redd said sternly.

Feya pulled back, looking into Olette's eyes, watching as her lips quivered. Some blood had dripped from her chin to Olette's neck. Brushing the blood away, a bright red swatch smeared across Olette's neck.

"Yes, father?" Feya sighed.

"Don't do it," he whispered.

"Did I ever introduce you to the gentleman who found me in that dark, lonely forest?" Feya said to Olette, ignoring her father's warning. "Olette, Aethelredd. Aethelredd, Olette."

Olette stammered, "Nice to meet you."

"There I was, bleeding out in the forest all alone. When Aethelredd found me. He completed the transformation." Feya said, bopping her on the nose.

"Be honest," Feya whispered. "Why did you do all this?"

Olette bit her lip.

"Answer my question!" Feya screamed.

"Feya," Redd said more sternly.

She looked at him, pouting. The laugh came out before she could control it. The blood always made her feel giddy and drunk when she had this much.

"How do you think Elwyn would feel if he knew you drank his mother dry?" he said, softly.

She watched as his eyes gentled and he smiled at her. She looked down at Olette, then back at him. Knowing he was right, but wanting to play with Olette longer.

"I think he will get over it in time, daddy," she said, demurely looking at him batting her eyes.

He laughed, shaking his head. The light of realization shining in his eyes as he realizes the game plan.

"I think you should let me have her blood," he said, his eyes twinkling brightly. "That way, Elwyn won't be upset with you, little one. Plus, he dislikes me already. If I drink his mother, it won't matter, anyway."

Olette started crying in earnest. Her sobs ricocheted through the room.

"Where was this when you had innocent males murdered? Where was your compassion for them?" Feya screamed.

Feya felt the rage build back up inside her. She had no pity or compassion for this vile woman. Breathing heavy she tried to rein her temper in.

"I... I... I..." Olette stammered.

"Shut up," Feya screamed in her face. Her nails are digging into Olette's chin. Feya smelled the fresh blood as it filled her nostrils. The sweet scent made her mouth salivate as the blood rage sat on the fringes of her mind.

"Feya," Redd growled, his voice lowering. It was the voice he used when he was lecturing her.

Feya took a calming breath. Resting her forehead on Olette's. Closing her eyes, she listened to her own heartbeat. Counting the beats till she had calmed down, one, two, three, four.

"Let the court of fae decide her fate, little one," Redd said.

"Please," Olette pleaded.

"She knows what I am, father," Feya said. She pulled back and looked coldly down at Olette. "We can't allow her to talk."

"She knows that there will be a fate worse than death if she opens her mouth," Redd said, kneeling down next to Olette. "Look at the man behind you, Olette. He is a walking zombie. Neither vampire nor fae. A shadow forever more. Trapped in his own mind, obedient to every whim we have. That will be you if you talk."

He bent down, placing his face next to hers. "You do not want to know the torture I will put your body through. While you are locked away in your brain. Seeing, hearing everything, but not being able to do anything about it."

He had a calculating smirk as he tapped his finger against her forehead.

Olette swallowed as fresh tears streamed down her face.

"Tell me you understand," Redd whispered.

Feya released Olette's chin as she tried to bob her head yes.

"Say it, out loud," Redd said, swiping a drop of blood from Olette's chin. He licked his finger slowly as he tasted her blood. Closing his eyes to savor the flavor.

"I... I... I understand," Olette mumbled.

"What was that? I didn't quite hear you." Redd laughed.

"I understand," Olette screamed, her voice strained from the tears clogging her throat.

"Alrighty then," Redd stated. "Feya, get up. Let's tie her up and take her in. Send the guard to a bar or something for the night."

Feya stood up looking for something to tie Olette up with. No rope or anything that looked useful was around. Looking down, she saw her father's shoes.

"Give me one of your shoelaces," Feya held her hand out to her father. She saw her hand tremble as she tried to tamp down the thirst. Clenching her hand into a fist, she shook it, hoping it would help.

"I am not giving up my laces," Redd growled. "Keep looking."

"Where else do I look? The table with no drawers? Underneath the bloody rug? What do you suggest?" Feya growled back.

"Take his laces," Redd said, flicking his hand at the corpse in front of the door.

"I am not taking his shoe laces off," Feya grumbled, pouting. "You take them off."

"Just do it," Redd growled.

"What is wrong with you both?" Olette cried.

"Can I slap her at least, dad?" Feya growled.

Redd looked from Feya to Olette and nodded. He turned and started removing the blood-soaked shoe laces from the corpse.

"I'm sorry," Olette cried as Feya took a threatening step towards her.

"Here," Redd said, tossing the shoe lace at Feya.

She caught the shoelace as she glanced down at herself. Blood drenched the front of her clothes. Redd was also covered in blood. They could not turn Olette in like this. Redd could not even turn her in to begin with. She turned to look at the guard, who was still under her control. HIs collar had two trails of blood on it from her fangs.

"We can't turn her in looking like this, but," Feya said, jerking her head towards the guard. "Maybe?"

Redd nodded, grumbling. "Probably for the best. He can play a hero and then vanish into the sunset. Give him the instructions."

"We would need him to change," Feya stated. "Look at his collar."

"Hmmm," Redd said, rubbing his chin. Shrugging. "Send him shirtless."

"The bite marks?" Feya grumbled, unsure if that was the best way to handle this. Knowing it had been her idea, she was still unsure if it was the right one.

"Good point," Redd muttered. "Give him the instructions and let me think."

Feya walked over, looking into the guard's eyes. "Flip her over and put her arms behind her back."

The guard manhandled Olette as he harshly obeyed. The guard yanked and twisted Olette's arms behind her back, causing her to inhale in pain. Feya wrapped the shoe string using a handcuff knot to restrict her. Once the knot was tied, she tested it to make sure Olette could not get free.

"Help her stand up," Feya said. As she calmed down, the lust vanished. She knew her father was right and she should not drink Olette's blood. It was hard doing the right thing sometimes.

The guard roughly jerked her up to her feet. Feya looked

around the room. There was no way people would not know that a vampire had been here. Blood was all over the floor, it had soaked into the rug, and the walls were covered in splatters of it.

"We're going to have to clean up," Feya groaned.

"I can clean up," Redd shrugged.

"Sun up is in an hour," Feya grumbled. "Go back to the wing. I can handle this."

"I can stay," Redd whispered.

"No," Feya stated. "I can handle this. I can turn her in and clean this up. Go."

Watching as her father left, she waited till he climbed the stairs. Looking down at her bare feet, she wiggled her toes on the cold stone floor. Feeling for the earth beneath the stones. She pressed down on her feet as she felt the earth shift, lifting the stones of the floor up. The stones floated around her as she let the bodies of the three guards and the rug sink into the earth. Flipping the stones over, she tried to press them back in place, but they did not fit anymore. Frustrated, she looked at the uneven floor as she tried to figure it out. She groaning, she realized she would need to shave a few stones down. She chipped a few, cracked a few, but got it mostly level. Shrugging it was good enough.

Glancing at the guard, she said. "Give me your shirt and jacket."

Using the shirt, she wiped off the best she could. Calling for some dirt, she used that to smear on the blood spots to cover the scent as best she could. It would have to do.

Olette stared wide eyed at Feya. Eyeing Olette, Feya had an idea.

"Do you have a change of clothes?" Feya asked.

"Yes," Olette demurred, smiling connivingly. "I would like to wear my blue dress then."

Rolling her eyes, Feya asked. "Where is it at?"

"There is a bedroom upstairs off the main hall," Olette said, cheerily.

Feya stared at her. Did she really think Feya would let her dress up?

Laughing, Feya said. "Wait here. Knock her out if she tries to run."

"Yes," the guard whispered.

Chapter 32

$\mathscr{F}$eya turned and walked up the stairs. She found the room Olette mentioned after two tries. On the bed was Olette's bag of clothes. Luckily, the bedroom had a bathroom for her to get ready in. Jumping in the shower, she rinsed off with her clothes on. Picking her wet clothes up, she went back to the room. She dumped Olette's bag out on the day's bed. Standing there naked, she hoped one of these would work. Spotting the blue dress. She shrugged and threw it over her head. The knit sundress stretched and fit snuggly.

Walking down the stairs, she smiled at Olette when she entered the room.

"That's my…" Olette started.

"I suggest you not finish that thought," Feya interrupted.

Smiling brightly, Feya eyed the guard. She knew she had control for a few days. Should be long enough to turn Olette in and have him run far away. That way, Olette did not learn that her father had fibbed a bit. She would need to have him hide in their wing till the vale opens up. He deserved a chance. He had just followed orders.

"Let's go," Feya said. "Drag her if she refuses to walk."

"I am going," Olette sneered.

They made the trek to the castle quietly. Sneaking through alleys and shadows. A few times, ducking to hide from passing

patrol. As they got closer to the castle, the patrol increased, meaning they had to be extra careful. Jumping from shadow to shadow, they slowly trekked forward to the castle. Listening to the heartbeats, she knew where every guard was and the direction they were heading.

When they were close to the kitchen garden, Feya texted Brady. Feya hoped Brady's phone was charged and she would receive her text. There was only one outlet in the wing to charge phones on.

I need you to bring a change of clothes for a male out and hide a fae in the rooms. I'm outside by the herb garden.

Looking towards the horizon, she knew she had been gone too long. The sky was a fire with the flames of sunrise. Hints of oranges and reds splashed across the horizon.

She had not brought her sunglasses because she had not thought she would need them. Her phone buzzed in her hand.

"Who are…" Olette said.

"Cover her mouth," Feya stated.

She heard mumbling noises behind her as the guard muffled Olette's mouth with his hand.

Glancing at her phone, she read.

Heading down.

Feya sighed, thankful that Brady had gotten the message. She would be happy when she handed Olette in. How she went from whiney fear baby to narcissistic bitch in the drop of hate Feya would never guess. The last dig of wearing the dress Olette wanted was petty, but she was loving it. The look on Olette's face when she walked into the room was truly priceless.

Feya watched the kitchen door trying to will Brady to come out. After five minutes, Brady came outside. Elwyn followed close

behind her. Biting her lip, she did not know how he would handle seeing his mother covered in blood, tied up, and a random Ailil soldier holding his hand over her mouth. Sighing, she closed her eyes, hoping this would not end in a fight.

Elwyn stopped a few feet away as he took in the situation.

"Here me out," Feya whispered.

"Let's get this done," Elwyn stated. "Are you wearing my… Olette's dress?"

"Yeah," Feya sighed. "There was a thing…"

"Do I want to know?" Elwyn muttered. Running his hand through his hair.

"No, dearie," Brady interjected. "What am I to do with this fella?"

"Change his clothes," Feya stated. "Get rid of the uniform and take him up to hide in the wing."

"Why?" Elwyn growled.

"I'll explain it later," Feya said through gritted teeth. "We should turn your… Olette in."

Feya took a breath. She needed to remember to not call Olette his mother. He obviously was trying to avoid saying it. She could hear the pain in his voice when he tried to avoid saying it.

"I'm tired and want to get this done," Feya sighed. "That way, I can go upstairs and rest."

"Fine," Elwyn grumbled.

Turning to the guard, Feya said. "This is Brady. You follow her directions. Hand Olette over to me."

The guard did as he was told without question.

"Oh, my love," Olette said, as the guard released her mouth. Her eyes shined bright with crocodile tears as she looked at Elwyn.

"Don't say another word," Elwyn growled at Olette.

Olette shrank back at the rage radiating from Elwyn. The fire of his rage was almost palpable in the air. Feya smirked at Olette before turning back to Elwyn.

Reaching up with her free hand, Feya toyed with a strand of Elwyn's hair.

"Does he know?" Olette whispered.

"Did I not make myself clear?" Elwyn growled.

"He knows," Feya whispered. Standing on tiptoe, she planted a kiss on his lips. "He has always known."

Olette inhaled as she tugged against her restraints.

Feya tugged her closer. "Don't fight. You remember what my father told you?"

Feya watched as Olette's eyes widened, and her head bobbed yes.

"Good," Feya stated. Turning back to Elwyn. "You can go. I can handle this."

"I am going with you," he stated.

Feya nodded, then dragged Olette behind her as Elwyn took up the tail end. As they approached the kitchen door, the guards on duty approached.

"Halt!" one of them exclaimed.

Elwyn stepped forward, saying. "We have the Olette Gadelica."

"Oh," the guard said. Turning to the other guard. "Let the captain of the guard know."

The other guard took off running into the castle.

"Are we supposed to wait for him to come back?" Feya grumbled, looking towards Elwyn. "I just want to go inside."

Elwyn looked to the horizon, where flames licked the sky.

"Yeah," he said. "Let's go in."

Elwyn pushed past the guard. The guard grabbed his arm roughly.

"Excuse me," Elwyn said. "Do you know who I am?"

"Yes, Brigadier General," the guard said.

"Then why is your hand still on me?" Elwyn growled. "You will move out of my way."

The guard released Elwyn and saluted.

Elwyn opened the door, and they walked in. As they entered the kitchen, a group of guards came running with General Wallace.

"Take her," General Wallace barked.

Feya released Olette as the guards grabbed her and drug her off. Grabbing Elwyn's hand, she tugged at him.

"I want to go to bed," Feya whispered. "I am tired."

Elwyn nodded. "Wallace, I'll let you take this from here."

Wallace nodded, before turning back to the guards restraining Olette.

Elwyn turned, dragging Feya off. Brady and the guard were still not back.

Feya sighed as she flung herself onto the bed.

"Can we please remove Olette's dress from your body?" Elwyn grumbled.

Laughing, Feya nodded. Letting it drop to the ground, standing there naked in front of Elwyn.

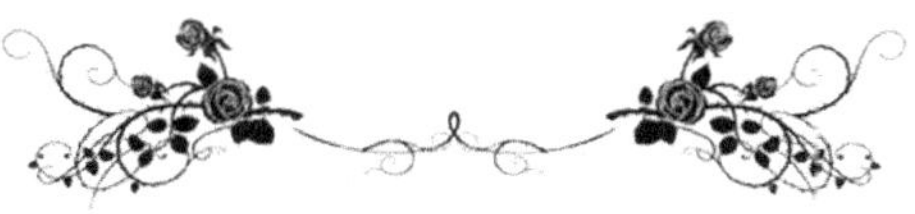

Feya woke up alone in bed. Reaching over Elwyn's side of the bed had grown cold. She could not believe she slept through him leaving the bed. The room also she realized when she could not hear his heartbeat. After consuming a lot of blood, she usually slept deep. She had slept the day away.

Climbing out of bed, she glanced out of the curtains. The sun was setting when she looked out the window. The night sky coming out, a smattering of stars dotting the sky. A hunter's moon illuminated the ground in its soft gray light.

Throwing on some khaki shorts and a black shirt on. Walking out of the room, she stopped to listen. She heard Redd's, Aguya's, and Brady's heartbeat, but not Elwyn's still. Walking to the dining room. Everyone was sitting around the table talking.

"Finally," Redd growled, as she walked in. "We need to leave tonight. The mission is done. We turned Olette in. We should have left a long time ago. They opened the vale up this afternoon sometime."

"Alright," Feya nodded. Sadness settled in her soul. She knew she would always miss Elwyn. "I need to say goodbye."

"Fine," Brady whispered. Standing, she went and rested her hands on Feya's shoulders, gently massaging them. "He is downstairs talking with the queen and her crew. Just wait here and you can…"

"Thanks," Feya said, turning she left the room before Brady could finish.

Mindlessly, she walked through the halls as she made her way to the queen's office. Sorrow settled into her core, knowing the time to leave had finally come. Closing her eyes, she stopped in the hall. Tears welled up behind her eyes. Taking a deep breath, she pushed it away. Opening her eyes, she decided to go wait outside the queen's office for Elwyn. Maybe her father would allow her to spend a bit of time with Elwyn before they left. Hopefully, he would not be in her office too long.

As she got closer, she heard Elwyn's heartbeat amongst the others. Several guards stood in the antechamber to the queen's study. As she stood there, she realized Elwyn was in her study.

"Good evening, Miss Annwen," a guard she did not recognize said. It took her a moment to realize he was talking to her. She had forgotten that they all thought that was her name. "I will let the queen know you are here."

Turning he went and entered the queen's office.

Feya had just thought she would wait here for Elwyn not to have to talk to the queen again. Sighing, she wished she had dressed more formally. The door opened again; the guard sweeping his hand for her to enter. Entering the room, she felt self-conscious. Elwyn sat in a chair in front of the queen's desk, looking irritated. Wallace stood stiffly behind the queen, who was sitting at her desk.

"It's high time our little vampire made her appearance," the queen said sternly. "At least this time she is wearing shoes."

Feya's heart stopped as she stared at the queen. She knew the queen knew, but her hope was she would not have to have this conversation with her ever. Fear sank into her soul, as she knew she could not fight them all or run without being caught.

Chapter 33

"Yes, your highness," Feya whispered. The words barely escaped her throat because of the fear that clogged it.

"Feya," Queen Cassada said. "You have done our people a great service. I have been waiting for you to come down so we can have a discussion."

"Alright," Feya choked out. Fear and anxiety eating at her. Looking down, she stared at her white tennis shoes. A grass stain on one toe looked like the shape of a bunny. Fixating on that stain, she tried to figure out how she could escape.

"Did you not think I would not figure out what you truly are?" the queen asked.

"I am confused," Elwyn growled. "You have Feya mixed up with someone else."

Feya wished she could have kept Elwyn out of this. Maybe he could escape with her family. She wished she could get a message to her father to take care of Elwyn. She needed to figure out how to get him out of the room.

"Elwyn," the queen stated. "You are dismissed."

"Alright," Elwyn stated. Jumping up, he walked towards Feya. Grabbing her hand, he started dragging her out of the room.

"Elwyn!" the queen yelled. "I dismissed you, not Feya!"

"If she stays, I stay," Elwyn said, icily. "If I go, she goes."

"Elwyn," Feya breathed. "Just go. I'll be fine."

"I am not going anywhere without you," Elwyn stated. Staring into those blue eyes that were washed in loss and despair. She wanted him to be safe and to go, but she knew he would not leave her.

"Go," Feya tried again.

'Nope," he stated, leaning over and brushing his lips against hers. Her eyes locked with those blue eyes. "I am not going anywhere without you."

"You think this is cute?" Queen Cassada growled.

"Nope," Elwyn stated.

Elwyn stood tall, his gray uniform starch and stiff. The rage and anger he directed at the queen was written in his eyes as they turned dark blue from rage.

"Please finish what you had to say, your highness," Elwyn chimed in.

Feya's hand trembled in Elwyn's. Squeezing her hand. She hated he was there, but still leaned on him for comfort.

"This conversation is to not leave this room," the queen said.

Feya nodded, not even sure if she would make it out of the room alive. Trying to control the trembling of her hands, she counted her heartbeats. It was not helping. Her heart was racing so fast she could not keep up.

"You are not the first crossbreed who has survived," the queen stated. Feya inhaled in shock. "And you will not be the last. With the change comes a great power and how you weld it defines who you are. We have always ended those that went through this due to them not being able to control the hunger or the powers. This time you have proven yourself worthy, but make no mistake, what you did on the battlefield was dangerous. It had ramifications that spread further than the battlefield you stood on. Several villagers and their homes were damaged from the earthquake you created. You will need to rein that power in. Once you have honed that power, I will call you forth if a need arises. That is the only way you will leave this room alive."

"You want me to pledge that I will come running back if you call me?" Feya said, confused.

"Not just any promise," Queen Cassada stated. "A celestial contract."

Feya inhaled, knowing that once she agreed to this, she would be bound to the queen and her whims. A contract that could not be broken unless the queen released her. Feya would be drawn to the queen if the queen even breathed her name.

"No!" Elwyn growled.

The temperature in the room went up as Elwyn's anger was close to snapping. This was the first time she had felt his magic. He was always in control of his powers. She had just assumed they were weak. She could see the sweat doting on the brow of the queen as she reached for a handkerchief.

"Elwyn!" Wallace yelled. His dark brown eyes turned blue as his room cooled down. Feya felt a frosty chill on one side and heat on the other. The two males' powers vying for dominance in the room.

Queen Cassada slammed her hand on her desk.

"I will send both you males out if you cannot stay out of this conversation," Queen Cassada said curtly. "Well, Feya, what is your choice?"

Feya stood there, knowing the queen meant it. Her life or being in debt to the whims of this woman. A woman she barely knew.

"Maybe," the queen stated. "I can explain more to you and ease your mind. As you may know, I am my late husband's second wife. His first dying in the Great War. I had hoped the peace would last. Many still suffer nightmares from the war. As with many things, peace was not destined to last. Many have been dissatisfied with my rule since I took over. So recreating that peace you will be my ace in the hole. I need to know with certainty that you are loyal to me, the crown, and the kingdom. Since I am sparing your life."

"You will wear this necklace at all times," the queen continued, sliding a black jewelry box over. "That way I will know where you are and can call you forth if the need shall arise."

Feya took a step forward, but was jerked back by Elwyn. He pushed her behind him as he walked over to open the box. Inside the box was a blood binding stone. A bloodstone nestled in an intricate silver filigree of the tree of life. The opaqueness of the dark green stone mixed with red spots that resembled blood splatter looked pretty if she had not known what that stone stood for.

Her life or her freedom? Plus, it would not just be her, the queen would be after. The queen would go after her family and anyone who hid her all these years. She had to choose between sacrificing her freedom and saving Elwyn and her family from murder. There was no choice. She had to save those that she loved.

Pushing Elwyn aside, she grabbed the necklace. Holding the stone tight in her right hand.

"No," Elwyn stated. Grabbing her arm and turning her to him.

"Its fine," Feya growled. Reaching up with her left hand to stroke his cheek. Turning back to the queen, she locked eyes with her.

"Repeat after me," Queen Cassada said.

Feya raised an eyebrow. She mocked. "Repeat after me."

Queen Cassada stared at Feya with annoyance.

"Promise beyond promise," the queen said.

"Promise beyond promise," Feya repeated.

"I pledge my troth to Queen Cassada and the fae kingdom," the queen continued. "By air and earth, fire and water, so may you be bound, by thee and thine. By moon and sun, by sky and sea, power be bound and light revealed. Now be sealed, this promise."

Feya repeated the celestial contract spell, the stone growing hot in her hand as it burned the contract into her soul. She wanted to drop it and throw it in the queen's face. Instead, she stood there holding the stone, glaring into the queen's eyes.

"Now you wear," Queen Cassada stated. "The crest of the fallen."

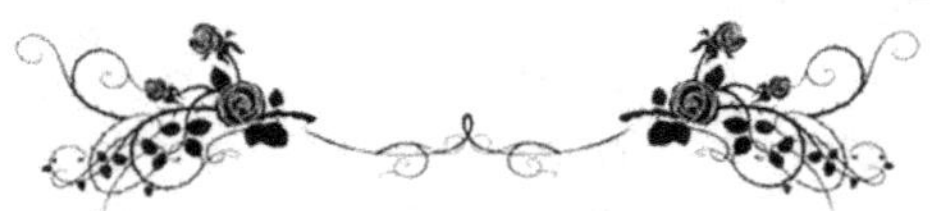

Feya stood there staring at the bed she had shared with Elwyn. Elwyn pacing the room. She knew it was time to leave. The sun would be up in about four hours. They would need to get her father to safety, plus Leo was probably worried. She did not know how much they had informed him of what was going on.

"I need to leave Elwyn," Feya whispered. A numbness settled inside her.

She had not told her father about what had transpired with the queen. The necklace sat in her pocket, a heavy weight that was dragging her down and drowning her. She had tried to leave it in the queen's antechamber, but she could not set it down. It was bound to her, and she was bound to the queen.

"I know," Elwyn grumbled.

"I mean right now!" Feya said. "I need to leave with my family now!"

Elwyn stopped pacing and stared at her. Nodding, he said, "Maybe we can wait…"

"No," Feya interrupted. "I need to leave now with my family."

"I need a few days to clean…" Elwyn stated.

"You stay," Feya stated. "I need to go now."

Elwyn nodded. "I will find you in a few…"

"Fine," Feya growled. She tried to reel in the rage building up inside her. The numbness gone now as the ramifications of what she had just done sunk in.

"I would understand if you were mad at me." Elwyn gulped. "I brought you…"

"Stop!" Feya yelled. "I am not mad at you. It was a matter of time before they caught me. I have spent so much of my life hiding and fearing the consequences. Now I know what they are and I just need to leave. You stay doing what you have to do. I need to leave now."

"Fine," Elwyn said, coming over and pulling Feya into his arms. "I blame myself."

"Don't blame yourself," Feya sighed. Stamping down on her anger, she buried her face in Elwyn's neck. She was not sure when she would see him again. A mix of rage bubbled inside her and sadness. Kissing Elwyn's neck, she wished they had more time.

"I'll find you soon, Fe," Elwyn whispered, kissing the top of her head.

"I know you will, Ellie," Feya said without conviction.

"You sure you're not mad at me?" he asked, lifting her chin up.

"I am not mad at you," Feya grumbled. "I don't blame you at all. Just mad at the situation and the queen, to be honest."

"Ok," Elwyn said. Sucking her lip into his mouth and gently biting it. He scraped his teeth across it as he slowly released her lip. "I don't want you to go."

"I don't want to leave you either," Feya whispered.

Brushing her fingers through his hair, she grabbed a chunk and pulled his mouth down to hers.

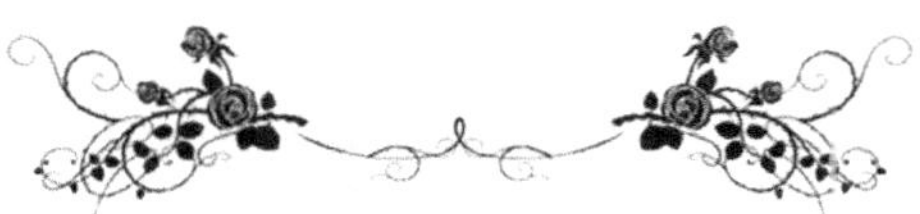

As they walked through the village heading to the vale exit, faes ran around like they were back to their normal routine. The atmosphere was different, though. Everyone seemed on edge. Neighbor side eyeing their neighbor. No one quite sure who to trust. The queen was still vague about what had happened. Only doling out what information she thought was pertinent to her subjects to know. Which turned out to be as little as possible.

Feya looked around, wondering if any of these faes were the ones the queen said she had hurt. She had not realized the extent of her powers, having thought it was just a section of the battlefield affected. She was too scared to ask Elwyn what damage she had caused

Elwyn's hand felt warm in hers. Realizing how much she would miss that little warmth from just his touch. So funny that something so simple could come to mean so much.

With each step they took towards the exit of the vale, her heart seemed heavier at the same time as her steps seemed lighter. She was both running away from her and running towards it. She still needed to tell her father what had happened. He would be upset that she had made the deal with the devil, aka the queen.

Crossing the fortress gates, it seemed an eternity since when she had walked through them just days ago. No one questioned as they walked out, a cloaked vampire, a fire witch, an Ailil soldier, 2 faes, and herself.

The air shifted as they got closer to the vale entrance. The charge made the hair on her arms stand on end. Everything looked the same as when she first arrived. It just felt off. Or maybe she was just off. Standing in front of the exit, she could almost see the blurring of the edges where it began.

Glancing up at Elwyn, this was it, the big goodbye.

"Don't drag it out, Feya," Redd grumbled as he stood there.

Glaring at her father, she already knew they had little time. She was not a fool. They needed to get somewhere before the sun came up.

"Go away, Redd," Elwyn said, smirking as he shoved Redd through the vale. "I quite enjoyed that."

"Elwyn," Brady scolded before she stepped through. The Ailil soldier following behind.

"I wish I could have done that," Aguya said before stepping through.

Laughing, Feya shook her head. "You could not play nice for even one more minute?"

"Nope," Elwyn laughed. "Plus, now I am alone with you."

"I can't stay long," she whispered.

"I know," he said. "Just one more minute."

Pulling her to him, he wrapped her in his arms. Lifting her head, she met his mouth. Gently, his tongue licked her lips as she parted them and he entered. One last taste before goodbye.

Pulling away, she stared into those blue eyes, not knowing when she'd see them again. Not saying a word, she turned and walked through the vale.

Chapter 34

Feya sat in the hotel room looking through an old arcane spell book, while her dad talked to Alvero as they discussed ways to break the celestial contract. Alvero had brought over several dusty old text books. Some looked like they were older than her father. She had come to terms that her life was not fully her own anymore. She would just enjoy the time away as much as she could. If only she did not have to spend every waking minute going through one book or another. Discussing and over discussing the celestial contract. Repeating what she said over and over and over. The two males were driving her more nuts than the idea of being hailed by the queen at any moment was. As per usual, her father made her go over the contract repeatedly.

Aguya, still mad at Alvero for some slight that happened fifty-ish years ago, refused to stay in the same hotel he was in. Aguya refused to talk about what happened. Alvero would just ignore Aguya. A small part of her was curious about why they hated each other so much. She wondered if she could sneak off and join Aguya in her hotel. Then she could stop staring at the dusty old fae books.

Turning a page, she glanced at her dad and Alvero. Luckily, they had not realized she was not actually reading the book on fae lore. Turning another page without seeing a single word on it.

Pausing as she heard a heartbeat. For a moment, she thought her ears were deceiving her, but then there was a knock

on the door. Elwyn was here.

Redd, distracted, did not realize whose heartbeat it was. Feya jumped up, running to the door to get it before her dad did, but her dad got there first.

He stared at her a moment before the light of realization shined in his eyes. Growling, he said, "What do you want, boy?"

Pushing Redd away, she opened the door. Grinning like a fool, Elwyn stood there. His blue eyes shining bright, his brown hair tousled, hanging in front of one eye. Feya's eyes gobbled him up as she realized how much she had missed him.

"Looks like…" Elwyn started.

Redd pushed Feya back and slammed the door in Elwyn's face.

"Father!" Feya exclaimed.

"He deserved that," Redd said, raising an eyebrow.

Rolling her eyes, Feya pushed him away and opened the door again.

"Sorry," Feya said, giving Redd the stink eye. "My father is rude."

"It's all good," Elwyn laughed, walking into the room. "Like I was saying, it looks like you're stuck with me."

Winking, Elwyn grabbed Feya and pulled her into his arms. Before he could kiss her, Redd put his hand on Elwyn's mouth, pushing his head back.

"Not today, boy," Redd said. "We are trying to get rid of the curse she has because of you."

"Well," Elwyn said, pushing Redd's hand away. "I am here with news about that, too."

"Oh," Feya said.

"It turns out that Olette has escaped," Elwyn stated. "She had some friends in the queen's personal guard. They sent me here to let you know, if you weed out who is loyal to the crown and find Olette, we can negotiate to get the contract broken. Plus, I have ended my tenure with the queen."

"Boy," Redd growled. "No one gives a shit what you do. We need more than to renegotiate the terms of the deal."

"What that means, grandpa," Elwyn growled. "Is that we hold the information the queen needs until Feya is released. I swear you are going senile in your old age. Do we need to put you in a nursing home?"

"Go away, dad," Feya growled, done with the childish battle. She wanted to be alone with Elwyn now. Reaching up, she brushed the stray strand of hair out of his face.

"This is my room," Redd said, lifting an eyebrow.

"Fine," Feya said, grabbing Elwyn's hand. "I'll go away."

Feya dragged Elwyn out of the room, crossing the hall to her room. Unlocking the door, Elwyn pushed it out of her hand as he turned her around and picked her up.

Laughing, she heard the door slam before he tossed her onto the bed. Elwyn followed her down onto the bed.

As soon as her head hit the mattress, his mouth smashed into hers. The hunger pouring from her almost devoured her as he tasted her. She heard his heart racing as fast as her own.

Pulling back, he looked down at her, brushing a strand of hair out of her face. Grabbing the back of his head, she tried to pull him back.

Laughing, Elwyn said, "Patient, Fe."

Groaning, she rolled her eyes at him.

Leaning down, he kissed the tip of her nose. "I missed you."

"I missed you, too, Ellie," she whispered back.

"I want to talk for a minute," he whispered, his teeth scraping across her chin.

"Do we have to?" she groaned. The embers of a fire igniting in her core.

"Yes, we do," he said, leaning back.

Sighing, she geared up for whatever bad news he was going to tell her.

He grabbed her hand and brought it to his mouth, kissing her knuckles.

"I'm not sure how to start," he laughed.

"Just blurt it out," she growled.

"Alright," he smirked. "There is my impatient little Fe. I've decided…"

Grabbing her he rolled her on top of him.

She waited for him to finish, but realized he was taking his dear sweet time to annoy her.

"Ugh," she said, annoyed. "Spit it out."

"Maybe," he said. "Just maybe I am nervous and trying to figure out how to say it."

Pushing off him, she rolled away. Grabbing her, he pulled her back. Pushing her head into the crook of his shoulder.

"Much better," he muttered. "Last time I tried to talk about this, you got all…"

"All what?" she growled. Anger rising inside her. Maybe she did not want to talk to him after all.

"I am making this so much worse," he laughed.

"Then just spill it," she muttered. "I am ready for this convo to be over."

"Fine," he stated. "Just give me a second."

She laid there waiting for him to speak. She tapped her fingers on his chest to let him know she was getting bored waiting. Placing his hand on hers, he stopped her tapping.

"I don't want us to be apart like that again," he whispered.

"You will have to go back to court," she whispered. "I can't stay there."

"I wasn't done," he said. "This mission with you is the last one I will do for the crown. Again, I don't want to be apart from you like that again. I…"

Waiting for him to continue, but he did not. She said, "I didn't like being apart either."

"You really missed me, Fe?" he said, uncertainly.

"Yes," she said, biting his shoulder gently. "I really missed you and your annoying cheeriness."

Laughing, he rolled her back over so he could loom over. Staring down, she could tell he wanted to say more, but was hesitating. She stared into those blue eyes, willing him to say it so they could get down to the other business.

He gently grazed his knuckles across her cheek. "I love you, Feya."

Staring into those eyes, she hesitated for a second. Fear ate at her. She reached up, tracing a finger along his cheek. Taking a deep breath, she dove in.

"I love you too, Elwyn," she whispered back.

Smiling, he turned and kissed her palm. Before leaning down and bringing his mouth to hers.

Crest of the Scorned

Sneak Peak of book 2 in the Ascelin Series

Johnna Dee

Chapter 1

Aguya looked down at her bleeding hands covered in dirt. She had tripped again and scratched them up. She could hear them coming closer, practically feeling their breath on the back of her neck. The sun was setting, and the path was getting harder to see. It was a moonless night, which could work both for and against her. She could not continue to outrun them. She was tired and running out of energy, having been running since this morning. They were stronger and faster than her, and there were more of them. She needed to find a place to hide. Looking around, she saw a small fox hole. She might squeeze her 5 foot tall frame into it if she curled up into a ball.

Curling up, she squeezed in tight. Whispering a prayer to Prauime, goddess of the sacred fire. Holding her breath, she waited. Squeezing her eyes shut, she heard the stomping of their feet as they ran past her hiding spot. Tears streamed from her golden brown eyes at her own sister's betrayal. Her entire clan had turned on her. She was alone now, lost and scared.

This morning she had woken up to do chores like every other day. When her sister, Alse, came to talk to her. She said Aguya was being called to the council's chamber. She had been so confused why they wanted to meet with her. Asking her sister if

she knew why, Alse just shook her head.

When she entered the chamber, an austere room with dark wooden panels. The only furniture was a massive, dark wooden table with chairs for the council behind it. One for each member of the council, six in total. Today, only five members filled the seats. A wad of bloody cloth in the center of the table.

A ball of fear grew in her stomach as she searched the faces. Elder Gordon, Elder Corrine, Elder Elise, Elder Morgane, and Elder Riche sat behind the table. Looking at the faces of the elder witches, she realized which one was missing: her stepmother, Cerridwen. A soft crying was coming from her right, turning she saw Alse crying. The ball grew bigger. She thought it might consume her.

"We are giving you the chance to explain yourself," Gordon said calmly. Empathy seeping from his brown eyes.

"I... I... I don't know what you mean," Aguya stammered, brushing her golden blonde hair behind her ear. Searching the faces for some clue what she was in trouble for.

"Don't play games!" Corrine exclaimed, slamming her hand on the table. The rage in Corrine's eyes sent a shiver down Aguya's spine. All the other elders had grown silent, letting Corrine take over.

"You need to understand," Alse said, a dramatic tear sliding down her pale cheek. "Our stepmother was both physically and emotionally abusive to us. Aguya was probably just pushed too far."

Aguya inhaled as she looked at the bloody cloth on the table. Had something happened to her stepmother, and she had accused her of it? Confused, she tried to figure out what she was being accused of and why her own blood was going along with this lie.

"I have done nothing," Aguya stated. Finding her voice again. She would not sit here like a meek kitten and let them run roughshod for something she did not do.

"All we will get out of this witch," Corrine sneered, waving a hand towards Aguya. "Is lies. She has murdered one of our own and cannot even just be honest."

Aguya felt the world shift around her. She looked at her sister and realized her sister, Also, had murdered their stepmother and was blaming her. The worst part is the council believed her. Taking a step back, Aguya tried to figure out what she would do. Corrine opened the wad of bloody cloth and in it fell out Aguya's ritual dagger. Looking at the cloth, she realized it was her nightgown covered in blood. Most likely her step mother's blood.

"Your sister has told us everything she saw," Corrine scowled. "Everything! We know what you did and there will be consequences."

Aguya stared into Corrine's blue eyes and knew she was damned. Corrine had never liked Aguya since she had burned her son's hand when he got handsy with her.

She took a breath as she never turned away from Corrine. She knew there was only one way out and it was to run. Cautiously, she tried to power up her magic. She tried not to make the room temperature change around her. Her fingertips tingled with the flames waiting to escape. Rubbing her fingers together, the flickers of fire just below the surface. Holding it in check for just a moment longer.

Corrine turned to look at the council members saying. "She will not talk. I am not surprised she did this. It is in her nature to lie and deceive."

Looking at her sister, she saw the look of triumph in those baby blue eyes. That's the moment she realized it, with certainty. No one would believe her over her sister. The beautiful, sweet Also with the honey blonde hair, baby blue eyes, perky little nose, and sweet disposition had crooked crossed her. Betrayal seeped into her soul and stabbed her heart. The one person she thought she would never have to watch her back against had stabbed her in the back.

Calling forth every ounce of fire she possessed, she let it rain down around her. The surrounding room caught on fire as she ran out the door, running towards the forest.

The sting of betrayal burning in her soul had given her an

extra burst of energy, making her run faster. She knew her sister hated their step-mother just as much as she did. Ten years back, their father had remarried an ice witch named Cerridwen. At first she had been so sweet and kind, but once she got pregnant, that all changed. She tortured both Alse and herself at every opportunity. Freezing sections of their skin with her powers, locking them in ice chambers she created for hours, and so forth. The punishments continued on and on. Cerridwen put up such a good front no one believed she could do this, including their father. Their father would always say she would never hurt them like that. When their father left for business, Cerridwen began the punishment. This last punishment pushed her sister over the edge. Spending 48 hours in the icebox with no food or water. What most don't realize as a young fire witch these punishments hurt ten times worse than usual. There was no spark to call forth your own flame as it dwindled inside you. A flame that was their life's blood itself. When Alse came out, she had been quiet, but Aguya saw the rage and hatred burning in her eyes.

Staying cramped up in the foxhole, she waited till the sun came up before leaving. Watching as the hints of fire touched the tree line, she hoped it was safe to leave. Slowly, crawling out, she listened to make sure she heard no steps or voices. If they found her, they would surely kill her for falsely thinking she had killed a member of the council.

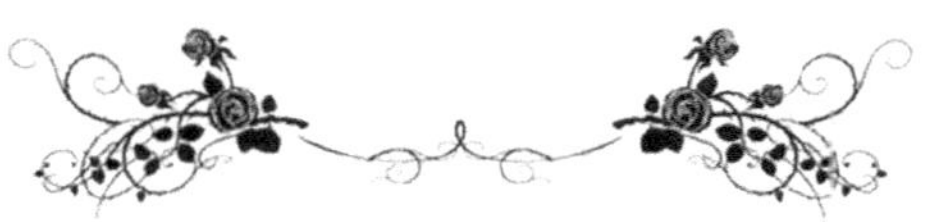

July 1886

Aguya had been on the run for two years now, never staying in one spot for long for fear they would find her. She could not even tell you the name of the human town she was currently in. Avoiding any towns that magicals lived in for fear they would search those places first. She would go stay for a few weeks to earn enough gold to move to the next human town.

The human landlady of the inn was tapping her foot, glaring at Aguya. Upset that Aguya did not have the money to pay for her stay anymore. She was four days behind on rent.

Her money had dwindled down to nothing. She did not even have enough money to buy food. For the last two days, she had to scavenge for food in the nearby forest. She had tried to find a temporary job in this town, but none were to be found. No one wanted to hire a strange woman from out of town. She knew her personality did not help. They all thought she was shrewish, as one human had said. She had tried to be nice and sweet, but it was so out of her nature and she could only act for so long.

She glared back at the landlady, trying to figure out how she would get out of this situation. Maybe she should just start a fire and leave, but fear the wooded shelter would go up like a tinderbox stopped her.

"There you are," a little fae with jet black hair and the greenest eyes she had ever seen walked up and grabbed her hand. A floral scent wafting around the child.

Looking down in shock at the little hand of a child in hers.

"We have been looking for you all over," the little fae stated.

A hand then rested on the fae's head. Looking up, she saw a vampire. His brassy red hair and amber eyes glowed in the firelight. The glint of his slightly elongated fangs gave away what he truly was.

He smiled a cat-like grin at the landlady, saying. "How much does my daughter's nanny owe you?"

Aguya watched as the vampire and landlady talked. Then he paid off her bill. The little fae never released her hand. She stood there as fear sunk into her core, freezing her. They found her and hired a vampire to end her life. The surrounding conversation faded as her brain buzzed with her impending doom. She had been so careful all these years and still they caught her. She tried to calculate a plan for how she would escape. Were there others outside waiting for her?

A tugging on her hand pulled her out of her reverie.

"I said I'm hungry. Are you also?" Aguya looked down at the little fae and nodded.

At least she would get one more warm meal before she fought for her life. She would need the strength for the battle to come. The little fae tugged her over to a table in a corner of the tavern below the inn.

"What do you want, little one?" the vampire asked, looking at the fae.

It donned on Aguya how strange this situation was. Was the vampire going to kill herself and the fae? Aguya understood she had to fight for her own safety and that of the fae child now. She could not let him kill this innocent little fae. She would hold off until they were outside and rely on her magic to defeat him. Determination to set fire to the vampire before he could harm the child or herself set in.

"Hmmm," the fae said. "I think they only have one option, daddy. It smells like beef stew."

"That's my sweet Feya," he said, tapping her nose.

Daddy?!?! Aguya thought.

Everything in her froze, as she was even more confused. Watching her face, the vampire smiled at the little fae.

"You look quite confused," he started. "My name is Aethelredd Ascelin. My daughter, Feya, is learning to weld her magic and I am having trouble training her. We saw you in town and figured we could hire you to teach her what you could, little witch."

A giant wolf shifter walked up to the table, nodding at her. The scent of wet grass filled the area, his blue eyes gentle as gentle as the wind and his gray hair just as wild as the wind.

"Uncle Leo!" the little fae, Feya, exclaimed. "You were gone so long, I thought you got lost."

The wolf shifter shook his head and ruffled Feya's hair.

"Well?" Feya said, smiling at her. "Will you help me? I am a fast learner and well behaved."

The vampire raised an eyebrow at the fae's statement. Leo snickered as he sat down.

"I guess," Aguya said tentatively.

"Your accent is quite thick," Feya stated. "Where are you from? Why did you leave? Do you have—"

"Feya," the vampire said curtly.

Rolling her eyes, the little fae went quiet.

"We are going to be traveling home," the vampire, Aethelredd, said. "You will, of course, have a room of your own next to my daughter. We will—"

"How is she your daughter?" Aguya finally spoke, cutting him off. Curiosity overriding fear.

"She is part vampire and part fae," Aethelredd stated. "Luckily, most only sense the fae part."

Nodding, Aguya looked at the little fae again. She could not sense or see the markings of a vampire. With Aethelredd, the fangs gave it away. Just a hair longer than humans was the only distinct feature. The shifter could smell the wolf on him, the wet grass and earthy essence. Nothing gave the child the appearance of being part vampire. Only the smell of a fae. The smell of flowers that permeated the surrounding air. Most people thought it was just a perfume they wore.

"We will be family soon," Feya smiled at her. "How old are you?"

"I am 25," Aguya stated.

"I am 10 years of age," Feya stated. "Daddy says his age does not matter and to tell people he is 35. Uncle Leo just says to say 34. We live in a manor house. It is enormous and you will love it. Though daddy likes to keep the windows closed during the day and it smells dusty—"

"Feya," Aethelredd growled. "You are over talking again."

Rolling her eyes, the little fae stuck her tongue at Aethelredd. Aethelredd laughed and tapped a finger on her nose. The loving look he gave Feya astounded Aguya. It was such a soft and adoring look.

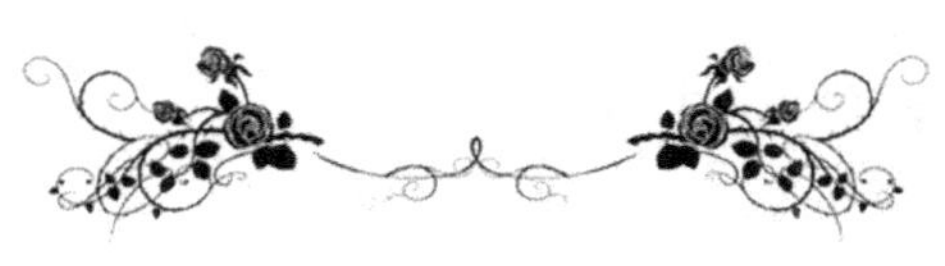

Aguya had been traveling with the vampire, wolf shifter, and little fae for two weeks now. Feya's magic was quite strong, but she had zero control over her powers. Aguya was trying to teach her that control, but she had never been a good teacher. She felt quite annoyed at the lack of getting it the first time she explained it. The child constantly complained about not being able to understand her because of her accent. She doubted they would keep her around long since she was quite failing.

The carriage bumped along the road as they traveled back to the manor house. The wolf shifter, Leo, drove the carriage as she sat inside with the vampire, Aethelredd, and the little fae, Feya. Sun would come up soon, and they were almost to the next town, but not quite. She knew they would not make it before sunrise.

"Redd," Aguya said.

She had been trying to get rid of her accent and talk like them. Like a proper Brit. She had always lived the life of a gypsy. Having no idea where she was born. She knew her father was from Lithuania.

"Yes?" Redd stated.

"We will not make it by sunrise," Aguya said. Even to her own ears, her voice sounded funny. She was having issues matching their accent.

"You're right," he stated. Tapping the roof, the carriage stopped.

She could hear Leo jumping down and coming towards the door. She did not know why they did not just yell. The wolf had extraordinary hearing and probably heard the conversation already. Since meeting him, she had heard Leo speak two words. Where Feya never stopped talking. She doubted she was part vampire. She had yet to see the little fae drink blood. So far, she only ate normal food.

"We need to park," Aethelredd said to Leo when he opened the door. "Can you guide the girls to town to eat?"

Nodding, Leo turned and jumped back onto the cart. The trail grew rough as he took the carriage off the road to find a shady spot in the forest.

"Aguya?" Feya said, sitting next to her on the bumpy ride.

"Yes, Feya?" Aguya queried.

"Why did you leave your clan?" Feya asked innocently. "I will tell you about why I left mine, if you want."

"They threw me out," Aguya started before pausing, not sure what to say. Maybe the truth was best saved for another time. "Because, I refused to follow orders. Maybe you should learn to listen better."

"Feya," Redd stated. "You stay with Aguya and Leo. Do not wander off. Do not talk to strangers. Do not—"

"Do not sass," Feya laughed. "Do not smile. Do not have any fun!"

Feya fell to the carriage floor, giggling at her own joke.

"Take what I am saying seriously, little one," Redd growled.

Nodding and wiping the tears from her eyes, Feya sat up. "Of course, daddy."

"Keep her safe with your life," Redd glared at Aguya.

Aguya nodded, knowing she would keep her safe. She did not want the child to know it, but the little twit had wormed her way into her heart. She is not sure how it was possible since she was quite annoyed listening to her over-talking constantly.

The carriage came to a stop. A moment later, the door opened. Feya jumped out before anyone could talk.

"Little one," Redd yelled. "What are the rules?"

Sighing, Feya said. "Stay close. Don't talk to strangers. Don't stand out. Blend in and be boring. Got it daddy."

Feya skipped off. Aguya jumped out, running to keep up with Feya. Feya at ten was just a few inches shorter than Aguya's 5 feet tall. The fae child would outgrow her soon.

Leo secured the carriage, then came running after them. He came up on them stealthily. For such a big shifter, it surprised her how quiet he was, his manors, his steps, his voice even.

They walked the two miles to the town to look for dinner. Aguya was so ready for a hot bowl of whatever. They had been eating jerky and fruits for days. Plus, hopefully, there was some fresh bread, too. She would kill for fresh bread.

They entered the human tavern in town. The dimly lit room had a few humans drinking, some playing cards. She could smell a rabbit stew brewing in the pot in the fireplace. It smelled delicious, especially after days of traveling fare.

They sat down and ordered stew. They were told the bread was one day old. Aguya was excited to eat.

The tavern wench brought the food over. She did not know if it was due to days of the same foods or if this was the most delicious food she had ever eaten.

As her bowl emptied, she realized the temperature in the room was rising. She did not know how long it had been happening, but she knew they had found her. Dropping her spoon, it splattered the bit of stew left.

"Take the child and run," Aguya whispered to Leo.

"We don't run," Feya stated, stuffing a piece of stew soaked bread in her mouth. "I am surprised it took you so long to realize they have been watching us for a while."

"Feya," Aguya grabbed her hand, forgetting her attempts to sound like the others. "They are very dangerous. I need you to run with Leo."

"Feya is right," Leo growled. "I do not run from a few fire witches."

"I will take care of this," Aguya choked, fear clogging her throat. It shocked a part of her, she had just heard the most words Leo had spoken since she met him.

"I am done eating," Feya whispered conspiratorially. "We should go outside to avoid the humans seeing."

Feya jumped up. She stopped to glare at Corrine and her daughter, Clairy. She then smiled and skipped outside. Leo grabbed Aguya and pushed her towards the door. Maybe he was going to grab them and run.

"Uncle Leo," Feya smiled when they were out front. "I am thirsty."

Leo nodded and pointed to the forest. They walked to the edge of the forest. She could hear the footsteps of the witches following behind them. Leo held her arm as he guided them.

They entered the dark forest and Leo said. "Here is good."

"For what?" Aguya whispered.

"Hold on to the tree tight," Leo said.

Looking up at Leo, she was confused. Then she saw Feya stomping her feet and laughing. The ground trembled as she stomped her feet. Grabbing the tree as she almost stumbled. She looked over to see Corrine and Clairy stumble to the ground.

"Roots!" Feya yelled as a tangle of roots came up and pinned the witches to the ground.

Smiling, Feya looked at Aguya, waiting for something.

Aguya stared back, confused, as the earth stopped trembling.

"She wants to know if she can have a drink," Leo grumbled.

Nodding, Aguya was more confused.

Feya bent down and lifted Clairy's head. Opening her mouth, she then chomped down on her neck. Clairy's eyes glazed over as Feya drank. Corrine started screaming. Leo ran over, clamping a hand over Corrine's mouth.

"Both?" Leo grumbled.

Feya lifted her head up and shook it, blood dripping from her chin.

"Do you want them alive?" Leo said, looking back at Aguya.

"No," Aguya whispered. Knowing if they left here, they would tell everyone where she was.

Leo twisted his hands, and Corrine's neck snapped like a twig.

Watching as Feya's finished drinking her fill of Clairy's

blood, some of it dripping from her mouth. Realizing this was the first hint of the child's vampire side. Clairy never once fought as she died, quietly.

"What do we do when we are done eating?" Leo stated, standing over Feya.

"We clean our mess," Feya giggled.

She placed her bloody hands on the earth next to the bodies and the dirt shifted and moved as the roots drug the bodies down. The earth was bare and looked like it had been freshly dug up.

"She was not a good witch," Feya whispered. "She killed many people. We have made the world a better place. That would make Father Thomas happy."

"Plus," Leo said. "They were after one of ours and no one hurts one of ours."

Nodding, Feya smiled at Aguya. "I told you, you would be family soon."

Aguya nodded, realizing that this was where she was going to stay. Relief washed over her as she realized she was no longer alone. A small part of her held that fear that she would be betrayed, no matter how she tried to push it away.

Looking at the upturned earth, it was now time to do a better job hiding the grave Feya had just created. Something else they would need to work on.

♦ **Alfheimr** - [ɑ-lv-hɛimẕ] In Norse mythology is home to the Light Elves. The Light Elves are said to be the fairest of them all.

♦ **Arianrhod** - [aaR-iy-AENRaaD] Arianrhod is the Welsh goddess of the moon and stars. She is also referred to as the silver wheel since the dead were carried on her oar wheel to Emania (Moon land or land of the dead). Which belonged to her as deity of reincarnation and karma.

♦ **Croi na Tine** - [cree-na-tīn] translates to Heart of the Fire.

♦ **Hippalectryon** - [hip-pa-lec-tron] In Greek mythology a hippalectryon is a half horse half rooster.

♦ **Rougarou** - [roux-ga-roux] In the Cajun legends, the creature is said to prowl the swamps around New Orleans, and the sugar cane fields and woodlands of the regions. The Rougarou is described as a creature with a human body and the head of a wolf or dog.

♦ **Balor** - [Bay-lor] In Irish mythology, Balor is leader of the Fomorians, a group of malevolent supernatural beings. He is often described as a giant with a large eye that wreaks destruction when opened. He has been interpreted as a personification of the scorching sun.

Honey cake

- 6 large egg yolks at room temperature
- 3 large egg whites at room temperature
- ½ cup Greek yogurt at room temperature
- 2 sticks unsalted butter at room temperature
- ⅔ cup honey, separated in half (Plus a little bit for drizzling)
- 1 1/2 tsp vanilla extract
- 1 ¾ cup all-purpose flour
- ¼ cup cornstarch
- ¾ cup granulated sugar
- ¾ teaspoon baking powder
- ¾ teaspoon salt
- ¼ teaspoon baking soda
- 2 tbsp. granulated sugar

1.	Preheat the oven to 350 degrees. Spray a 9×13 with nonstick spray.

2.	In a small bowl, combine ⅓ cup of honey with the egg yolks, the yogurt and the vanilla. Whisk it together until smooth. Set aside.

3.	In a large bowl, sift together ¾ cup sugar, flour, cornstarch, baking soda, baking powder, and salt. Mix to combine.

4.	Add the butter to the flour mixture and mix until butter is incorporated. Mix batter looks crumbly. Add the other ⅓ cup honey to the mixture. Mix until the batter lightens.

5.	Add the egg yolk mixture ½ at a time.

6.	Beat egg whites on high until they form soft peaks. Add in the 2 tbsp. of sugar and beat on high until stiff peaks form. Gently fold egg white mixture into the batter.

7.	Bake for 25-30 minutes.

8.	Frost and drizzle with honey.

Everpeach Drink

- 2 tablespoons lime juice
- 1 cup fresh orange juice, strained
- 1 tablespoon simple syrup
- 2 cups peach juice
- Fresh sliced peaches, optional

1.	In a small pitcher, combine lime juice, orange juice, simple syrup and peach juice. Stir to combine.

2.	Pour into a cup over ice. Garnish with a peach slice.

 Grilled Brie Sandwiches with Pistachio Pesto

For Pesto:

- 1/4 cup honey
- 1/3 cup shelled, roasted pistachios
- 1 1/2 teaspoons lemon juice
- 3/4 teaspoon salt
- 1/2 teaspoon grated lemon zest
- 2 tablespoons extra-virgin olive oil
- 1.5 cups chopped fresh basil
- For Sandwich:
- 2 tbsp. prepared pistachio pesto (recipe above)
- Bread of choice
- 4 ounces Brie
- 4 tablespoons salted butter, divided

1. For the pesto - Combine all ingredients in a food processor and blend very well until smooth. Taste and adjust salt as necessary.

2. For sandwich - Spread 2 tablespoons of pesto on each slice of bread; set aside.

3. Slice the Brie and place on slices of bread, put the Brie on pesto covered bread.

4. Heat a large skillet over medium heat and melt 2 tablespoons of butter in it. Add the sandwich to the skillet. Cook the sandwiches until golden brown both, approximately 3 to 4 minutes. Add two more tablespoons of butter when flipping the sandwich.

5. Cook until the cheese is fully melted and the bread is crisp and golden brown on each side. Remove from the skillet and enjoy!

Johnna Dee

by day is an office worker by night writer, crafter, and baker. Her keyboard is her weapon of choice, unless in the kitchen, then it's mixing bowls. Living in the blistering sun of beautiful Phoenix, AZ. Hiking, archery, and exploring the world are some of her favorite hobbies.

Poetry is how she got her opening into writing. There, she determined to branch out into books, and is the co-writer on the fantasy romance The Calpa Series. Writer of the fantasy romance The Ascelin Series.

Socials

- https://linktr.ee/johnnadee
- https://www.kickstarter.com/projects/johnnadee/crest-of-the-fallen-book-1-in-ascelin-series
- https://www.facebook.com/johnna.buttrick
- https://www.instagram.com/johnnadeeb/
- https://www.tiktok.com/@johnna_dee
- https://clapperapp.com/johnna_dee
- https://www.goodreads.com/author/show/23048317.Johnna_Dee
- https://www.goodreads.com/book/show/123244269-crest-of-the-fallen

www.ingramcontent.com/pod-product-compliance
Lightning Source LLC
Chambersburg PA
CBHW061147210726
48294CB00006B/1603